ALSO BY ROSANNE BITTNER

RIDE *the* HIGH LONESOME

ROSANNE BITTNER

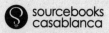
sourcebooks
casablanca

Sourcebooks and the colophon are registered trademarks of
Sourcebooks.

Published by Sourcebooks Casablanca, an imprint of Sourcebooks
P.O. Box 4410, Naperville, Illinois 60567-4410
(630) 961-3900
sourcebooks.com

Printed and bound in Canada.
MBP 10 9 8 7 6 5 4 3 2 1

ONE

August 1869

KATE DUCKED INTO THE TALL GRASS AS SOON AS SHE heard men's voices. She slowly crawled to get close enough to listen, then parted the dense, yellow blades to see five rough-looking men gathered around a lonely, half-dead cottonwood tree. One of the men raised up in his stirrups and flung a rope over the biggest branch left on the leafless tree, while another, guarded at rifle point, sat astride his horse with his hands tied behind his back.

Dear God, are they going to hang *that man?*

In the distance, about twenty head of cattle and a pack horse grazed, unconcerned about the terrible event about to take place. All five men shouted at each other, but Kate could distinguish only bits and pieces of their conversation.

"Hang…son of a bitch!"

The man whose hands were tied was angrily and desperately yelling back at them. "I didn't steal—"

"Makes no difference—"

"Murdering bastards!"

If she were a man, with a weapon and a horse, Kate could at least ride down to the site to see what was going on and maybe talk the men out of the hanging, but whether what was happening below was lawful or lawless, what could a thirty-two-year-old woman, with nothing more than the clothes on her back, do against five men? She didn't even dare show herself. This was pure outlaw country. There wasn't a man around who could be trusted to help and not harm.

Was the poor soul about to be hanged innocent or guilty? And did it really matter in this lost world of lawlessness? All around them, massive and endless mesas stood guard over a valley that stretched so far into the distance that she couldn't even see the end of it. It would probably take a week of nonstop riding to escape this place. How many weeks would it take to flee on foot—her *only* way out?

She'd never seen such big country, such endless horizons, nor had she ever felt so far removed from civilization…so dreadfully and completely alone. She'd read somewhere that canyons and strange rock formations like this were formed by water cutting a path through the land—probably a million years ago, when dinosaurs roamed the earth. She felt caught up in that past. Did civilization still exist beyond this vast chain of buttes and mesas?

She watched with a sinking heart as one of the men led the man with his hands tied under the noose and placed the rope around his neck. Kate put her head down, unable to look. Strangely, the worst part of this was wondering how close she might be to food and water, to men who might be able to help her find her way out of this god-forsaken country and back to safety. But she'd rather die from thirst and hunger than to suffer the things four desperate, lonely men might decide to do with her if she showed herself. They might even kill her for witnessing what they were about to do.

She heard more shouts and strained to hear the doomed man swear his innocence.

"I *paid* for those cattle!"

"Thief!"

"Rustler!"

"*You're* the outlaws!" he snapped.

Kate jumped and almost cried out when a gun was fired. A couple of horses whinnied, and she felt literal pain in her stomach at the thought of what had just happened. Everything grew quiet, until one man yelled loudly, "Goddamn it! He isn't dead yet."

"He *will* be in a couple more minutes," someone answered.

"Let the son of a bitch suffer."

"Let's go!"

Kate hadn't watched any of it. With her ear to the ground, she heard the pounding of horses' hooves, a sound that seemed to carry like thunder for miles through the earth. She'd learned from the wagon train guide how to listen for oncoming horses or buffalo this way. That guide was dead now, along with all the others she'd traveled with—even two children. She would always remember the guide telling her that out in this land a man could hear the thunder of horses' hooves from miles away. Too bad old Gus hadn't listened to the ground the day of their attack. They would have had more time to circle the wagons and prepare for a fight.

As the thundering began to fade, she raised her head slightly. She heard whistles and shouts that sounded more like war whoops, but they sounded far away.

She dared to lift her head higher. Three men were charging after the cattle in the distance, while one kept trying to grab the hanged man's horse. It kept rearing up and yanking itself away, until finally the fourth man rode off after the others, who'd already stolen their victim's pack horse. Kate thanked God they were all riding away from her rather than toward her. She noticed then that the hanged man's feet were still kicking, and she grasped her stomach at the awful sight. "God have mercy on his soul," she said softly.

She again looked into the horizon of dry, yellow grass. The four men were still riding hard behind the cattle. They headed around the bend of a mesa, and soon men and cattle all disappeared. When Kate turned her attention back to the hanged man, she noticed that his feet were *still* moving. "Oh my God!" she groaned.

Did she dare get up? Outlaw or not, she couldn't bear the fact that the man was suffering horribly as his last bit of oxygen left him. He couldn't possibly be a danger to her at the moment. He was, after all, just one man, and he would likely die before she could reach him. Besides, she needed his horse and supplies. A canteen hung from his saddle horn, and she saw a rifle strapped to his gear. The saddlebags lying over the horse's rump were surely full of needed supplies. A gun belt lay on the ground. The horse and its supplies were her only hope of staying alive and finding her way out of this cruel, unforgiving country.

It was now or never. She couldn't let the man suffer any longer, and she had to grab his horse before it decided to run off. She stood up, lifted the long skirt of her dress, and started running through the tall grass. The sole on her right shoe had loosened from so much walking, and she stumbled as she ran.

Everything around her was rocky and steep and treacherous.

Finally, she reached the horse, which had already wandered several yards from where its owner still hung. She grunted as she climbed into the saddle, so weak she barely had the strength to pull herself up. She didn't bother to shorten the stirrups. She just let her legs dangle and kicked the horse into a hard run, heading for the hanged man. She reached his limp body and gasped when she heard a horrible gurgling sound come from his lips. His face had turned purple, but his feet jerked gently in a sickening signal of dwindling life.

The man's eyeballs rolled back. Kate desperately searched for a way to get him down, then noticed that though he wore no gun, there was a knife in his belt. She leaned over and yanked it out of its sheath, then reached as high as she could and grabbed the end of the rope near his head.

She strained to vigorously cut at the rope, and finally the knife sliced through. The man's body fell with a thud onto a sandy patch of ground.

TWO

Kate dismounted the horse and quickly tied it to a low branch of the hanging tree. She knelt beside the suffering man, who was still choking and gasping for breath. She yanked the rope from around his neck and threw it aside, noticing he was a big man, tall and solid. Could he even breathe?

He made a chilling gagging sound, and although she didn't know him, she wished she could take away his misery. "Mister? I want to help you."

He couldn't find his voice to reply.

Kate scrambled to retrieve the knife she'd dropped and then hurried back to where the man lay. She rolled him to his side and cut the ropes that held his wrists together. She pulled one arm forward and gently rolled him onto his back, then pulled the other arm out from under him. She reached under his neck and helped him arch his head back to open his airway as much as possible.

He gasped in ugly grunts, a deep, grating groan that made Kate ache for him. "Try to relax," she urged. "You're getting air, so relax and slowly breathe in, mister. Keep breathing and let your throat open back up." She sat down and moved her legs under his head to keep it raised, then began massaging the sides and back of his neck, trying to relax his muscles while at the same time avoiding the scraped, blood-tinged skin where the rope had produced an ugly ring around his throat.

He struggled to put one hand to his chest and dig the other into the sand. His chest heaved as he forced himself to breathe in, over and over.

"That's it," Kate told him. "Just breathe." She studied his face, noting the purplish hue had eased. His skin was tanned, and the outer corners of his eyes were creased from weeks, months, maybe years of sun exposure. Who was he, and why was he out here? Was he guilty of rustling cattle, or maybe something worse? Could she trust him once he reclaimed his breath and strength?

As she wondered, she observed him still. Beyond what must be only a day-old beard, his features were strong: square jaw, straight nose, full lips, a prominent brow. The high plains were cool today, and he wore a wool jacket over his broad shoulders. His hair needed cutting, but what man out here *didn't* need a haircut? Towns with barbers and bathhouses were hundreds of miles apart, and in between, there was little access to water. Even so, this man didn't smell of someone who seldom washed. She'd encountered that nose-twisting odor too often during the trip out here, and now she wondered about herself. After walking for three days through dry, hot country, she had no business worrying about someone else's hygiene.

For the moment, her priority was to get this man back to normal breathing. His dark-brown hair was almost shoulder-length, and she brushed errant strands from his face, wondering if it was the thickness of his hair at the sides and back of his neck that had protected him from the rope. His hair and the collar of his jacket might have saved his life.

She shivered, the air suddenly chilling her. She remembered others telling her that the weather could change in an instant in high country, and that sometimes it even snowed this time of year. She was afraid to leave the man on his own yet, so she just hunched closer and kept coaching him to breathing. As she bent closer to stay warm, he opened his eyes and looked straight into her eyes.

They were inches apart. They just stared at each other a moment until Kate suddenly straightened, not sure just how aware the man was of his surroundings, or of her.

"Do you know where you are?" she asked him. "Do you remember what just happened?"

He kept staring at her as though she were a creature from another world, confusion and pain in his gaze. "You...an...angel?" He gasped the words in a deeply strained, grating voice.

Kate rubbed the sides of his neck again. "No," she replied. "You are indeed alive, mister, and I'm lost out here. My name is Kate. I came across that awful hanging and hid until those men left. I saw that you were still alive, so I cut you down."

The man gasped again and made a sickening choking sound, then turned sideways and coughed up blood before turning back and relaxing his head on her legs again. He swallowed. "Sorry."

"You can't help it."

"Your...dress."

"It's already torn and filthy. You can't hurt it. Just relax and keep breathing. Don't get up yet. What's your name?"

He gasped for his next breath and bent one knee, then opened his eyes again and just stared at her a moment, still looking confused. He was silent, as though he wasn't sure of his name, then closed his eyes again. "Luke," he grunted. "I...need...water."

"Oh, of course! Can you sit up?"

"Try..."

"See if you can help me scoot you against the tree," Kate told him. "You're too big for me to do this by myself." She helped get him to a sitting position, then moved behind him and grasped him under the arms, pulling at him while he used one leg to help push himself backward until he could lean against the tree. He started gasping for breath again, and Kate hurried over to his horse, taking a canteen from where it hung around the pommel of the saddle. She knelt beside him and uncorked the canteen, holding it to his lips. "Here. Try to drink, but be careful. You don't want to start coughing if you can help it. I imagine it would hurt to cough and might even injure your throat even worse."

She tipped the canteen a little and let some water dribble into his mouth. He took hold of it then himself and took a bigger swallow.

"Be careful," Kate warned.

Luke lowered the canteen and closed his eyes again, taking a deep breath.

"Mister, I have to drink some of this, too. I've gone all day without water. The one canteen I managed to salvage three days ago ran empty last night."

Luke watched her as she took a long swallow of water.

"I hope you have more than just this one canteen," she told him as she recorked it and wiped at her lips.

"One...more," he managed to choke out. "Inside... that satchel...tied to my...horse. Don't want...other men to see it. Out here...men steal...water...horses... money...cattle...anything." He groaned with pain then, grasping at his throat and bending over to take more deep breaths.

"Is that what those men were doing?" Kate asked him. "Stealing your cattle?"

Luke nodded. "Bastards! I'll...kill...every last...one of them!"

Kate wondered just how many men Luke had already killed. He seemed to have no qualms about killing four more. Maybe he would have no qualms about hurting or killing her, too. "First you have to learn to breathe again and get your strength back," she told him, hoping kindness would save her. "I saw another jacket tied to your supplies. Do you mind if I put it on? I'm cold."

He studied her a moment, looking her over in that way a man had of telling a woman he liked what he saw. Kate scooted away a little, wondering if she'd gotten herself into worse trouble by helping him.

"Sure," he answered. "You...saved...my life, lady."

Kate rose and walked to his horse, untying the

sheepskin jacket and pulling it on. It was far too big, and its sleeves hung down over her hands, but the sheep's wool lining brought welcome warmth. She walked over to where Luke's gun belt lay and picked it up, taking it to the horse and hanging it over the pommel of the saddle. She hesitated then, wondering if she needed protection. She took out the heavy six-gun and dropped it into a pocket on the jacket.

The gun weighed down that side of the jacket awkwardly, but she had no choice for the moment. This was dangerous country, full of dangerous men. She turned to see Luke watching her.

"No need...for that," he managed to tell her.

Kate walked around to gather some pieces of dead wood from under the tree. *We'll see*, she thought. "I'll build a fire," she said aloud. "It will be dark soon, and it looks like we have no choice but to camp here for the night."

"I'm...grateful," Luke said. "I...owe you."

"You don't owe me a thing. I might have saved your life, but you've saved mine just by being here. I'm hungry and worn to the bone from walking, and I was getting desperate and terrified. I'm completely lost, so you need to live in order to help me find my way out of this godforsaken country."

Kate glanced over at the tree to see the man had slipped sideways and was lying on the ground again. She grabbed a blanket from his horse and hurried over to bunch it up under his head and helped him lie flat. "Don't die on me, Luke," she said. "I'll never find my way back to civilization without you. I hope you know where you are and how to find help."

"Don't...steal my...horse," he whispered, his eyes closed. "Don't...leave me here without a...gun and...a horse."

Kate couldn't help feeling sorry for him. She leaned closer. "I need that horse, but I also need the man who owns it," she told him. *Unless I can't trust him.* "So I won't steal it. Besides, why would I ride off after just saving your life?"

She rose and walked back to her little pile of wood, then looked out at the violent landscape that was growing dimmer as the sun set. In the distance she saw a herd of wild horses running through the valley, so far away she could see them, but could not hear them. She got on her knees and put her ear to the ground.

The guide had been right. She could hear their pounding hooves, even though they were unshod and so far away she could barely see them in the evening's dim light. She raised up to watch them disappear into a deep shadow created by the sun settling behind a grand mesa. Somewhere in the unreal landscape; a wolf howled, its cry echoing across the valley.

"Can you eat?" she asked Luke.

He just lay there, making no reply.

Kate fished through the man's supplies and found some biscuits. She ate two and decided that would have to do for now. She remembered someone telling her once that a person shouldn't eat too heavily on a severely empty stomach. Maybe it was when she'd helped with wounded men during the war...that awful war that had robbed her of everything she'd ever loved.

She checked Luke once more, touching his shoulder. "Luke? Are you okay?"

He opened his eyes. "Just…cover me and…leave a canteen," he choked out.

Kate did as he asked, taking another long drink first. She left the canteen near Luke, then laid out his bedroll near the fire. She found leather straps for hobbling the horse, led the gelding out to better grass, and wrapped his front legs into the straps. She took Luke's rifle from his gear and walked back to the fire, where she practically collapsed onto his bedroll. Exhaustion overwhelmed her as she crawled inside the bedroll, thinking to rest just a few minutes and then check on Luke again. She figured she shouldn't let herself sleep too hard. After all, Luke was yet a stranger, and for all she knew, he still could be dangerous. He could recover faster than she anticipated.

She laid the rifle and Luke's six-gun beside her and closed her eyes. *Where in God's name am I*, she wondered, *and what kind of man am I with?*

THREE

SOMEONE NUDGED KATE AWAKE. SHE GASPED AND reached for the rifle she'd left beside her the night before, but it was held in place by a big, booted foot.

"Don't be...shooting me out of fear." The words came out in a grating rasp. "I'm just giving you time... to get your bearings."

Kate blinked and jumped to her feet to face Luke, who stood there in the early morning light with his six-gun in hand. Kate felt mortified. Rather than sleep just a little, she'd apparently slept through the night and wasn't even aware that Luke was up and better and had possession of both guns.

"I—you—"

"You're fine," he told her. He'd already strapped on his gun belt, and he slipped the six-gun into its holster. "I just don't want you to shoot me from being startled awake," he repeated.

Kate noted his eyes were bloodshot, and his entire neck and part of his jawline were bruised. His shoulder-length hair stuck out in disarray from under his hat. He stepped back, taking his foot off the rifle, then leaned down to pick it up. "Sometimes when a person is lost and scared, he or she will shoot at anything." He took out his handgun again and handed it out. "Take this...if it makes you feel better."

"It's okay, I guess." Kate pushed a tendril of her hair behind her ear, thinking she must be as much in need of a bath and clean clothes as Luke. She was suddenly too aware of how she must look. Her red hair always tried to go in six directions at once. Now it was disheveled from the wind and sullied with dust and grit.

She looked around the camp, realizing Luke had rebuilt the fire.

"I...I intended to get a fire started...make some coffee or something before you were even up," she told him, realizing only then that the man was taller than she'd first surmised—certainly big enough to have his way with her if he so chose. Yet he'd offered her his six-gun. "I didn't think you would be up and around so soon."

"Don't worry about it. I aim to get going soon as possible and get my cattle back." He re-holstered his six-gun.

Kate frowned. "But you must be in terrible pain. You should rest another day. And I need to find a way to civilization. I need a horse of my own, supplies, clean clothes. I was hoping you'd lead me to a place where I can get those things before you go after those men."

Luke shook his head. "I can't let them get too far ahead." He sniffed the air. "There's clouds hanging in the west. Look like rain clouds, something you don't see out here often." He cleared his throat and choked a little. "It's going to get colder instead of warmer. There's no predicting the weather in this country. We'll warm up a little and rest up more… just to get the ache out of our bones. Then we'll need to get going. I aim to go after the men who hanged me. I want them dead, and I need to get my cattle back. Or my money. Both, if possible. You needing to ride with me will slow us down, so the earlier we start, the better."

"Where will we go?"

"There's a town a good thirty-five miles north of here called Lander. I'm sure that's where those men are headed. We'll find a good place for you to hole up while I ride to Lander and get what's mine. It will all go faster if I do this alone. I'll also get the supplies we need—food, clothes, and a horse for you."

Kate watched him look around for more firewood. "I don't even know your last name," she told him.

Luke kept his rifle in one hand and leaned down to pick up an unburned stick. He stirred the coals under the fire. "Bowden," he answered. "Luke Bowden. How about you?"

Kate helped pick up more wood, glad he'd mentioned finding her a horse and supplies, and doubly glad to realize he seemed to know his way around this country. "Kate Winters."

They both laid more wood on the fire at the same time, momentarily raising their heads and looking into each other's eyes. After helping nurse wounded men during the Civil War, Kate knew enough about men's pride to know Luke Bowden was feeling more than a little shame at how she'd found him, at the mercy of other men, a noose around his neck, hanging, kicking, and dying.

"I reckon I owe you my life, Miss Winters. Or is it Mrs.?"

"It's Mrs.," she told him. "My husband was killed in the war." She quickly rose, feeling a little embarrassed at their faces being so close. "And I suppose you do owe me, but I can't take too much credit, Mister Bowden. I didn't want to see you suffer, but I also needed your horse and supplies. The wagon train I was with had dwindled down to only three wagons because of sickness and breakdowns along the way. We were headed for Oregon when we were attacked by a gang of ragtag soldiers and renegades, probably leftovers from the war. I never even got a good look at them. The three men I traveled with—a preacher and two farmers, plus the guide—they hid me under a blanket beneath my wagon."

Kate wanted to cry at the memory. "They were all killed. All supplies stolen. The wagons burned. Mine collapsed right on top of me. By some miracle I was able to burrow deeper into a little dip in the ground, and I just let it burn around me. The wagon bed didn't burn, and I was able to crawl out after the awful men who attacked us rode off with our small remuda of horses and the supplies. They killed the oxen." Her heart ached at the memory of the friends she'd made, including the rugged old guide who'd taught her to listen to the ground. "I just started walking, hoping I'd find someone to help me."

Luke shook his head. "Why in hell did your guide

leave so late in the year for Oregon? It's too late to get over the mountains. It's already snowing up there."

"We were going to lay over in Utah at a Mormon settlement."

"The fact remains, you're in outlaw country now, and you won't find much help among the kind of men who live out here. They call this the Outlaw Trail. Runs from Canada practically all the way to Mexico." He fanned the flames with his hat. "You've likely figured out that men come here to hide from the law. No lawman will show his face in this country."

Kate knew it to be true, but her heart fell a little more at hearing it. "Are *you* an outlaw, Mister Bowden?"

Luke managed a light laugh. "Depends on what you consider an outlaw. Once I catch up to those men who hanged me, I reckon I'll end up being called a murderer. Just rest your mind that I'm no woman-beater, and I don't kill men without good cause. And I sure as hell wouldn't harm someone who just saved my life, so get that worried look off your face. And call me Luke, not Mister Bowden. Can I keep calling you Kate?"

"Of course."

"Well, Kate, grab that blanket you slept with last night. Sit by the fire for a while. We'll eat a couple of biscuits and then leave."

"Luke, it's a terrible thing you went through yesterday. I think you should rest one more day."

He shook his head. "No, ma'am. Time is of the essence. Those sons of bitches—pardon my language—but they stole what's mine and tried to kill me. A man doesn't forget something like that." He coughed again and rubbed at his throat. "I want to hunt them down." He coughed again. "I'm sorry, but that comes first, and I'll travel faster alone. I know a place where you can stay and wait. I'll leave you food and water and blankets."

Kate rubbed at her eyes. "Right now, I need to you to look away while I go behind that big rock to… well…"

"Everybody needs to pee when they wake up, ma'am. I already took care of my own needs. Go ahead. Then get over here and warm yourself more. I'm surprised you were able to sleep at all with only my old coat and my bedroll to bed down with. It gets damn cold in this country at night. You must kind of hurt all over after what you've been through." He met her gaze. "How long ago was the attack?"

"Four days, I think. I've been wandering so long and was so hungry and thirsty and worn out, I lost track. I'm afraid I ate some of your biscuits last night."

"No problem."

Kate wanted to ask so much more. Where was he from? What was he doing out here herding cattle by himself? Where was he headed when the outlaws stole his herd? Was he married? Did he have family somewhere? Was he even telling the truth about not being an outlaw and not being a threat to her? And how did he think he was going to take on four men all by himself?

She stood up and walked to the boulder, glad it was just big enough that he couldn't see her kneel behind it and lift her skirts.

Just as she started to rise, a quail fluttered upward
from where it was hidden in tall grass. Kate gasped
in surprise and quickly pulled up her drawers. She
jumped and let out a little scream when a gun went
off. She hurried around the boulder to see the quail
drop to the ground some distance away.

Luke turned to her, rifle in hand, and nodded.
"Our supper," he told her. "Now if we can find some
water, we won't starve or die from thirst."

Kate walked back to the fire while Luke walked off
to find the quail he'd shot. *Well, Luke Bowden, you are
apparently a strong and able man when it comes to survival.
And at least you seem to know this country.*

Whether or not he could be trusted was still to be
proven. Right now, he was weak and grateful. Men
changed when they got stronger, and she was already
aware from some men's attitudes and remarks what
some men thought a widowed woman needed. She
prayed Mister Luke Bowden was not a drinking man,
or that a meaner side would not show itself as he grew
stronger. Right now, he was all the hope she had of
getting out of this place alive.

FOUR

Luke buttoned the collar of his wool jacket closer around his neck, then pulled his left foot from the stirrup. "Put your foot in the stirrup and climb up behind me," he told Kate, reaching down for her.

"Are you sure you should be doing this?" Kate asked. "You don't look good. Getting hanged isn't like having a cold or something. You're seriously injured."

"I'll manage."

His voice was so pitifully raspy that Kate couldn't help feeling very sorry for him. She threw a blanket over the horse's neck, then grasped Luke's hand and put her left foot into the stirrup. "Are you sure this isn't too much weight for your horse?" she asked.

Luke helped hoist her up, and she settled in behind him, surprised and impressed with how easily he'd pulled her up. He was a strong man, but she couldn't help worrying how easily he could use that strength against her.

"You don't weigh much," he replied. "Ole Red will be fine, especially since we managed to make up a travois from some of those tree limbs to carry the supplies separate." Luke handed her the blanket she'd draped around Red's neck, and she laid it over her legs and huddled against his back.

Luke had been right. Even though it was still August, the morning had already grown colder instead of warmer, and the sky was getting darker instead of brighter. She could hardly believe the change in the weather, after sweating so much the past four days.

She had no choice now but to wrap her arms around Luke's solid middle and hang on tight as he kicked his horse into motion. She glanced back at the doused camp fire they had shared, wondering where on earth life would take her from here. Although Luke Bowden was a complete stranger, she was grateful to have finally found some kind of help.

She'd smoothed the wild curls of her hair back at the sides as best she could and secured it with the three combs she'd managed to hang on to after the wagon attack. That day her hair was piled on top of her head with several combs. It had fallen down, section by section, as she walked mile after mile, looking for help, not even knowing which direction she'd taken. She desperately needed a bath, a real bed, and a decent change of clothes.

"Tell me again where we are going," she said.

"A town called Lander, but I need to find a decent place for you to wait while I take care of the men I'm after and get the supplies we need. There's a cave where men sometimes hole up on the way there. Hoping to reach it by nightfall."

Kate looked around at nothing but more wide-open

valley surrounded by miles and miles of the same high, flat-topped cliffs. How a man found his way in country like this, she could not imagine. It seemed impossible there could be a town anywhere even remotely close, and everything looked identically empty and endless. She saw no signs of life. She did see trampled grass ahead of them. The stolen herd of cattle had left an easy path. She looked down at it when the horse stumbled.

"Easy there, Red," Luke soothed.

Kate noticed the quail he'd shot was bouncing against the horse's rump, where Luke had tied it upside-down after gutting and beheading the bird to let the blood drain as they rode. The travois, tied to the back of the saddle, dragged and bounced behind the horse and made scratching and tearing sounds as it was pulled through the grass and over patches of gravely ground.

"Luke, we can't travel like this for more than a couple of days. It's too hard on the horse and too awkward for us."

"I am well aware of all of that," he answered, his voice hoarse.

"I'm sorry," Kate told him. "Are you sure you know what direction we are going?"

"North. Trust me. I used to hunt in wild country with my pa a long time ago. Learned how to track things. Besides, I've been living out here the past couple of years. I know this country, and I know north from south."

Kate wondered why he'd chosen to stay in such desolate country, but she didn't ask. It was too hard for the man to talk, and it really was none of her business anyway. They rode a while in silence. Kate looked up when she heard the cry of an eagle and saw the big bird floating on an air current, making it all look so easy. She thought how, from above, she and Luke Bowden must look like nothing more than two specks against the yellow grass, no bigger than bugs against a landscape so magnificently vast.

Red plodded along, his riders rocking back and forth with the horse's gait, the horse snorting and tossing his head at times. Luke had given the animal a little water before they left, but the poor animal needed more. All *three* of them needed more.

"Who were those men who hanged you?" Kate asked Luke, feeling she needed to break the awkward silence in spite of how difficult it was for Luke to talk.

"I'll explain later," he answered.

A cold wind suddenly picked up and rushed through the valley with surprising speed, making Luke duck his head. Kate lowered her own head behind his broad back, feeling guilty that she could use his body as a shield while Luke had to take the brunt of it. A light, cold rain began to fall. It was soon mixed with snowflakes, then solid snow.

"So it's true," Kate muttered. "It *can* snow in August."

"This country is higher than you think."

They plodded on, bent against the wind and snow, still able to follow the tracks of Luke's cattle in spite of the fresh snow that would normally have covered them. The trampled grass left an indention that, even snow-covered, was easy to follow. They continued the miserable ride for what seemed hours, stopping once behind a huge boulder for shelter. They ate another biscuit each and drank a little water while letting Red rest. It was late afternoon when Luke drew Red to a halt and stared intently at something. He pointed and leaned back, talking close to Kate's ear because his pain kept him from yelling above the howling wind.

"There's the cave," he told her. "We'll hole up there."

Kate nodded, thinking how good it would feel to get out of the wind. She shivered into the sheepskin jacket as Luke headed across to the east side of the valley. It took far longer to reach the cave than Kate first expected, but she was learning that nothing in this wild land was ever as close as it looked. The wind and snow let up a little as they drew closer.

They were perhaps a half mile from the cave when Red stumbled, and his front legs seemed to collapse. Both Kate and Luke went flying forward into the snow. Luke quickly rolled away and got to his knees. He noticed Kate took a moment to answer. She rolled over, holding her head.

"You okay?" Luke asked.

Kate finally managed to sit up, wet snow on her face. "I think so."

Luke noticed a spot of blood on a snow-covered rock. "Jesus," he muttered. "Sit still a minute." He reached over to Red. The horse whinnied and stood up again, shaking his mane and stumbling slightly.

"What happened, boy?" Luke got up and checked the horse's legs. "I think he's okay—just worn out," he told Kate. He walked up to her and reached out a hand to help her up, then frowned. "Ma'am, your forehead is bleeding."

Kate put a hand to the painful spot. "I hit my head on that rock."

"He put an arm around her waist and helped her toward his horse. "Put some snow on it," he said as he grabbed the reins. "The cold will slow the bleeding. I'll find you something to hold against it." He let go of her and turned back to Red and ran his hands over the horse's shoulders and front legs again, then checked the ground around them. "There's a big hole here," he said, pointing to a spot just behind the horse. "The snow hid it." He turned back around to see Kate crumple to the ground as her legs went out from under her. "Kate!"

Kate tried to gather her thoughts and steady herself, but a terrible dizziness made that impossible. She fought a black fog that scattered her thoughts as Luke gathered her in his arms.

"I'll get you to that cave," he told her. "I'm sorry, but I'll have to drape you over Red unless you think you can sit up on the horse."

Kate couldn't find the words to answer him. She was aware of being draped over a horse's back and covered with a blanket. "I know this is uncomfortable, but we have to get to the cave," Luke said. "I'll lead Red so he doesn't step into anymore holes. I don't want to put my weight on him till I'm sure he doesn't have an injured leg."

Kate instinctively reached down with her hands and grabbed the right stirrup, hanging on to it to keep from slipping backward off the saddle. The slow walk the rest of the way to the cave seemed to take forever.

"It's just ahead now," Luke told her.

His voice was the last thing Kate remembered.

FIVE

KATE AWOKE TO THE CRACKLING SOUND OF A FIRE, HER head on something soft, two blankets covering her. She thought she smelled coffee, and the smell reminded her she was hungry. She opened her eyes to a dimly lit room. Except it wasn't a room. The walls were made of rock. The only light was that of the fire.

A horse whinnied, and now she saw a man wearing a gray wool jacket sitting on the floor of the cave and leaning against the rock wall only about five feet away. He appeared to be sleeping. She lay still, thinking. She remembered falling…someone telling her she was bleeding…something about a cave…lying facedown over a horse.

Her head hurt. She put a hand to her forehead and realized it was bandaged.

The fall! A snowstorm! She gasped and sat straight up. The blankets fell away, and she looked down to realize she wore only her camisole and ruffled panta-loons. Where was her dress? And *where* was *she*?

A man's voice spoke up. "So, you finally woke up."

Kate jerked the blankets up to her neck and looked

over at Luke Bowden. She glanced at the fire then around the room, then back at the man. "Where are we? And why am I half dressed?"

Luke got up and walked closer to the fire, where he sat down across from her and poured coffee into a tin cup. He handed it out to her. "Here. You need this."

Kate stared at the cup, thinking how good a cup of coffee would taste. "Answer my questions first, Mister Bowden."

Luke sighed. "So, now it's 'Mister Bowden.'" He shook his head. "Look, Kate, we are in that cave I told you about. You were blacked out from that blow to your forehead. The bottom half of your dress was soaking wet. I took care of that wound, and I took off your dress so it wouldn't be wet under those blankets I made up into a bed for you to warm you up. As far as the coffee and blankets, they're from my supplies, but this cave is stocked with a little food. It's shared by outlaws who sometimes leave things stored here for the next men that come through these parts. Lucky for us, there's firewood in here and extra blankets. I even found that coffeepot and a couple of wrinkled potatoes. They're kind of soft, but they're still edible. I figured I'd cook them for our supper along with that quail. We each won't get more than a bite of the meat, but mixed with the potatoes, it should hold us over for a while."

Kate glanced at the fire, weighing all he'd told her. She was mortified that he'd taken off her dress, but she understood it was likely necessary. Still, had he taken any privileges while she was unconscious? He was a man, after all, and God only knew how long he'd been traveling alone. She cautiously took the coffee from him and sipped it. She had to admit, the strong, hot, black brew tasted wonderful.

"I know what you're thinking, but I didn't take advantage while you were out," Luke said. He poured himself a cup of coffee. "You are a handsome woman, Kate, but I'd never bring you harm. I was just aiming to make sure you don't end up with consumption and die on me. How does your head feel?"

Kate struggled to keep the blanket around her neck with one hand while she drank the coffee with her other. She wasn't sure how to take his remark about her being a *handsome woman*. She'd never been what she thought of as beautiful and was sure he couldn't have meant it that way. If he did think of her as handsome, she wasn't sure how to react. It meant he'd been looking at her as a man usually looks at a woman. What if he thought that just because she was a widow, she needed a man in every way?

"I...it still hurts," she answered, "but I'm not dizzy anymore. At least I don't think I am. I haven't stood up yet." She met his gaze, realizing only then that she'd not even taken note of the color of his eyes. By the firelight they looked dark. "What about you? Your voice sounds hoarse but not as raspy as it was before."

Luke ran fingers between his wounded neck and the scarf he wore around it. "I put a little whiskey in my coffee. It took away some of the pain. I found this scarf in my supplies and put it on so's you wouldn't have to look at this ugly scar all the time. I usually wear the scarf against dust when I'm herding cattle, anyway."

Kate glanced at a flask of whiskey he'd set nearby.

"Don't worry. It takes a lot more than one or two

swallows of whiskey to get me drunk," Luke told her. "I did have a pretty bad drinking problem when I first came out here...for personal reasons. Now I generally drink only for medicinal reasons or because I'm extra happy, and I haven't been extra happy in a long, long time."

Kate noted the sadness in his words.

"The snow let up," he added. "That's how it is out here. It could even be warm again by tomorrow."

Kate finished her coffee and lay back down. "There's still so much I don't know about you, Luke. How old are you? Where are you from? How did you end up out here with a bunch of cattle, getting yourself hanged? Are you married? What do you do for a living?"

"I could say the same for you. All I know is that you're a war widow whose wagon train was attacked. What's a widow woman doing traveling out here in the first place?"

Widow woman. There it was again—a term she was getting tired of hearing, especially with the slanted way men said it.

"I'm not looking for a man, if that's what you think," she told him.

Luke shrugged. "I wasn't thinking that at all. It's a simple question. This isn't a place for *any* woman— single, married, or widowed."

Kate stared at her coffee. "I know this is no place for a woman, but ending up here certainly was not my choice. And I grew up on a farm in Indiana, so I am used to hard work and hard living. I'll manage until we reach civilization."

Luke frowned. "You haven't fully explained why you were with that wagon train in the first place."

Kate forced back an urge to cry over her predicament, not wanting to show any kind of weakness in front of this man she barely knew and who might think he could take advantage.

"I'm from Indiana, as I said," she told him, "and I've been living alone for four years, trying to run my husband's supply store. He and my father were both killed in the war. My mother had died years before that, as had both of my husband's parents." She rubbed at her eyes, her head aching. "The store was failing. I wrote a brother-in-law in Oregon about helping him and his family with a big farm he has there. He answered right away, his letter glowing about how perfect the Oregon weather and the soil is for farming. He said he and his family could use my help. I couldn't afford to travel by train, so I packed up and joined a wagon train."

Kate curled onto her side, keeping the blankets close around her and feeling more and more humiliated by the fact that Luke Bowden had seen her bare shoulders and a good share of her breasts not covered by the camisole.

"As you already know, the Oregon Trail goes right through outlaw country," she continued. "We knew an attack was possible, but I didn't imagine someone would murder all of us, steal everything, and burn our wagons. She shook her head. "When I crawled out from under that wagon, there was no one and nothing left. I needed food and I found only one canteen of water, so I just started walking. On the third day I came across your hanging. When those men rode off and left your horse, I knew that horse and the supplies on it were my only chance of survival."

Luke grinned. "So, you meant it when you said that your intention to claim my horse and supplies was the main reason you came down that hill, not to rescue me."

Kate met his gaze. "No. I mean, initially, yes, it was, but I saw your feet moving, and I couldn't bear the thought of how you must be suffering if you were still alive. I spent part of the war helping nurse wounded soldiers. I can't turn my back on a man or woman needing help, stranger or not. I was just afraid I might regret my decision this time, since this is outlaw country. And that leads me to my own questions. Just how innocent *are* you, Luke Bowden?"

He shrugged. "I'm not perfect, but I didn't do anything to deserve a hanging. I bought those cattle from some outlaw who stole them from somebody else. I knew they were stolen, but I paid for them right and proper. Out here, most men survive that way. Fact is, a lot of them come here to get away from the law or bad memories from the war. I was a lieutenant in the war. I'm from Ohio. After the war I came out here to get away from things too familiar...and too painful... back home."

He lowered his gaze, an obvious bitterness in his voice. He poured a splash of whiskey into his coffee cup and swallowed some, grimacing from pain. "I've been wandering around out here, working odd jobs ever since, mostly for no-good, law-breaking men who are out here for the same reason I am. I figured maybe I would start my own ranch, maybe in northern California," he continued. "Turns out the man I bought those cattle from ended up dead, at the hands of other outlaws who *did* steal those cattle first from a legitimate rancher. They took the money I'd paid the dead man and then came after me. They didn't care that I *paid* for those cattle. I even had a bill of sale. They hanged me anyway, even though they are cattle thieves themselves. They just figured they could take back the cattle and keep my money and claim I stole the cattle." He drank a little more whiskey. "I aim to make those men pay me what they cost me, plus pay for trying to kill me. They didn't need to do that. They could have just tied me up and taken my money and the cattle. But they thought it would be fun to hang a man."

He coughed with a pitiful gag then, and Kate could tell he was still in pain. She wondered what he'd meant earlier by saying he wanted to get away from things too familiar. It seemed there were few people left who were not affected by the awful conflict that had torn the country—and families—apart. He still hadn't fully explained what drove him to come out here in the first place.

"So you bought cattle from a man who had stolen them from outlaws who'd already stolen them from a law-abiding rancher. And it's the first bunch of outlaws who came after you."

Luke nodded. "That's right. Now do you understand the kind of men who live out here?"

"Yes, and it's very disturbing." Kate shivered into her blanket again. "A person doesn't know who can be trusted."

"Exactly." Luke held his cup up to her. "But you can trust me. You ought to know that by now."

Kate shook her head. "I feel like I don't know *anything* anymore."

Luke swallowed more coffee. "Well, to help you a little more, you asked my age. I'm no spring chicken. I'm thirty-five. And no. I'm not married. Never have been."

Kate felt obligated to reply in kind. "I'm no spring chicken either," she told him. "I nursed a sick mother for years and didn't have time for men. I was already twenty-two when I met and married my husband, Rodney Winters. He'd moved from Michigan to our small town in Indiana and opened a supply store. He left two years later for the war. My father went with him because my mother had died, and he wanted to get away from too many memories. Neither of them ever came back. That's when I decided to write Rodney's brother in Oregon." She felt her cheeks flushing at her next remark. "Rodney and I had no children. Now I'm glad, because it would have been difficult trying to raise them on my own."

Luke sighed. "Yeah, well, life can take us in strange directions sometimes." He looked her over. "I have to say, ma'am, that you look a lot younger than you say, but no woman would lie about something like that. And I suspect you're a lot braver than you give yourself credit for. You likely would have found a way to handle a child on your own."

Kate looked away, a bit embarrassed by his compliment but not sure why. *You're a handsome woman,* he'd said. She wasn't quite sure what to think of that remark. "So, what do we do now?" she asked, wanting to change the subject. "I desperately need clothes and to clean up and feel human again."

"We both need that." Luke swallowed the rest of his coffee, then rubbed at his throat.

Kate looked around. "Where is my dress?"

"Draped over that rock behind you. You are right about that dress being a mess, but what's left of it should be dried out by now."

Kate suspected he'd not touched anything he shouldn't when he'd undressed her, but she didn't doubt he'd looked. "I would appreciate it if you turned around while I put my dress back on," she told him. "You might have been the one to take it off, but that doesn't mean I am willing to stand in front of you half-dressed when I am wide-awake."

Luke looked her over appreciatively, which made her even more uncomfortable. "Doesn't make much sense now, but I'll turn around." He did so, and Kate quickly got up and draped her dress over her head. She'd long ago ditched her slips somewhere in the endless valley as she'd walked through it. The slips had only made her even hotter.

Now that Luke Bowden seemed to be getting better, she felt vulnerable and frustrated. She quickly buttoned the front of her dress, her cheeks feeling hot at the thought that the near stranger who sat across the fire had *un*buttoned it while she was passed out.

She sat back down on her bedroll. "Thank you," she told him. "You may turn around now."

Luke obeyed, smiling. He poured himself more coffee and added more whiskey.

"Please be careful with that whiskey," Kate said.

Luke shook his head. "Don't worry." He drank down more. "Lucky for us there were even a couple of extra blankets in here. That's why I could cover you better. I have no idea how clean they are or if they've got bugs in them, but in this weather and this land, you have to make do." He reached around and turned back with a black fry pan in his hand, which he set over the fire. Then he picked up one of two potatoes he'd set on a tin plate near the fire and began slicing it into the pan with his knife. "There's a little lard still in this pan, and lard doesn't spoil, so I guess it will have to do."

He took the bloody, skinned quail from a tin plate nearby and threw it into the pan with the potatoes.

"I plucked the feathers off this guy while you slept," he told Kate. "This bird and one potato each should help fill our bellies. We're running out of biscuits, so we'll save them for tomorrow. I did have a pack horse with a lot more supplies, but those men took that, too, so we have hardly any food. But I have a plan."

"To leave me here?"

Luke nodded. "You can stay here and wait while I leave in the morning and keep following that cattle trail to Lander. They will try to sell those cattle there. I'll find them, get my money and my revenge. Then I'll get us some supplies and bring them back here along with an extra horse and get you out of here to some-place where you can feel like a human being again."

Kate still didn't fully trust him, yet she didn't want him to leave her. "How do I know you'll come back?"

"Because you have my word. I don't break promises, and I have no use for people who do."

Kate watched the potatoes begin to sizzle. "But I won't be safe here. You said outlaws use this cave."

"They do. It's just a chance we have to take. I can travel a lot faster without you along. I'll leave what supplies I have left, and you have blankets and more wood. There's water farther back in this cave that trickles out of the rocks, so you have that, too. And I'll leave you a gun for wolves...or for men, if necessary." Luke glanced at her. "You up to it?"

"Up to shooting a man?"

"Yes ma'am."

"If it means my honor or my life, yes, I could shoot a man. You might want to remember that yourself."

Luke finished slicing the two potatoes and shoved his knife back into its sheath. "Kate, look at it this way. If I was going to take advantage, don't you think I would have done so already?"

"How do I know you didn't?"

"You'd know."

Kate looked away, embarrassed at what he meant by the remark. "The fact remains that you almost died not long ago," she said. "I guess you aren't exactly in any shape to take advantage if you wanted to."

Luke sighed. "Kate, there is a code out here when it comes to how a woman is treated. Most men in these parts respect a good woman. And I'm obligated to you. Rest easy tonight and get any thoughts out of your head about me taking advantage when you were passed out. I just didn't want you taking sick on me. Is that understood?"

Kate met his gaze and saw honesty in his eyes. "Yes." She could tell he was a man who meant what he said. "And I appreciate your help. But I also want you to understand that a woman alone is not totally helpless and unable to survive without a man."

"Seems to me like you *are* a bit helpless and *do* need a man at the moment," Luke answered.

Kate met his gaze. He was smiling again.

"I'm just trying to get a smile out of you, Kate. How many ways can I say I'm here to help, not hurt, and to get you to relax?"

Kate couldn't help but return the smile. "All right. We will change the subject. You keep saying you intend to kill those men. Is it that easy for you? To kill men?"

"Yes, when those men try to kill me first. The war kind of hardened me to killing." He stirred the food once more. "Besides, if those men learn I'm still alive—and they will—they will keep coming after me. I don't intend to have to worry about that."

"You just don't seem like a man who could kill so easily." *The war—or something that happened after that—changed you.*

"Don't underestimate me, Kate. But don't be afraid of me either. I'm fair and good to men who are fair and good to *me*."

Kate nodded. "I think I understand."

"Good. And if you do need to use the gun I leave you, *use* it. Don't think twice about it. There are always the no-goods who just plain don't respect a woman for *any* reason. Sometimes it's kill or be killed out here. Now let's eat and get some sleep. I'll make sure things are set up good for you before I leave in the morning."

Their gazes held, and Kate felt a growing closeness

to the man. "Do you have a family somewhere, Luke? Or a woman waiting somewhere?"

He looked away then and drank more coffee. "Not anymore."

There was the bitterness again.

"War changes a lot of things," he added, all-out anger in the words.

Kate decided not to press the issue. Right now, she didn't relish the thought of sitting alone in this cave in the middle of the most God-forsaken country she'd ever seen, worried about wolves, and not just the four-legged kind. They both remained silent while they watched the potatoes and quail meat turn brown. After a few minutes Luke turned to a gunny sack and took out two forks.

"These have probably been used by somebody else, but we don't have much choice." He handed her one and pulled the pan off the fire. "Let's eat. We can share right out of the pan."

Kate took the fork and stabbed a few slices of potato. "Thank you, Luke, for everything," she said.

He drank a little more coffee. "You can thank me when and if I get us out of this mess."

"I think you will. You seem to be a strong and able man."

"And I got myself hanged." Luke stabbed at the quail meat. "I won't get over that shame until I find those men and make them pay."

"You shouldn't feel ashamed. You could hardly have stopped them. But if it will make you feel better, then I will pray that you find them and get your revenge," Kate told him.

"Well, since you are a Christian woman, I take hope in your prayers," he answered. "Right now, let's finish eating and get some rest. Maybe another whole night of not talking will help my throat feel better. You're welcome to a little of that whiskey if it will help you sleep."

"No. Thank you. I've never tasted that demon drink and do not wish to start. I am worn out enough to sleep just fine."

"No headache? That's a damn big bump on your forehead, and it's purple and topped off with a scabbed cut."

"It doesn't hurt too much. Is Red all right?"

"He's fine."

They finished eating, and Luke made up his own bedroll. "I'm done in," he told Kate. He added some wood to the fire. "It's near dark. Fire should keep the wolves away," he said before lying down and resting his head on his saddle, turning his back to her.

Kate thought how, if nothing more, Luke Bowden was a practical man who knew survival. She turned back to her own bedroll and settled in as the fire snapped and spit bigger flames, the smoke wandering on a draft that pulled it somewhere into the back of the cave to places she decided she'd not bother exploring.

She did not look forward to watching Luke Bowden ride out of her life in the morning. If something happened to him, she would likely die right here in this cave, never to be heard from again in the outside world.

SIX

LUKE URGED RED THROUGH THE DEEP BUT MELTING snow, glad for the fact that the weather had changed yet again, this time for the better. Warmer temperatures returned, and he removed his heavy jacket and tucked it under the rope that held his bedroll. He'd traveled a good twenty miles or more, pushing poor Red almost to the gelding's limit.

He was headed up a steep hill, walls of rock guarding both sides of the awesome, yellow valley that continued on for miles between cliffs and mesas. Big, lonely country it was. He'd grown used to it, and to the kind of men who lived here, most of them as lonely as the land…and as lonely as he was.

He supposed it was time to move on with life, time to get over the war—and Bonnie.

He was surprised to even have such thoughts, and he wondered if it was because of being around Kate Winters. She'd awakened his baser and very neglected needs—that desire to have a woman in his life, have children, get back to living a normal life, if he even knew what was normal anymore. He'd just met Kate and still hardly knew her, yet he found himself worrying about her the way a man would worry about a woman he truly cared about. He felt guilty for leaving her behind in that cave all alone and couldn't forget the look of doubt and fear in her eyes when he left at sunrise. But this way he could get the help and supplies they needed much quicker, and he couldn't buy supplies without money. The men who'd attempted to kill him had robbed him, too, left only a few coins in his pants pocket. He had to get to Lander as fast as possible, and Kate and the travois would slow him down too much. Besides, Red could not have gone on carrying both their weights and pulling more weight behind him. The poor animal would die—and being caught out here with no food and no horse would mean sure death for him and Kate both.

Kate had enough food for about three days, and at least there was a water supply inside the cave. Still, all sorts of dangers lurked for a woman alone in outlaw country. Would she be smart enough to use the gun he'd left behind if she needed to? A woman was more prone to hesitate than a man, and hesitation could cost her in a lot of ways that were as bad or worse than death. He worried about wolves and bears, but he worried more about men.

The woman had grit, and under all that dirt, messed up hair, and torn, dirty dress was a lovely woman. How was he supposed to forget the round, pale breasts he'd seen when he'd removed her dress? He could tell by the slim shape of her legs and hips that she'd be beautiful naked.

"Shit," he muttered. He'd been too long without a woman. He couldn't get her off his mind. She was alone back there at that cave, and what she needed was a hot meal, a warm bath, clean clothes, and a real bed. He'd damn well make sure she got that much, but he couldn't take too much time doing it.

He told himself to stop thinking so much about a woman he barely knew. Once he got help for her, he'd make sure she found a safe way to keep heading west, and they would part ways. It was probably his broken heart that was bringing on these feelings. He reminded himself that maybe even a woman like Kate couldn't be trusted any more than Bonnie. But then Bonnie had been so young. Still, it sure as hell didn't take her long to turn to his brother once he'd left for the war. By the time he got home, she'd married Matt, and they already had two sons. That was five years ago, and it was time to get over it. Still, it wasn't the woman herself he couldn't forget. It was her *betrayal*.

He shook away the thought. He needed to concentrate on matters at hand, and that was finding the men who'd hanged him. He knew he was close. Earlier today he'd come across the fresh remains of a camp, the ground all around trampled to the point where there was no snow left, just wet, scrunched grass. There was no doubt who'd camped there. He was damn close, and the town of Lander was just over this hill. He'd made it here in record time, and he hoped to settle things before dark so he could leave in the morning and get right back to Kate. He never would have reached Lander this soon if he'd not left her behind, and now he owed it to her to waste no time getting back to that cave. The sooner he settled things in Lander, the sooner he could help Kate.

He reached the top of the hill and halted Red. There below, less than a mile in the distance, lay Lander, which was nothing more than a few centered buildings surrounded by a scattering of sheds, houses, and a few other supply businesses. Corrals were spread out all around, full mostly of stolen stock, he was sure. His own cattle were down there somewhere, and if he couldn't get them back, he'd damn well get back the money he'd paid for them. Lucky for him, those men had done a piss-poor job of trying to hang him, but that mistake would be very *un*lucky for them!

He headed down the hill and straight for the corrals, reaching them in about twenty minutes. In the distance he heard the clanging of a blacksmith's maul. A few men moved about, but other than that, the town seemed fairly quiet. It was late afternoon, and he figured most men were already in the saloons.

He led Red in a slow walk around several pens, realizing his herd could be mixed in with others by now. One white-faced Hereford looked the same as the next, except for a young bull he'd named Scout. Scout had an odd black spot shaped like the number seven on his white forehead. He figured the bull would be a good breeder and had paid damn good money for him. If he could find Scout, he'd know the rest of his cattle were here, which meant the men he was after were also here. They would take plenty of time now to relax, visit the bathhouses, and get their fill of whiskey and whores.

"Lookin' for somethin', mister?"

Luke glanced up at a man who sat on a fence with a rifle across his lap, obviously hired to watch for thieves.

"Looking for a young bull that would have been brought in with twenty other cattle yesterday," he answered. "He's easy to pick out—has a black spot on his forehead that looks like the number seven."

"What's it to ya'?"

"That's my business. Have you seen it?"

The guard pushed his hat back a little, then nodded toward a far corral Luke hadn't visited yet. "Over there. How'd you know about him?"

"That's also my business. Thanks for letting me know." Luke turned his horse and rode to the corral the guard had indicated. "I'll be damned," he muttered when he spotted Scout in a pen that separated him from the female stock. A small herd browsed in a nearby corral, some eating feed out of a trough, some lying down in the morning sun. He counted them. Nineteen.

He couldn't believe his luck. He had no doubt they were his. One of the cows had one leg that was far darker than the rest of her body—another mark that helped him identify them. He trotted Red back over to the guard. "Those cattle been sold yet?"

"I don't know. You'll have to ask in town."

"Oh, I'll ask all right." Luke turned Red in the direction of town. *I'll do more than ask.*

"Try the Royal Flush saloon," the cowboy yelled out to him. "That's the most popular stop here."

Luke nodded and headed up the street.

SEVEN

Silence. Nothing else. Kate sat at the edge of the cave, looking out at the unending expanse of red rock that walled the meandering valley ahead. If not for the wind that made the tall grass ripple and sway, it would be like looking at a painting of cliffs and mesas and yellow grass—here and there a boulder or one lonely tree, and no explanation for how they got there.

Did God have fun creating this part of the country? Did he pick up rocks and trees and plants from some-place else and just toss them into the valley and leave them where they landed?

She breathed deeply, longing to be able to wash and brush out her hair, which she'd again pulled back at the sides and secured with combs. She hated feeling so filthy, hated not being able to change her clothes. She couldn't cook because there was nothing to cook. She didn't make a fire because it had warmed up and she didn't want to waste the wood. She couldn't bathe. She couldn't wash these clothes because there wasn't enough water and she had nothing to change into. She couldn't brush down a horse because she *had* no horse. She hadn't even seen any more wild horses since those she saw the day she freed Luke Bowden from a noose around his neck. Nor had she spotted an eagle, or even another quail.

She'd spent a restless night, unable to sleep because she knew Luke would leave this morning for Lander. He'd left at the crack of dawn and should have reached town by now. She worried he wouldn't come back, either on purpose or because he'd be killed today by the men who'd hanged him. That was a distinct possibility and could mean her own death. She'd had no choice but to put her life in the hands of a complete stranger.

Now she worried wolves would come for her tonight. She almost wished they would, because shooting at wolves would give her something to do. Their barks and growls would be music to her ears compared to this utter silence so intense it actually hurt her ears.

Alone was not a strong enough word for this feeling. If only she had something to read, a newspaper, the Bible. She decided to occupy her time by coming up with a word that better fit her situation.

Desolate? Forlorn? Deserted? Isolated? Abandoned?

She touched her sore forehead. The swelling had gone down, but there was a small, scabbed cut there, and she didn't doubt it was bruised. She shook away an urge to scream and began thinking of more words—this time words that described the landscape spread out before her.

Astounding. Breathtaking. Vast. Immense. Magnificent. And again, *desolate.* Desolate seemed to fit both her and the land.

All senses came more alive when she spotted a rider in the distance. She stood up and shaded her eyes to see better. Luke couldn't possibly be returning this soon, unless something had gone wrong. Her heart beat a little faster at the possibilities. Was he a thief? A rustler? A killer? And was he headed for this cave to rest for a day or two? She tried to guess how far away he was, and how much time she had before he would reach the cave, if that was where he was headed. Right now, he was just a dot on the landscape—a dot that was moving in her direction.

She'd learned on the way out here that nothing was ever as close as it seemed, and what looked like distant clouds turned out to be mountains. What looked like water was just a hazy, rippling atmosphere created by heat.

Still, what seemed to be a man riding in her direction now truly did appear to be just what she thought it was. How much time did she have? An hour? Two hours?

Luke, where are you? Is that you coming? Did you change your mind? Maybe he would never come. Maybe he would ride on without her. Why should he bother coming all the way back here, and why did she trust he would? She was no one to him. There would be saloons and other men and gambling and whores where he was going. What man would turn all that down to hurry back to a woman who could die up here and never be missed. Even if she was found, no one would know who she was—or care. She could be thrown over a cliff and left for the wolves and buzzards.

She stepped away from the ledge, afraid the oncoming rider might see her and ride even faster to find out who was in this cave. Maybe he would just ride on by. Yes, that was a possibility! She would hide in here until he was gone.

Then what? More loneliness? More waiting? More maddening silence? For all she knew, he was a decent man who would have food with him and would help her like Luke had. What if Luke never came back and she passed up this chance for help? How could anyone make such choices in a place like this, where everyone a person met was a stranger…and likely an outlaw?

She had no choice but to wait this out and pray the person coming had a heart and decent intentions. If she had to defend herself, she had nothing on her side but the element of surprise—and one six-gun.

EIGHT

Luke longed for a bath and a good meal, but that would have to come later. He headed down the main street of Lander, glancing around cautiously for any man he might recognize, or any who might recognize him in return. The air hung rich with the smell of cow and horse dung, but he'd grown used to such odors out here.

He'd hoped to find his prey before the sun settled behind the mountains, which wouldn't be much longer. Walking around after dark would make his search more difficult, and his own life would be in more danger from a gunshot in the back.

He halted in front of the saloon and dismounted, tying Red to a hitching post out front. He shoved his spare six-gun into his pants belt. He'd given his gun belt to Kate for protection. He untied and opened a saddlebag, pulling out two small drawstring leather bags and hanging them around the pommel of his saddle. He fished into one of them and grabbed a handful of bullets for the spare handgun, shoving them into a pants pocket. He reached into the other bag and pulled out some rifle cartridges, dropping them into his other pants pocket. He yanked his rifle from its boot and mounted the steps to the boardwalk, then stopped to take a deep breath before heading into The Royal Flush. As soon as he was inside, the air changed to a blue haze of smoke with odors of whiskey and cigarettes and unwashed men. Several of those men turned to look at him, all of them probably wondering if the newcomer was someone out to get them, maybe even a brave but stupid lawman.

Luke quickly scanned the room for a familiar face but saw none. Most men were bunched together in groups, every table filled with card players, the bar crowded with drinkers standing amid spittoons, some with booted feet perched on a scraped-up foot rail along the bottom of the long, dark-wood bar.

Fancy-dressed prostitutes mingled with all the men. One woman looked him over and smiled before turning to a handsome, dark-haired man sitting at one of the card tables. He wore all black and looked dangerous. Because the table hid the lower part of his body, Luke couldn't tell if he wore a gun, but if anybody looked the part of gunslinger, this one fit the bill. The saloon girl leaned down and kissed his cheek, but he gently pushed her away. She turned to flirt with a different man.

The man wearing black glanced at Luke, and Luke saw by the look in his eyes that he was someone who didn't miss a thing and who read other men with keen insight. It left no doubt in Luke's mind that the man in black was not one to mess with.

Luke scanned the room once more, then walked up

to the bar and ordered a shot of whiskey. The barkeep set a bottle and a shot glass in front of him, and Luke paid the man, who then filled the shot glass with what Luke hoped wasn't cheap, watered-down firewater. He slugged it down, pleased with the taste, and asked the man for one more shot, which was all he could afford for the moment. He drank that down and asked the bartender about the best restaurant in town.

"Pretty good eatery across the street called Biscuits and Gravy," the man answered. "Opened just a couple of months ago. The owner used to run a restaurant back East, but he got in some kind of trouble. Some say he killed a man he found in bed with his wife. He came out here to get away from the law."

"Haven't *most* men come out here for that reason?" Luke asked.

The barkeep nodded. "Expect so." He glanced toward the table where the dangerous-looking man sat. "That man over there playin' cards—the dark, good-lookin' one—that's Jake Harkner. He's wanted for a lot of things, and he's in a piss-poor mood most of the time on account of he's got a wife and family some place back in California and he misses 'em plenty. He's good to the whores, but he doesn't sleep with them on account of his wife. Least ways, I've never seen him go upstairs with any of them. He can be real sociable, or he can be an ornery son of a bitch and kill a man at the drop of a hat if that man rubs him the wrong way." The barkeep leaned closer. "How about you? You wanted?"

Luke grinned. "Not that I know of. I'm just here looking for some men, but I don't see any of them."

He smiled inwardly, amused at how much a man could learn from a bartender. Most of them knew everyone in town and loved to talk.

"Maybe the men you want are in Atlantic City," the bartender suggested. "It's bigger and only about twenty miles southwest of here."

"No. They're here. I'm sure of it. I'm looking for four men who stole my cattle and money and then tried to hang me." He pulled down the scarf from around his neck, and the bartender's eyes widened.

"Damn, mister, that's a hell of a thing! How come you ain't dead?"

"Long story." Luke looked around again. "I'd like to find those men and pay them back for what they did to me. Those cattle were rightfully mine. I found them in one of the corrals, so I know those men are here, and I aim to repay them for what they did."

"I don't blame you." The bartender put out his hand. "Name's Hank. I'll keep an eye out, but so far the men in here are pretty regular."

"Thanks." Luke turned as someone new walked in. Again, most men in the room warily watched the new man enter. He wore a tan jacket and a badly stained, wide-brimmed hat. He had a full, black beard... and Luke instantly recognized him as one of the men who'd hanged him—his friends had called him George. George had placed the noose around Luke's neck and had been the most adamant about wanting him dead. Luke kept his head down and cautiously watched the man walk inside and sit down at a card table, right next to the outlaw Jake Harkner.

"Shit," he muttered softly. It was one thing to face

down the man called George and something else if the gunman sitting next to him decided to take the wrong side in the showdown. He couldn't believe his luck in finding the man, but maybe it wasn't luck at all, since Jake Harkner could get involved in this.

He pushed his hat back a little, hoping Harkner lived by the rule most obeyed in this country, which was that men in these parts usually let another man take care of his personal beefs without interference. He picked up his rifle and headed for the card table.

The whole room quieted, and every man turned to look when they heard Luke cock his rifle. Luke didn't look at Jake Harkner, but he could feel the man watching him. He figured if he kept his eyes on George, Harkner would realize it was George he was after and wouldn't shoot him "at the drop of a hat," as the barkeep had said the man was known to do.

"Remember me?" Luke asked George as loudly as he could with a sore throat and raspy voice.

Every man at the table ducked away, except Jake Harkner. Men anywhere within Luke's rifle range also headed for the side of the room and out of the way. The whole room grew even more quiet. Jake Harkner still sat calmly at the table.

"Who the hell…?" George frowned, studying Luke for a moment.

"Maybe this will help," Luke told him. He kept the rifle in his right hand, still steadily aimed at George, his finger on the trigger. With his left hand, he untied his neck scarf and tossed it aside, revealing the ugly, still raw scar around his throat.

George's eyes widened. "Jesus Christ, you *lived*?"

"I sure as hell did, you son of a bitch! Get up! I'm not wanting to kill a man still sitting!"

"You goddamn cattle thief!" George shot back, rising.

"*You're* the thief!" Luke kept his eyes on George but raised his voice as loud as possible, in spite of the pain it caused him. "This man and three others tried to hang me!" he told the rest of the men in the room. "I bought a few head of cattle from a rancher south of here and paid good money for them! I didn't know till this man and his bunch caught up with me that those cattle were stolen from them. Him and his friends killed the man I bought my cattle from and stole my money from him, then came after me and accused *me* of stealing them. They *hanged* me, just for the fun of it, but they did a piss-poor job of it. If it wasn't for somebody who came along and cut me down, I *would* be dead!"

He glared at George the entire time he spoke.

"A man doesn't soon forget a *rope* around his neck choking him to death. I don't mean any man here any harm. But I intend to kill this man and his friends and get my money back."

"You ain't gonna kill me, you motherfucker! You ain't got the right! Where's the proof you paid for those cattle?"

"In my right coat pocket."

George grinned. "You'll have to put that rifle down to find it, you lyin' bastard. And before you reach in that pocket, I'll *shoot* you."

"No, you won't." The words came from the gunman called Jake, who still sat calmly in his chair.

"This might be outlaw country, mister, but we still have a code out here of what's right and wrong. You go for that gun, and this man standing here won't *need* to kill you. *I'll* do it."

George glanced at Jake. He swallowed nervously. "I know who you are, mister. You're a professional killer, and I ain't drawin' on you. But you ought to stay out of this. It ain't your business."

"Well I'm *making* it my business," Harkner answered. "I'm not real fond of vigilante-type hangings." He looked up at Luke. "Go ahead and take out that receipt," he said.

For some reason Luke trusted Harkner without even looking at him. Keeping his eyes on George, he put down his rifle and reached into his pocket, handing the receipt to his right. Jake took it and looked it over while Luke picked up his rifle again.

"Looks legitimate to me," Harkner announced loud enough for everyone to hear. "This is a receipt for the sale of twenty head of cattle to a Luke Bowden, signed by a Casey Link. Anybody in here know the man?"

"*I* do!" came a voice from the balcony behind Luke.

It all happened at once then.

George went for his gun.

Luke fired his rifle.

At the same time there came a loud boom from the right. Jake Harkner had drawn and fired. Luke whirled, and a man's half-naked body came crashing down onto a card table behind him, splitting the tabletop and sending money, cards, and drinks flying. A naked woman who'd been standing near the man on the balcony screamed and fled back into her room, slamming the door shut.

The barroom remained quiet, the men backed away. Luke turned to face Jake Harkner, whose gun was still smoking. Harkner rose and calmly put the gun back into his holster. He grinned when he faced Luke. "Must have been one of his friends. You need help finding the other two?"

"Could be. The person who cut me down was a woman. She's waiting for me in a cave about twenty miles south of here and is in bad need of food and clothing, plus she's hurt from a fall. I can't waste any time getting back to her."

Jake frowned and picked up Luke's receipt, handing it back to him. "Then let's go find the other two and get your money back. You don't want to be leaving a woman out there alone."

Luke shoved the receipt into his pocket. "Why in hell are you helping me?"

Jake took a cigarette from a pocket on his shirt. "Because I know how it feels to worry about a woman who might be needing your help." He lit his cigarette with a large match that burst into about a six-inch-long flame when he flicked it with his fingernail. "Go look at the man I shot. Make sure he was one of them. I'll rummage the pockets of this one here by the card table."

Others in the saloon began moving back to their chairs as though the shooting was just an everyday matter to be ignored, while those whose table had been destroyed by the body that had fallen into it began scraping up cards and money. One of them dragged the dead man's body over to the side of the

room and left it there as though it was just a piece of
trash. Luke knelt closer to study the dead man's face.
An ugly hole gaped right in the middle of his forehead.
Thank God Harkner had sided with me, he thought. He
recognized a big, dark mole near the man's chin. He
was definitely one of those who'd tried to hang him.

"This is one of them," Luke told Harkner. He
remembered that one of the other two men who'd
hanged him was Mexican, and the fourth one was
older, with white hair and beard, and a patch over one
eye. He wore a red vest that looked new. He should
be easy to spot.

"Somebody get those damn bodies out of my
saloon!" the bartender barked.

Harkner, as tall and broad-shouldered as Luke,
reached for a long black duster that hung on the wall
behind him and pulled it on, then took a black, wide-
brimmed hat from the same wall. "How many more
are there for sure?" he asked Luke.

"Two," Luke answered.

"Let's go," Jake put his hat on and turned to a
shorter and slimmer, nice-looking man standing against
the wall. "Come with us, Jess," he told the man.

"I don't never turn down a chance to see Jake
Harkner in action," the man answered. He looked at
Luke and put out his hand. "Name's Jess York. What's
yours?"

"Luke Bowden."

Jess nodded. "Let's go get the other two, Bowden."

Luke walked out with the two men, wondering at
the fact that he'd just killed a man with no feelings of
regret. He'd killed plenty of men in the war, but that

was different. Seemed like he should feel bad about killing one point-blank, but he didn't. Jake Harkner also seemed unaffected by shooting the man on the balcony, even though he wasn't even a part of what had happened to Luke. Apparently, he figured it was just something that needed doing.

Luke supposed most men in these parts felt that way. A man rubs you wrong, you shoot him and go on about your business. He never thought he would end up living this way, but the war, and the horror of being hanged, had hardened his heart. In lawless country, it was every man for himself.

NINE

AN HOUR. IT FELT AT LEAST THAT LONG SINCE KATE first spotted the rider heading in her direction—just a speck then, but now much, much closer. He'd stopped for a while, but she wasn't sure why. She could tell that he was definitely headed for the cave. It was a climb up a grassy slope to get here, but it was not difficult. He'd be here within ten minutes.

She'd not fully shown herself at the entrance, hoping he would just ride on by. That wasn't possible now. This was a shallow cave, and in exploring the back of it for ways to hide, she'd discovered it went only a few feet beyond the wall where water trickled down. The stranger would certainly want the water. Beyond that area, the ceiling sloped downward and was too low and shallow to be livable, as well as impossible for hiding from whoever was coming. She would have to face her intruder squarely and hope for the best.

She grabbed Luke's gun belt and put it over her shoulder, then stood against the side of the cave opening and waited, gun in hand. She soon heard a horse's hooves clattering against the rocky ground just outside. Her chest tightened with dread. She would be lucky if Luke returned by tomorrow, so anything that happened now was up to her.

If you need to use that gun, use it, Luke had told her. *Don't hesitate. Sometimes out here it's kill or be killed.*

Kate didn't doubt that in her case, she could be defending herself against something worse than death. She heard a man cough—the loose, wheezing kind of cough some older men made when they'd smoked too much all their lives. Her throat went dry and she felt warm all over from nervousness and fear when she heard the clink of spurs as a man walked around outside a moment.

"I'll get you some water, girl."

The man's voice was deep, and Kate guessed by the sound of it that he was perhaps around fifty years old. She held the six-gun out straight, waiting for him to walk in. She heard more footsteps, more clinking of spurs, and then he entered the cave. He didn't notice her at first, but rather headed for the water at the back of the cave. Kate noticed he wore a gun. Moments later he came out carrying a hat full of water. It was then he noticed Kate.

They just stared at each other a moment. The man was dusty from the long ride, and old sweat stains showed on the underarms of his shirt and around his neck. He looked about the age Kate had guessed, and like most other men in these parts, he needed a bath and a shave.

The man slowly lowered the hat full of water and set it on the floor, then rose with his hands up. "Who the hell are you?"

Kate swallowed and used both hands to keep the
gun steady. "Kate Winters. My husband and I are
using this cave," she lied. "He went hunting and will
be back soon."

The man grinned. "That so?"

"Yes."

He put his hands on his hips and looked her over.
"I figured I might come upon another man out here,
but I sure as hell didn't figure on a woman. You
should have greeted me at the entrance so's I knew
you was here. You're damn lucky I was carryin' that
water for my horse, lady, or I might have drawed on
you the minute I spotted you. It ain't wise for a person
holdin' a gun to surprise a man in these parts. We're
all pretty jumpy, you know."

"No. I *don't* know. I only know that my husband
will be back soon and we will be on our way. We
mean no man any harm. We just saw this cave and
decided to use it for a couple of nights, so you need
to leave."

"Oh, really?" the man asked mockingly. "You
gonna' shoot me if I don't?"

"I just might!"

"*Might?*" The man sighed and shook his head.
"Look, lady, when you pull a gun on a man, you
either shoot him or you don't. There ain't no *might*
about it. Now, I've been ridin' all day. Me and my
horse need to rest, and I don't mean you no harm. Let
me take this water to my horse, and let me at least sit
over there by your fire for a while. I'll make myself
somethin' to eat, and if you'll allow, drink some of
your coffee, and then I'll sleep outside just for tonight

and be on my way in the mornin'. Are you really gonna' deny a man a little food and rest?"

Kate thought a moment. This man could be as harmless as Luke had been. Shouldn't she give him a chance? It wasn't in her blood to be so rude. Still, Luke had told her not to hesitate using her gun if she had any doubts at all. "You can make your own fire outside."

The man scowled. "Aw, come on, ma'am. You already have a perfectly good fire there, and you said yourself your husband would be back soon. I don't mean you no harm, honest to God. I'm just tired and hungry and want some sleep."

Kate studied his eyes. He seemed sincere. "At least take off your gun belt and leave it here with me," she told him. "And if you walk back in here with a rifle from your gear, I'll shoot you."

The man shook his head and scowled, as though defeated. "Deal," he answered. He unbuckled his gun belt and tossed it across the fire. It landed on the other side of Kate's bedding. "Thank you," he said. "My name is Buck. Just Buck." He leaned down and picked up his hat full of water, glancing at Kate's revolver again before heading out of the cave to water his horse.

Kate lowered her gun, which had begun to feel heavier and heavier. She walked over to the fire and took Luke's gun belt from her shoulder, feeling as though she'd lifted a hundred pounds from her neck. She sat down to wait, wondering how on earth she and the stranger called Buck were going to spend the rest of the day and night together. She realized now that she would have to come up with an excuse for when it got dark and Buck realized her "husband" wasn't coming back tonight at all. She decided she'd tell the man her husband had said he might spend one night away if he had to ride too far to find game. *But he could show up any time,* she would warn. Deep inside she'd like nothing better than to see Luke Bowden come back sooner than expected. Now she would have to try to stay awake all night. Then again, if wolves came snooping around, Buck could help her fend them off. She could end up glad she'd let him stay after all.

She hated being constantly afraid and never knowing who to trust. Maybe she couldn't even trust Luke to come back. It irritated her that Buck had come along at all. How likely was it that one lone man would happen by in this great big country and decide to use this one cave set amid a vast valley that stretched for hundreds of miles?

Just as likely as you and Luke coming upon it, she thought. Fate was fate.

Buck came back inside with his saddle over his shoulder and plunked it down with a thud. Kate kept hold of Luke's gun, resting it in her lap as she watched him. He'd brought no rifle with him.

"That coffee hot?" he asked.

"Yes. But I have nothing else to offer," she answered, her stomach beginning to pain her because of hunger. She had one biscuit left. "My husband and I were attacked. Everything was taken, so we don't even have food. That's why he went hunting." She hoped that if she kept talking about a husband who could return at any time, it would keep Buck at bay in case he was having wrong thoughts.

Buck dropped a leather supply pack near the fire and sat down across from her, then picked up a tin cup and poured himself a cup of coffee. Before he drank it, he reached into the supply pack and took out a flask of whiskey. He uncorked it and poured some of it into the coffee, glancing slyly at Kate. "A man needs a little whiskey after a long, hard ride," he told her. He drank down the coffee and whiskey in one gulp, then poured straight whiskey into the cup. "You know, somethin' don't add up," he said. "You look damn thin and hungry and tattered. No man around. No sign of any kind of supplies at all, other than what you probably found in this cave and that one supply pack nearby...and that gun." He slugged down the second cup of whiskey. "I don't think you have a husband at all, lady. Could be you're some whore a man brought out here with him for a good time, then abandoned once he was done with you."

Kate stiffened. "You are very wrong. It's like I told you. We were attacked and lost everything, wagon and all. We had one horse left, and my husband used it to go hunting. Surely you saw the fresh horse dung outside."

Buck nodded. "I saw, but that could have been left by the cowpoke who brought you here and got his jollies, then left."

Kate kept hold of her revolver and lifted it a little. "Believe what you want. Just know that I am a respectable woman who knows how to use this gun. If you want food, you'll have to get it from your own supplies or go hunt for it, like my husband is doing right now."

Buck chuckled and shook his head, pouring himself

a third cup of whiskey. "Whatever you say, lady. Seems to me you talk about your husband a bit too much, which makes me think there *ain't* no husband. What's his name?"

"Luke. Luke...Winters," Kate told him, remembering she'd already told the man her own last name. "We were on our way to northern California."

Buck slugged down the third cup of whiskey. "Too late for that. It's already snowin' up in the Sierras. You'll have to hole up someplace out here for the winter."

"We already know that."

Buck leaned closer over the fire and grinned, showing crooked, yellowed teeth. "Could be your husband, if he really exists, is runnin' from the law. That's how it is for most men out here. Why else would he just now be comin' through country like this so late in the year, tryin' to make it to California? What did he do that the law is after him?"

"Whether he is running from the law or not is none of your business. And I do not appreciate you getting drunk," Kate told him.

Buck poured himself more whiskey. "Well now, ain't that just like a woman, tryin' to tell a man what to do." He slugged down the drink. "I had a wife once who did that. I got tired of her bitchin' and I slugged her." He set the flask aside and looked Kate over again in that way that told a woman what a man was thinking. "Trouble is, I slugged her a little bit too hard, and she went and died on me. That's what brought me out here. I'm wanted back in Missouri for killin' her. What do you think of that?"

"I think I made a bad decision letting you stay

here. I think you're a reprehensible, despicable, filthy-minded murderer, and that maybe I should shoot you. My husband can bury you when he gets here."

Buck leaned his head back and let out a loud guffaw, then poured coffee into the cup rather than whiskey. Kate could hardly stand the sight of his teeth as he grinned broadly at her. She noticed then that several of his lower teeth were missing.

"I guess maybe then I should drink more of this coffee and sober up, huh?" he asked. "Whiskey tends to make a woman, any woman, look pretty good to a man, even one as untidy and unpleasant and bossy and skinny as you."

Kate felt all her nerves tingle with rage and dread. "And a woman would *need* whiskey to put up with the likes of you!"

Buck laughed again and poured another cup of hot coffee. In the next second, he threw it at Kate, catching her completely off-guard. She let out a scream as the hot water burned her cheek, neck, and shoulder. She instinctively knew the man was diving at her. She fired the six-gun, not even aiming it or knowing if she'd hit anything. Something heavy fell across her. She smelled whiskey breath and felt whiskers scraping her neck and cheek. Buck's body was on top of hers, and her gun was caught flat under his belly.

"Get off me!" she screamed.

"Ain't no man who hunts this late, lady. You're lyin' about havin' a husband, and I aim to poke you 'til sunrise, you fuckin' whore!" Buck growled the words, pushing his hand hard between her legs while he slobbered at her neck.

Desperate, Kate pulled the trigger on the six-gun, even though she couldn't raise and aim it. Buck jerked and grunted, and at the same time, Kate felt pain in her left leg.

Buck rolled off her. "What the hell!" he screamed. He raised up a little and looked down at blood quickly soaking his shirt at his belly. "You shot me!"

Ignoring the pain in her leg and her burned skin, Kate managed to jump up and away from him. "I told you I would, you filthy pig!" she screamed. "Get out of here! Get out!"

Buck got to his knees and tried to get up. "I...can't! You gut-shot me, you...bitch! You rotten bitch!" He reached for his own gun that still lay nearby where he'd tossed it. Kate fired again. A hole opened in the man's chest, close to where Kate guessed his heart would be. Buck never got a chance to pull his gun from its holster. He just froze in place for a moment, staring at her.

"I...didn't think...you'd do it," he muttered.

"You thought wrong, mister." Kate stood there shaking as she watched the life go out of him. Eyes wide, Buck finally slumped over in death.

Kate dropped her gun and grasped her stomach, looking at the man called Buck in disbelief. She'd just killed him. In that moment, she felt no better than Buck or Luke or any other outlaw in this country. In her mind, she'd become one of them.

TEN

LUKE SEARCHED TWO MORE SALOONS AND A BROTHEL for the other two men who'd hanged him. Jake and Jess followed him, watching out for back shooters. Every place they went, the women seemed to know Jake Harkner well.

"I thought you were married," Luke joked.

"I am, and my wife is the best damn woman who ever walked this earth," Harkner told him. He headed out the door of the brothel ahead of Luke. "But I was raised by women like the ones in that brothel. They often protected me from my father whenever the rotten son of a bitch tried to kill me, and that was pretty often."

"Yeah?" Luke asked. "What happened to him?"

Jake didn't look his way. "I finally ended up killing him instead, and that's something I'd rather not discuss. Let's go try The Shooter saloon. Maybe the men you want will be there."

All three men walked across the street, and Luke decided he'd better stay away from the subject of Jake and his father, since he'd been warned by the barkeep

and now by Jake himself. He figured nothing he heard
about the doings of men in outlaw country should
surprise him, and right now he had his own killing to
do. He knew it should bother him, but it didn't, so he
figured he was no better than Harkner.

The three men stepped up on the boardwalk in
front of The Shooter, and Jake leaned against a wall to
light another cigarette. "We'll go in and let you look
around," he told Luke. "You do what you have to do,
and Jess and I will back you up."

"I can't thank you enough," Luke told both men.
"Like I said, this helps me get back to Kate faster."

"That's the name of the woman you left back at
that cave?" Jess asked.

Luke nodded. "Kate Winters."

"That woman is the reason we're helping you," Jake
told him. "No woman alone is safe in country like this."

"I know that. She's already been through hell. She
was lost and looking for help when she came upon
those men hanging me. She hid till they left, then cut
me down. I didn't have any choice but to leave her
behind early this morning so I could travel faster and
get the supplies we need, but I need my money back
so I can afford the supplies. She'll starve to death if I
don't get right back to her."

Jake finished his cigarette and crushed it under his
boot. "I left California because of a shoot-out that got
a little too much publicity—decided my wife and kid
were better off without me around for a while. Soon
as I can find a job some place where no one knows
me, I'll be able to send for them." He gave Luke a
dark look of warning. "Look, Bowden, once we part

ways, you never saw me. *Remember* that. I'm wanted
back East."

"Harkner, if you help me find these men and get
my money back, why would I do anything to bring
you harm?"

"Because there's money on my head."

"I'm not a man to judge, and from what I saw back
there of how you handle a gun, I'm not about to get
on your bad side."

Jake nodded. "Just making sure we understand each
other." He looked toward the swinging doors that led
into The Shooter, then looked back at Luke. "If we
find the other two men, do *you* want them, or do you
want *me* to handle it? I'm not particularly fond of men
who would hang someone for no good reason."

"*I* want them, unless something happens and you
have no choice, like that guy on the balcony in that
saloon. You saved my life back there."

"I've had my share of being accused of things I
didn't do," Jake answered. "If I can help somebody
else in the same fix, I'll do it."

"Let's go," Jess told Luke.

The three men headed to the doors of the saloon
and charged through. There were only five or six men
inside, and they turned to look at the newcomers.

"Look around," Jake told Luke. "Do you see either
one of the other two men?"

Jess and Luke held rifles ready as Luke studied
each man. They all stared back warily, and one man
moved his hand to his sidearm. Just that quickly, Jake
Harkner's handgun was drawn and pointed directly at
the one who'd started to draw.

"Jesus, you're fast," Luke muttered to Jake.

"Any man who makes too quick a move for his gun goes down!" Jake announced to everyone inside. "No questions asked."

Jess and Luke held rifles ready.

"This here is Jake Harkner," Jess announced. "That should be enough to make all of you hesitate."

Every man in the place moved his hand away from his gun.

"Go on upstairs," Jake told Luke. "Jess, go with him. I'll keep an eye on the men down here."

"Sure."

Luke hurried up the stairs and Jess followed. Luke kept his rifle ready as he began kicking in doors. A woman screamed, "Get the hell out of here!"

"Sorry, ma'am," Luke shouted at the woman who was just getting into bed with a man Luke didn't recognize.

"Can't a man have his daily poke in peace?" the man yelled.

Luke left the door open and walked to the next, kicking that one open also. No one was in the room.

He hurried to a third room and kicked yet another door open. A man wearing an eye patch rolled off the bed. He reached up to grab a six-gun from the bed table, but Luke raised his rifle and fired first. A hole opened in the man's chest. He just sat there for a moment, naked and bleeding, his one good eye wide with shock.

"You...son of a bitch!" he groaned. "How'd you...?" His eye rolled backward until Luke saw only white as the man slumped all the way to the floor. The woman in the bed who never even screamed just sat staring at Luke, a sheet pulled up to her neck.

Luke turned to see Jess standing behind him. "He was one of them—wore an eye patch." He nodded toward a bed post, where a red vest hung neatly. "I recognize the eye patch and that red vest."

"One to go," Jess said with a grin.

Luke walked to the next door to see a man ducking out a window just as he kicked in the door. Luke turned and charged past Jess and down the stairs. "He went out a back window!" Luke yelled to Jake as he ran out the door. Jess was on his heels, and Jake joined them.

"Go around to the right!" Jake told Jess as they headed outside. Jake ran around the left side of the building, and the men reached an alley behind the saloon to see a man ducking around the corner of a supply store.

The chase was on. Luke headed back toward the street while Jess and Jake followed the man down a side alley. By then, other men had come outside to watch the fracas. Luke saw a man dart into the street. "Hold it!" he shouted, wanting to be sure he had the right man.

The runner turned and fired. A bullet whizzed past Luke's ear, and he saw long black hair and a black vest. It was him! The man started running again, and Luke raised his rifle. "Turn and shoot, you son of a bitch!" he yelled.

The man kept running. Luke decided he didn't want to have to worry about the man coming after him later, maybe while Kate was with him. He took aim and fired, hitting him in the back just as Jake and Jess came running into the street from a side alley.

Luke lowered his rifle, and they hurried toward the body that had fallen facedown. The outlaw suddenly rolled onto his back and sat up, aiming his gun at Luke, who raised his rifle again. Someone else's gun boomed before he could fire, and a hole opened up in the outlaw's head. Luke turned to Jake, a little taken aback by the very dark look in Jake's eyes. Yes, he had the heart of a killer.

Jake holstered his six-gun. "Go on back to those rooms at The Shooter and get your money from their belongings."

"Thanks for handling him," Luke told Jake.

Jake shook his head. "Your bullet did the job. He was already dying when he sat up and tried to shoot back. My bullet just finished him off faster." Jake lit yet another cigarette.

"I thank you for your help, and I hope you find a job and can rejoin your wife," Luke told him. He put out his hand, and Jake shook it.

"I miss her like hell," Jake said. He squeezed Luke's hand tightly. "It's a rough life out here, Bowden, so be on the lookout, and don't hesitate to use that rifle. You seem to be pretty good with that thing."

"My pa and I did a lot of hunting together back in the day."

A darkness came into Jake's eyes, and he let go of Luke's hand. "Sounds like you had a good father. My own father was born of Satan's blood." He adjusted his hat and turned to head for The Royal Flush. "I wish you luck, Bowden. I have a card game to get back to, before the other men at that table make off with my money."

Luke shook his head. "Do you really think any man would dare to steal from you?" he shouted as Jake walked away.

Jake just laughed and kept walking. Luke watched after him, thinking how the man had helped him as though it was merely all in a day's work. He headed back to The Shooter, thinking how people…strangers…moved in and out of a man's life—here today and gone tomorrow, especially in this country, where figuring out which of those men could be trusted was just guesswork. Men out here might help you one day and shoot you the next.

So far today he'd had a good run of luck, but it might not be that way for Kate. He had to get back to that cave.

ELEVEN

Kate refused to look at her left leg, as though not looking at it would help the pain. There were other things to be done before she gave in to the injury she'd suffered when she shot Buck. She ignored the horror she felt over killing a man, knowing only that she had to get his dead body out of the cave before it was too dark to see.

In spite her wounded leg, she pulled on her floppy, worn-out shoes, pretending her bloody leg couldn't be all that badly wounded. She grimaced and cried out as she pulled on the left shoe, wondering if there was a bullet in her leg or if it had just skimmed across her shin and taken a good deal of flesh with it. Fighting the terror that she could be bleeding to death, she reached down and lifted Buck's legs, turning to face away from him so she could drag him behind her. She positioned his booted feet under her arms and started walking, pulling his body to the cave entrance and then outside.

Buck's horse still had a bridle on, so she limped into the cave and took a rope from Buck's saddle. She walked back outside and tied the rope around the man's ankles, then around the horse's neck. She took hold of the reins and led the horse down the steep embankment to the grassier ground below, grasping the horse's mane at times to keep her own balance. She could feel blood in her shoe, and it was becoming more and more difficult to walk.

She continued leading the horse as far away from the cave entrance as she could stand to walk. She untied the rope from Buck's ankles, leaving his dead body behind as she guided the horse near the cave. She hung on to the animal's neck and let it help her back up the steep hill. She managed to find a scrubby little pine tree not far from the cave entrance and tied the horse to that, realizing she would need it if Luke didn't return. Feeling light-headed, she stumbled back inside the cave and struggled to keep her senses as she rummaged through Buck's supplies.

She took comfort in knowing that at least now she had a little food and some extra blankets. Surely Buck had a change of clothes in his saddlebags. Maybe somehow she could use those, too. A canteen lay near his saddle, so she could also carry more water.

She rifled through the man's saddlebags and found a clean shirt. Tired of feeling so filthy, she stripped off her dress and threw it aside, then removed her camisole and her pantaloons. She used the canteen to pour water over her burned skin, then over her entire body, giving her at least a little relief from the dirt and sweat she'd longed to bathe off. She poured more around her neck, down over her privates and to her bloody leg, squinting at the pain and still refusing to look at it.

Shivering, she pulled on the clean shirt, reveling in

how good it felt just to be wearing something clean. The shirt hung down to the middle of her thighs, covering what needed to be covered. She rolled up the sleeves, then took the combs from her hair, bent her head over and poured water into her hair for yet another bit of bathing and cooling off. She tossed her head back and pulled her hair tighter at the sides, securing it again with the combs. She glanced at her filthy clothes lying in a pile on the cave floor. She wanted to burn them, but she would instead need to wash them somehow and save them in case Luke didn't come back.

The pain from the bullet wound and from her burns was becoming dreadfully worse. She limped over to Buck's saddle and the bedroll he'd unpacked, and dragged them close to the fire. She managed to spread out the bedroll over her own blankets to make her bed a little softer against the hard cave floor. She pulled Buck's saddle close to the blankets so she could use it to rest her head against, then collapsed onto the bedroll, wondering if she would simply lie here and bleed to death tonight.

The pain and the trauma of her ordeal began to wash over her in a wave of deep depression and weariness. She climbed inside the bedroll, wrinkling her nose at the smell of an unwashed man. She'd killed that man point-blank. And now here she was, half-naked, her leg bleeding and probably swelling, her skin on fire. She crawled into the dead man's bedroll for warmth…and she was alone. So utterly alone. She decided that if Luke didn't make it back by tomorrow, she would have to find a way to wash her clothes and dress...and leave this place. If other men came along, she would surely be raped and murdered...or maybe they would hang her for killing the man called Buck. Hang her, as Luke had been hanged.

Maybe Luke was no longer even alive. Maybe he'd found those men and they had killed him. Her leg was getting worse by the minute. Maybe whoever came to this cave next would find her dead and just drag her out to bury her along with Buck.

She lay back, resting her head on Buck's saddle, longing to eat but too weak to fish around for food. She would do that later. First, she had to sleep. She closed her eyes, remembering. She'd killed a man and dragged his dead body out for the buzzards to take care of. God would surely send her to Hell for it. She burst into tears, then felt the need to scream. She screamed as loud as she could, over and over, begging God to forgive her for killing a man, then begging Him to please bring Luke back.

Finally, everything went black...a blessed blackness in which she felt no more pain. Her last thought was to not worry about wolves. The dead man's body below the cave entrance would distract them for the night.

TWELVE

LUKE GUESSED THE TIME TO BE FOUR OR FIVE O'CLOCK in the afternoon. It wouldn't be long before the sun dropped behind the mountains, and things would get dark fast. He'd ridden poor Red almost nonstop since it was barely light enough to see back in Lander, determined to reach Kate as soon as possible. He towed a riding horse for Kate, as well as two pack horses for carrying the supplies he'd purchased. He'd sold his cattle to a butcher in Lander, but he kept Scout. The valuable young bull was tied to the back of the pack horses and ambled along behind, last in line after the horses.

He had his money back plus what he got for the cattle...everything he needed for a new start in the spring. But first he had to get back to Kate and bring her to Lander to hole up for the winter. He was pleased about how much food he had, including bacon and beef packed in lard to preserve the meat.

He and Kate would have plenty of flour, sugar, and salt, as well as potatoes and even some dried apples. He also had plenty of medical supplies, a big bag of oats as an extra treat for the horses, and two small barrels of water plus four filled canteens. He'd brought along plenty of blankets, soap and towels, two dresses and a coat for Kate—a heavy, dark-blue winter wool coat with big white buttons. He was sure a woman like Kate would like it. He'd also bought her a sky-blue shawl for days that were just a little cool. The color would match her eyes.

A woman named Esther, who owned a clothing store, helped him pick out pantaloons and a camisole for Kate, and he smiled at the memory of how embarrassed Esther had been when helping him guess Kate's size. Thinking about it made him remember how slim and pretty Kate was when he'd taken off her dress in that cave after she got wet.

Maybe he *should* have seen a woman before he'd left Lander, because he still couldn't get the sight of Kate's slender legs and perfect breasts off his mind. He had no business thinking about Kate Winters in any way but as a stranger who needed help. She certainly deserved anything he could do for her, after saving him from that awful hanging.

No more being cold and hungry, he thought, getting anxious to show Kate all these supplies and let her finally bathe and change her clothes. He was within a half mile of the cave, but he drew Red to a halt when he noticed buzzards circling something below the cave.

"What the hell?"

Kate! What in God's name had happened? Circling buzzards nearly always meant a dead body. Was it Kate?

"God, no!" How would he forgive himself if he reached the cave to find Kate dead? He felt guilty enough having to leave her, but if something awful had happened while he was gone...

He kicked Red into a faster lope, but the horse was slow because it dragged three more horses and Scout behind him. After going only a few hundred feet, Luke halted Red and dismounted, then tied the first pack horse to a small pinion pine. Each horse behind that one was tied to the next, so all the animals were secure for now. He mounted Red and urged the horse into a full run. He reached the area below the cave where he'd seen the buzzards and realized they were snacking on a body. When the ugly carnivorous birds squawked and dived at him, Luke pulled his spare six-gun and began shooting at them, killing four and chasing the rest away, at least for the moment.

"Filthy bastards!" he yelled at them. He shoved the gun back into his belt and dismounted, keeping hold of Red's reins, afraid the smell of death would scare the gelding away. Red whinnied and tossed his head. "It's okay, boy." Luke walked closer to the already-bloated body to see it was a man, his eyes pecked out. "Jesus," he muttered at the gruesome sight.

What had happened here? He glanced up at the cave and saw no one. "Kate!" he screamed. There came no reply. He saw a horse at the entrance and realized it must belong to the dead man. How in God's name had the body ended up down here? He looked a little closer to see what appeared to be a deep graze down over the man's belly, but he couldn't tell what had caused it. A wound in his chest was definitely a bullet hole.

"My God!" he muttered. What had Kate been through?

He quickly mounted Red and pulled his rifle from its boot, kicking the horse into a fast climb to the cave entrance. Keeping his rifle ready, he dismounted. He glanced at the extra horse, a mare that had no brand and no saddle. She still wore a bridle and looked hungry and thirsty. He patted the horse's rump. "I'll take care of you in a minute, girl."

Keeping a close watch on the cave entrance, he kept gun in hand and carefully approached.

"Kate?"

No reply.

He ducked inside, letting his eyes adjust to the much dimmer light. "Oh my God!" he muttered. There lay Kate, partially covered by a bedroll, her head on a saddle. She looked thin and ashen. He looked around to see her clothes lying in a pile next to what looked to be the supply packs and saddlebags that likely belonged to the dead man.

"Kate!" Luke set his rifle aside and knelt beside her, noticing the left side of her face looked scalded. She stirred as he pulled away the top blanket of the bedroll. She wore a man's shirt. Had the man stripped and raped her, then made her put on the shirt?

He pulled the blanket completely off to see Kate's left hand also looked burned. Her legs were bare, even her thighs, which meant she wore no pantaloons.

"Son of a bitch!" he swore. This was just what he'd dreaded finding. He noticed her left leg was dark and swollen. He grasped Kate's shoulders and shook her lightly. "Kate! What happened, honey?"

She stirred more and opened her eyes, then slugged

Luke in the face and continued swinging wildly as she sat up. "Get away! Get away from me, you bastard!"

Luke grasped her wrists and forced her arms down to her sides. "Jesus, Kate! It's *me*. Luke. It's okay."

She struggled a moment longer, then finally focused. "Luke?"

"Yes, honey, it's me," he answered. "What the hell happened here?"

Kate sucked in her breath in an odd gasp and reached out to throw her arms around his neck. "Luke!" She burst into tears. "I thought you abandoned me. I thought you weren't coming back."

Luke sat all the way down and pulled her onto his lap. "Hell, I said I would, Kate. I told you I don't break my promises. I came fast as I could. I nearly killed poor Red with the ride to Lander and back."

"Don't go away again. Don't leave me here."

"I won't. I have lots of supplies, Kate. Clothes, blankets, medical supplies, food and water. You just need to lay back down and let me go get everything."

"No! Don't go!"

"Honey, everything is just below the hill. I just have to walk down to the pack horses and bring them up here. I promise it won't take me more than ten minutes."

"He might come back!"

"Who? That man below? He's dead, Kate. He's not coming back."

She began crying harder. "I shot him! I shot him! Luke, I killed a man. He was unarmed. Now I'm an outlaw, too! They might hang me like they did you."

Luke held her tighter. "Nobody is going to hang

you. I promise. For God's sake, Kate, it was self-defense. Anybody can see that. And out here, there is no law to say any different. I'll bury that man out there as soon as I can. I'm guessing he's a no-good drifter that nobody cares about, so nobody will be looking for him or ever miss him."

"He threw hot coffee on me. And he tried to…" She pulled away a little, shaking. "He was…on top of me, and I…shot him! I *had* to, Luke. The gun was between us. The bullet went into his belly and on down over my leg. Then I shot him again. I didn't really mean to kill him. I just wanted him to stay away!" She looked at her leg. "Luke, my leg. It hurts something awful. I finally fell asleep…but now that I'm awake…" She looked around. "Oh, dear God! It's light out. It must have all happened yesterday. I've been passed out this whole time."

Luke kept one arm around her. "You just calm down and save all the explaining for later, all right? First thing we need to do is take care of that leg. It looks pretty bad. I've seen wounds like that in the war. I'll have to clean it up—drain any infection you might have, and bandage it. And you need to eat something as soon as possible."

"Are you really here to stay?"

Luke saw the frightened, pleading look in her eyes. "I'm here to stay."

"Did you find those men?"

"We'll talk about that later." Luke stroked strands of her red hair away from her face, thinking what pretty blue eyes she had. "I'm damn sorry about all of this, Kate. You just lay back down here while I go get the supplies. I have some fresh cornbread with me. I'll come back and you can eat some while I make a fire and some coffee and let you rest a little bit before I take care of that leg. We'll talk about what to do next once we get you situated. I even brought you two dresses and some underthings and—"

She drew in her breath and pulled away more, her eyes wide with humiliation. "Oh, dear God!" She looked down and quickly jerked a blanket back over herself. "I'm not dressed! I...I couldn't stand that filthy dress another minute...and the dress and my underclothes were covered in blood after I shot that man. I managed to drag him out of here, and then I went through his things and found this shirt and..." She started crying again, looking away from Luke. "Oh, dear God." She put a hand to her head. "Luke, I think I'm going to pass out again."

Luke reached out and touched her shoulder. "You just hang on. You need to eat something."

"What will I do? We should go. I can travel..." She tried to get up, then cried out from the pain in her leg.

Luke gripped her shoulder more firmly and made her sit back down. "Kate, you're all confused right now, and you're in no shape to travel. Now you sit right here and wait for me to come back with those supplies. We'll get you cleaned up, and I'll fix you a meal and coffee. Let me go get that cornbread for you. You're too weak to do anything but sit here and let me take care of you."

She glanced at her left hand. The skin was blistered and pink. She touched her left cheek lightly then. "My face!"

"It will heal. In a couple of weeks nobody will ever know it was burned. The important thing right now is to take care of that leg."

Kate kept the blanket over herself, but her feet were sticking out. With a clearer head, she studied her leg again. "Oh my God, Luke, it's turning dark!" She met his gaze. "Am I going to lose my leg?"

"Not if I can help it." He gently pushed her back down. "Now you just lay back and wait for me to bring those supplies. We'll fix up that leg and you are going to sleep. We *both* need to sleep. I'm dead tired from all that happened in Lander and from the long ride back here. When we're rested and ready, we'll decide what to do next, and we'll get out of here."

"And you won't leave me here alone again?"

"After what you did for me? Not a chance."

"You're…you look different."

Luke smiled. "Probably because I'm clean and I shaved, and I look human again."

Kate put a hand to her hair. "I must look terrible."

"Honey, you're *alive*. That looks pretty good to me. Now lie back on that saddle and wait right here. Don't you try to move."

Kate obeyed, staring up at Luke as he rose. "Thank you for coming back."

Luke frowned. "Of *course* I came back. What kind of man do you think I am?"

"I don't know. When you left, you were still a stranger. After what that man out there did to me, who am I supposed to trust?" More tears trailed down her cheeks.

"You can trust *me*," Luke answered, "and that's the

God's truth." He turned to leave, feeling sick at what had happened in the short time he was gone. He walked out and mounted Red, then turned the horse and headed for his pack horses.

He had to take care of Kate's leg. If he didn't fix it right and proper, she could lose it.

This was all his fault for letting a thirst for revenge come ahead of taking care of a woman desperately alone in this world. *You're a damn asshole, Luke Bowden.* He couldn't believe so much had happened in just one night, but then this was mean country, full of mean people. And he figured, after yesterday, he was fast becoming one of them. Maybe being around a woman for the next few days would help get that meanness out of him.

THIRTEEN

KATE TUCKED HER BLANKET TIGHTLY UNDERNEATH herself, mortified at what Luke Bowden might have seen when he found her here unconscious. She'd been so shaken and in so much pain after killing Buck that she'd given little thought to stripping off her filthy clothes and pulling on one of the man's shirts. All she'd wanted was to feel a little cleaner. She must have passed out for most of the night after that. She honestly could not remember much of anything between killing Buck and being awakened by Luke.

Now she was not only humiliated at being mostly naked, but the pain in her leg was becoming unbearable. Would she lose the leg? And what did Luke Bowden know about taking care of such wounds? Had he seen men's feet and legs and arms being sawed off in the war? She'd seen that kind of horror herself, but never dreamed it could happen to her. Now she understood why some men had begged the doctors to just let them die.

She lay back and waited. Luke had come back from Lander, just like he'd promised. She'd truly had her doubts. She was nothing to him. He could have just left her here to die and no one would have known the difference. But he'd come back, and with all kinds of supplies, even clothes, or so he'd told her. He'd been kind. He'd even called her "honey." Was it just because he felt sorry for her terrible condition? Or did it have a more endearing meaning? But why would it? Counting today, they'd known each other all of four days—or was it three? Or five? All of it had been under such strange circumstances.

She was pleasantly surprised at how handsome Luke was, now that she'd seen him cleaned up and shaved. It made her feel embarrassed at her own condition.

She heard horses' hooves then and realized Luke was back with the supplies and the extra horses. She watched him carry armfuls of packages inside, followed by armfuls of wood, some of which he put on the fire. He stacked the rest against a wall of the cave.

"If we don't use all this, someone else will soon enough," he told her.

"Where did you get it?" Kate asked. "They sell wood in Lander?"

"They sell a *lot* of things there. I put the wood in four burlap bags and loaded two onto each pack horse to even out the weight. It's not that much, but it will get us through the next few days. What's left over will help whoever else stays here after us."

Luke left again, and in a few minutes he brought in a package wrapped in brown paper tied with string. Her new dresses? New underthings? How kind of him. He laid aside a new rifle, boxes of ammunition, some towels and a bar of soap, a gunny sack out of which he took some canned goods, some potatoes, and something wrapped in cheesecloth.

"Is that fresh bread?" Kate asked, her hungry stomach growling at the smell of cornbread.

"Yes. One loaf of regular bread and one loaf of cornbread. I'll cut you off some cornbread, and you can get some into your stomach while I build a fire and make coffee. I also have to heat some water to work on that leg," Luke told her.

"Oh, Luke, the bread looks wonderful!" Kate watched him cut off a generous piece of cornbread. He brought it over to her.

"I have plenty of supplies now, so we can stay here long enough for you to get stronger before we head for Lander."

"Oh, thank you!" Kate wanted to hug him but was in too much pain. Besides, that would be much too forward of her, and a little voice deep inside warned her to remember he was still very much a stranger and she was completely at his mercy. Still, she could not ignore the kindness he was showing her now. She took the bread and bit into it, sighing deeply at its fresh texture and delicious taste. "You thought of everything," she told him, secretly grateful to have a man around, one who so far seemed very able and respectful.

"I have some laudanum for pain," Luke told her as he unpacked more items. "Once you get something in your stomach and rest a little, I want you to swallow enough to numb you up some. I can't work on that leg without you being mostly out, or you won't be able to stand it."

"You said you saw such wounds in the war, but did you ever have to help bandage them?"

"Sure I did. I saw a lot of real bad things in that war, Kate…and I *did* a lot of bad things. War changes a man." He didn't bother explaining, and Kate wondered what all he'd been through in that awful war.

"I saw a lot of awful things, too," she told him before eating more corn bread. "I helped nurse some of the wounded."

Luke didn't answer. He stirred the coals under the fire and let it build to heat coffee and water. Kate kept eating her cornbread, relishing every bite.

"I brought flour and water and sugar and a Dutch oven," Luke told her. "I'm hoping you know how to make bread so you can make more once we run out. Have you used a Dutch oven?"

"Of course I have, and yes, I can make more bread," Kate answered. "How do you know about Dutch ovens?"

Luke shrugged. "Watching my mother when I was little, and the cooks used them in the war. I also brought us a good wrought iron frypan and some bacon packed in lard."

"My goodness! You thought of everything. You must have got all your money back to be able to buy so much," Kate said.

He kept unloading supplies. "I had a little help, but yeah, I got it all back. I got you a decent wool coat, too, one that would fit a woman well so you don't have to wear that big ole jacket of mine. You'll really like it. It's dark blue and has big, white buttons. Hopefully, you won't need it much the next couple of weeks. It warmed up good again outside." Luke glanced at her as she finished her cornbread. "I'm real sorry, Kate. I took care of things fast as I could, but the fact remains that part of the reason I left was to find those men and get my revenge. I didn't figure anything so bad would happen to you in just one night—I'd planned to get back here before anything could go wrong." He set some things aside. "I feel bad about that—you here facing that man all alone and all. Without the help of a couple of other men, I might not have made it back here at all, but I'll explain all that later."

Kate lay back, enjoying the feel of something in her stomach.

"We'll eat something better later," Luke told her, "once I take care of that leg."

Kate watched him, hardly able to believe all the wonderful things he'd thought to bring back with him. She felt guilty about how much money he must have spent. How much had those men stolen from him? And how did he get all that money in the first place? She still knew so little about him, what he normally did for a living, how far he intended to travel once they reached Lander, or if he would stop there for the winter.

Luke proceeded to organize things, then fished around in the supplies until he found a strainer for fresh coffee grounds. He filled the strainer and put it inside the pot of heated water, then left the pot on a grate over the fire. "I'll let that simmer and get good and strong, and I'll cook up some potatoes and fry some of that bacon once you're set up good," he told her.

Kate tried to ignore the pain in her leg, worried

about how painful it would be when Luke drained some of the infection. "You're a good man, Luke Bowden."

Luke sat back for a moment and met her gaze. "You think so, do you?"

"I *know* so."

Luke smiled and shook his head. "After some of the things I did in the war and what happened in Lander, I wouldn't be so sure."

"What *did* happen in Lander?"

Luke stirred the kindling under the bigger logs to make the fire a little bigger. He gazed at the flickering flames. "Like I said, we'll talk about that later."

And something happened in the war you aren't telling me either, Kate thought. *Something besides the fighting itself.* She remembered the bitterness in his voice when she'd asked whether there was a woman in his life.

She watched him take bandages and a flask of whiskey from the supplies.

He held up the whiskey. "Just to calm your worries, this is for your leg, not for me, although I'll probably take a swig or two in order to get up the courage to drain that wound." He reached inside a saddlebag and took out a small brown bottle, handing it out to her. "Laudanum, to knock you out a little," he told her. "It tastes bad, but it's worth the taste to not feel the pain. Do you want to get this over with now, or wait a while and have some coffee first?"

Kate took the bottle from him. "We'd better get it over with now because of the infection. How much of this should I drink?"

Luke sighed. "I'm not sure. Take a big swallow,

and we'll wait a few minutes. I can cut you some more cornbread if you want. You need food in your stomach when you're drinking that stuff."

Kate took a swallow and couldn't help making a face. "It's awful! Give me some more cornbread—and some water."

Luke obeyed. Kate drank some water from a canteen, then ate another piece of cornbread. By then, she was feeling even more dizzy. "Oh my," she muttered. "Is this what getting drunk feels like?"

Luke grinned. "Likely so. That stuff has a lot of alcohol in it, and you're already in bad shape after what you've been through."

"Now I know I'll never drink whiskey. I'll have you know I've never been drunk in my life."

"Well, it happens to most people at least once."

Kate noticed him taking a swallow of the whiskey. "Promise me you won't get drunk and take advantage when I'm passed out," she asked, feeling a little silly and bold.

"I promise."

Kate took another swallow of the laudanum. "You kept your promise to come back, Luke," she said. It felt like her words were coming out of someone else's mouth. "Make sure—" Everything seemed to spin around her, and for some reason she couldn't finish her sentence. She was aware of Luke coming closer with the bandages. Was that a knife he was holding in the flames?

"Got to...drain...infection..."

Was that Luke talking?

"But...I'm not dressed." Did *she* really say that?

Someone held her head up, and she drank more of the bad-tasting stuff. "You just lay back…I'll try… save…leg," a man's voice told her from somewhere. "Give the laudanum…few more minutes."

She wasn't sure how long she lay there before blackness began to envelop her and someone took the blanket away from her leg and grasped hold of it just under the knee. She felt pain then—an odd, deep pain that was a horror yet somehow bearable.

Someone was screaming. A woman.

"Just hang on," someone told her. "Get rid… infection."

She slipped into a deeper blackness, deeper and deeper, until the screaming stopped.

FOURTEEN

KATE STIRRED AWAKE AND STRETCHED. PAIN SHOT through her leg, but it was more topical now, not so deep. Everything seemed a little foggy, and she felt sick to her stomach. She put a hand to her eyes and moaned.

"It's okay, Kate," someone told her. "I think I got rid of all the infection."

Confused, Kate studied a man who bent close to her. "Luke?"

"Yeah." He smoothed some hair back from her face. "How do you feel, other than the pain in that leg?"

He was sitting right next to her. Had he sat close like this the whole time she'd been passed out? "I feel awful—mostly my head and stomach. The pain in my leg isn't so deep and unbearable as it was before."

"You feel awful because of the laudanum. I know what it's like to wake up with a hangover. You need something in your stomach." Luke wiped at her face with a damp cloth. "The pain in your leg is better because it's just a fairly deep flesh wound that's trying to mend itself now, but the infection is gone. I wrapped your leg good and tight, so the bleeding has stopped."

Kate watched him as he turned to rinse out the rag, then put it to her forehead again. "You're being so good to me," she commented, still not able to put all her thoughts together properly. "Are you a doctor?"

Luke grinned. "Hell no. I've just seen plenty of wounds, and watched and helped treat them at times," he answered. "There wasn't any bullet in your leg. It just skimmed over it and flew off. Took a little bone with it, so your shinbone will be pretty sore for a while, but there's no real, lasting damage done. You'll be up and around just fine in a couple of days, but it's still going to hurt." He put the rag back in the pan of water and stood up, carrying the pan to the cave entrance and tossing out the water. Kate watched him hang the rag over a scraggly bush outside before he came back to sit down near her again. "I have coffee and fresh biscuits. I even have a jar of grape jam. How would you like a biscuit with jam on it?"

Kate studied his dark-brown eyes...the look of worry and even a hint of adoration in them. She looked around the cave then, everything hazy, including her memory. "I'm not going to die or lose my leg?" she asked.

Luke reached out to touch her cheek with the back of his hand. "No, ma'am. You aren't going to die or lose that leg. Thank God I don't feel any fever. That would be the only bad sign, but so far your face is cool." He sighed and took hold of her hand. "I took care of the wound yesterday afternoon. It's morning now. That laudanum really knocked you silly. I've been waiting for you to wake up and checking for fever all this time. I was scared to death you'd die on me, because it would be my fault for not getting here quick enough, or because I didn't do a good job of getting rid of that infection."

He squeezed her hand as Kate thought a moment longer. She'd shot a man! Yes, now she remembered...remembered his awful stench...remembered what he'd tried to do to her...remembered...

She put a hand to her left cheek. "He...burned me..."

"It's not that bad, honey. It's just a surface burn. It will fade in no time."

Kate met his eyes again. Why had he called her honey? Was it just pity, like someone would say to an injured child?

"How about that biscuit?" he asked her. "I brought back so many supplies we could live in here for a week if we needed to."

Kate covered her eyes then, embarrassed at what she had to tell him. "I...I have to relieve myself."

"Go ahead. There is no way you should stand on that leg yet. I'm worried that any pressure this soon could start up the bleeding all over again, so I put some towels under you, just for today."

"You *what*?" Kate felt under the blanket and realized she still wore only the shirt she'd taken from Buck's gear. Other than that, she was naked. "Oh my God!"

"It's okay, Kate."

"No, it *isn't* okay! I'm not even wearing any bloomers!" She pulled the blanket over her face. "What did you do?"

She heard Luke sigh, felt him moving away from her. "All I did was save your life. The condition you were in, it couldn't be helped. You were already wearing that shirt when I got here, and it looked like you'd washed up a bit. Would you rather I'd left you laying there dying and in God-awful pain just because you wore only a shirt?"

"Of course not, but—"

"But what?"

"You saw things you had no right seeing," Kate answered from under the blanket, her humiliation knowing no bounds.

"Kate, I did what I *had* to do," Luke answered.

Kate peeked at him from under the blanket to see he was sitting on the other side of the fire and pouring himself a cup of coffee. "I'll allow you're in pain and confused, and you've been through hell since the day your wagon train was attacked," he said, "so I won't take offense. But I'll remind you that if I was like that man I buried out there, you'd be lying there raped and dead. I'll have you know I didn't touch one thing wrongly. I was scared to death you'd die on me, and I did what I could to save that leg. That's all I was thinking about. I didn't want you to wake up to find that I'd cut your leg off."

Kate breathed deeply to control her tears and embarrassment. She lay there with the blanket still over her head, contemplating all that had happened and what Luke had just told her. But the fact remained he'd seen everything there was to see while she was out cold. Through the small opening where she'd lifted the blanket enough to see him, she watched Luke light a pre-rolled cigarette. She noticed again that he was cleaned up and shaved. A blue shirt stretched across his broad shoulders. The sleeves looked a little tight against muscled arms, and he'd tied a red neck scarf around his throat to cover the scar left there from his hanging. His shoulder-length hair was washed and neatly combed, and he had a look of manly sureness about him. He glanced at her, and Kate pulled the blanket back over herself.

"Take that damn blanket off your face and look at me, Kate Winters. We need to talk."

He'd spoken the words like a man used to being in charge. Worried she'd angered him, Kate obeyed, revealing only her eyes.

"Do you really think I'm the kind of man who would get his jollies with a dying woman who'd saved his life just a couple of days earlier?"

Kate didn't answer right away.

"*Do* you? Cuz if you do, I'll still take you to Lander and drop you off, but you can fend for yourself after that. I don't intend to travel with a woman who's always wondering when I'll rip off her clothes and have my way with her."

Kate was glad he couldn't see how red her face was. "I...suppose you wouldn't."

"You *suppose*?" Luke shook his head. "You aren't exactly the first woman I've seen naked, you know. And under the circumstances, I wasn't much concerned with looking at things I shouldn't." He spoke the words with the cigarette between his lips. He took it from his mouth before continuing. "I just didn't want you to die or lose your leg. You can't be bashful about things like having a towel under you when you're as sick as you were." He drank some coffee.

"Now, do you want some coffee of your own? And a biscuit?"

Kate sat up, pouting. "Yes, but I will not do what you expect me to do with these towels." She reached under her blankets and pulled the towels away, throwing them aside, then kept the blanket wrapped around herself and struggled to get up.

Luke quickly tossed aside his cigarette. "What the hell—" He stood up and was instantly at her side. "Woman, you're being careless and stubborn! If you open up that wound, I've a mind to leave you here to bleed to death!"

Kate clung to a blanket to keep herself covered. "Just carry me outside and leave me. I can do this myself."

"Jesus," Luke muttered. He lifted her with surprising ease and carried her outside the cave and to an overhanging flat rock, then set her on her feet. "Grab hold of that rock for balance and do what you have to do. Just don't faint on me and go rolling down that steep hill and mess up all my good work."

Kate caught the anger and frustration in his words. Part of her was a little afraid he'd get *too* angry, and part of her felt sorry for him. The man had, after all, gone completely out of his way for her so far, and she knew deep inside he meant well using those towels. She glanced back to see he'd left her and had gone back into the cave. She quickly did what needed doing, in spite of extreme pain in her wounded leg. She stubbornly forced back a need to cry out with the pain, not wanting to give Luke the satisfaction of an *I told you so* moment. "Luke!" she called out, keeping the blanket around her again.

In seconds, she was in his arms again. Luke carried her back into the cave.

"Can I have a clean nightgown?" Kate asked him.

Luke set her on her bedding. "You can have anything you want," he answered, still sounding disgruntled. "Like I said, I have plenty of supplies. Let me see that leg first." He pulled her blanket away. "There's a spot of blood on the bandages. If it doesn't get any worse, you're probably okay. You'd better hope you haven't done any damage, and you need to quit being so damned stubborn and proper. Proper doesn't mean a damn thing when you could lose your leg." He rose to walk over and fish through the supplies he'd brought with him.

Kate hated him being so upset with her. "I'm sorry," she said quietly. "Surely you understand, Luke. I still hardly know you, and—"

"Don't worry about it," he interrupted. He kept searching through a canvas bag for the nightgown she'd asked for. "You've been through a lot, and I ought to be more understanding of how a woman would feel, I guess." He pulled out a nightgown. "I even got you a couple of dresses and some underthings," he said, seeming to be proud he'd thought of so much. "I had to guess about your size, but I think I did pretty good. I have soap, more towels, woman's skin cream, and some hair combs and rosewater." He pulled many of those items from the bag as he named them. He held something up then. "And I got a brush for that pretty red hair." He turned to her, still scowling a little. "I'll brush out your hair for you, unless you think that's too forward, too."

Kate sighed and dropped her blanket to her lap. "After all you have already done, what's left for me to be shy about?"

Luke finally grinned. "At least now you understand what I've been trying to tell you."

Kate couldn't help noticing he was even better-looking when he smiled. She put a hand to her eyes. "I think I'm more embarrassed at the filthy condition I'm in than over you seeing things you shouldn't. I'm a mess."

Luke brought over a nightgown and the brush, as well as a jar of cream. "Tell you what." He laid the nightgown beside her, then rose. "I'll go outside and take care of a few things while you put on that nightgown. Give me a yell when you're done. I'll come back inside then and fix you some coffee and a biscuit. When you're done eating, I'll brush your hair for you. You'll feel a whole lot better tomorrow. So in the morning, I'll fix you a pan of hot water and give you some bloomers and a dress, and I'll leave for a while and let you wash up on your own and get dressed if you want. I just don't want you using that leg any more than necessary."

Luke walked out then, and Kate watched after him, not sure how angry he might still be at the moment. Now she felt rather foolish. Wincing with pain, she studied her bandaged leg and decided Luke had done a pretty good job of wrapping it. She saw some small bloodstains, but nothing alarming. Quickly, she took off the shirt she was wearing and pulled on the nightgown, then managed to raise up a little and pull it down over her legs. She waited several minutes until Luke finally came back inside and sat down across from her again. He poured himself a second cup of coffee and then poured one for her, handing it out.

Kate took the coffee. "I truly am sorry," she said again, watching his gaze as she spoke. "I'm not exactly myself, and you can't blame me for still being afraid of everything and everyone."

Luke took a biscuit from a cloth bag next to him and stuck a fork into it, holding it over the fire to warm it. "Don't be sorry," he answered. "Life is life. You went through hell before we even met, and what happened with ole Buck out there must have been awful, let alone lying here alone with that leg going bad on you. You're a hell of a woman, Kate, brave and strong. I think I can imagine how hard it must be in your situation, us hardly knowing each other. But I'm an honest man and can be trusted. I think I proved that by practically killing Ole Red getting back here to you." He paused to put jam on the biscuit.

"You said you found those men?"

He nodded and handed the biscuit to Kate. "Found them and killed them. Had a little help with one of them, but I got the other three myself. Got my money back and my bull. I had enough to buy you a horse and saddle, plus two pack horses, and all the supplies we need. If I'd known I'd come back here to find a saddled horse waiting, I could have saved some money, but I guess it's just as well. Now we have an extra riding horse. In country like this, you can't have too much in the way of backup supplies. We have plenty of food and water—" He glanced at her and grinned. "And clothes," he added. "I'm sure you're glad of that."

Kate smiled, relieved he was in a better mood. She bit into the warm biscuit, relishing its flavor and the feel of food in her stomach.

"I respect you, respect your courage and the fact that you didn't have to save me at all," Luke told her between sips of coffee. "You could have ridden off on my horse and never looked back—could have left me for the buzzards. But you didn't." He lit another cigarette. "Life out here is hard on a man, let alone a woman. You might have found a way to survive, but fact is fact, and it's not easy. You saw what happened to me."

Kate finished her biscuit. She couldn't help wondering at how easily he'd talked about killing those men—like it was nothing. It was probably because of all the killing he'd had to do in the war. He didn't strike her as a man who'd always found killing an easy thing to do. She wanted to know more about his background. Had he ever loved a woman? Did he think about settling? And why did she suddenly hate the thought of the two of them parting ways eventually?

She finished her biscuit and coffee while Luke got out more supplies.

"I have the horses and other things to tend to," he told her, "so I'll have to leave you alone for a bit. I'll be right outside." He stood up. "I might go do a little hunting, but I promise I won't be far. Don't be alarmed if I'm not back in a few minutes, and don't worry if you hear a gunshot." He walked out, his big frame filling the cave entrance as he did so.

Kate lay back down and waited, drifting off a time

or two because of the grogginess left over from too much laudanum. She started awake when she heard three gunshots, but she reminded herself he'd said not to worry. Still, she couldn't help wondering if the gunshots were from Luke shooting at an animal, or from someone shooting at Luke. She realized then that she was becoming much too dependent on Luke Bowden. Not only that, but she was starting to care about him in womanly ways that seemed wrong for someone she'd just met. She couldn't help a sigh of relief when Luke finally returned with a skinned and gutted rabbit, the biggest one Kate had ever seen.

"I'll shove this big guy deep into a small barrel of lard to preserve it," he told her.

Kate watched, thinking how he seemed to know everything about survival. He'd mentioned once that he'd hunted and explored with his father, who'd taught him a lot of these things. Plus, there was the war. There was *always* the war. It had changed men… and women.

Luke washed up and walked around to Kate's side of the fire. "How's that leg feeling?"

Kate moved it a little. "It's still okay. No more blood stains."

"Good."

"I'm sorry to slow you up, Luke. I'm sure you want to get going."

He sat down beside her and picked up the brush he'd bought for her. "Can't get over the mountains any more this year anyway. No big rush, I guess. We'll have to figure out how we're going to hole up for the winter."

We. Did he mean together?

"We have a lot of plans to make." He began running the brush through her hair, pulling a bit at first to get the tangles out, then brushing through it more easily. "I'll have you know I've never brushed a woman's hair for her before, but I promised I'd do this for you after you ate. I just figured I'd better do some hunting first while it's still plenty light out."

"Thank you." Kate closed her eyes and enjoyed the brushing. It helped make her hair feel cleaner. "And thank you for getting me this nightgown."

"When we leave, you can wind this hair up into the combs I got you and get it out of the way, so it doesn't get all tangled again." He finished brushing her hair and handed her the brush. "There you go. Now lie down and get some more rest. I'm pretty done in myself. I'm going to sleep for a while. You need anything first?"

"No." Kate watched his eyes again. "Thank you for everything, Luke. For a while there, I was so terrified you'd never show up. I've never felt so alone in my life as I did the day you left, not knowing how long it would take for you to make it back, *if* you came back at all."

"I told you I'm a man of my word." He rose and walked around to his own gear, spreading out a bedroll. "I didn't want to leave you alone like that, Kate, but you weren't strong enough to make that ride to Lander. It was selfish of me to put revenge before your safety, but there's a part of me that's angry all the time—ever since the war, and for reasons I'd rather not talk about. Getting hung doesn't exactly help a man deal with the hate he carries inside over other things. I figured you'd be safer around me if I found those men sooner than later and got all that festering revenge out of my system. If I'd gone to Lander later and missed them, I'm not sure I could have lived with that. Just don't worry when I ride off. I can take care of myself, and I'll never leave you alone for long."

Kate lay back down and covered herself. She watched Luke remove his boots, and she decided that later she'd ask more about finding those men—what had really happened. He settled into his bedroll and covered himself. She soon heard a soft snoring.

Who are you really, Luke Bowden? Why are you out here in such dangerous, rugged, unlivable country? Life is hard enough without deliberately coming to places like this and staying.

She thought how ridiculous her situation was. Never in her life did she dream she'd be caught sleeping half naked in a cave in the middle of nowhere with a near stranger, a man who was full of dangerous anger and could break her in half if he wanted. She was completely at his mercy and completely dependent on him to get her out of this place, and he was under no obligation to do anything more for her than he already had. He could have his way with her and leave without ever seeing her again.

She closed her eyes and tried to sleep. She missed home, missed her old life, missed her dead husband. She wondered if she would ever make it to Oregon, yet suddenly it didn't matter. She had no idea if she even wanted to go there now. Wherever she went, it would mean saying goodbye to Luke Bowden, and she couldn't imagine why that bothered her. How could someone become so completely attached to a stranger in such a short time?

It's this country, she told herself. *It does that to a person.* Yes, that was it. She would have to be very careful of her emotions and her decisions until she was back to civilization and a normal life…whatever normal was.

FIFTEEN

KATE AWOKE TO SEE LUKE WAS STILL SLEEPING. SHE realized how tired he must be, since he'd apparently ridden hard and fast in order to get to Lander and back in the shortest time possible, let alone whatever he went through when he got there. She still didn't know the whole story. She couldn't help feeling grateful for so many supplies, and she wondered how on earth she would repay him for her share. He hadn't asked, but she felt responsible to give him something for all he'd done.

She had to relieve herself again, but she didn't want to wake Luke. He needed his sleep as much as she did. She threw off her blankets and grimaced with pain, struggling to make no sound as she got to her knees and used her right foot to push herself up. The effort was fruitless. The minute she stepped on her left leg, the pain was worse than she expected, and she let out a short, unintended yelp that woke Luke. He stirred and sat up as she tried to get to her feet again. Immediately he was beside her, helping her up.

"What the hell are you doing?" he asked.

"I didn't want to disturb you," Kate agonized. "I just needed to go outside again. I'm sorry!"

"Stay right there a minute," Luke ordered. His boots still on, he walked to his gear and fished out a package of Gayetty tissue paper. He handed it out to her. "Hang on to this, and I'll carry you out."

Kate felt the color coming to her cheeks. "They had this in Lander?"

"Yes. Supply wagons come through there twice a year." Luke picked her up in his arms as though she weighed nothing.

"I wouldn't think a place so remote would have anything this modern," she told him.

"Well, believe it or not, there are enough women there that things like toilet paper are in demand. God knows how fussy women can be." Luke carried her out of the cave.

Kate looked around in bright afternoon sunlight, afraid to put her head on Luke's shoulder for fear it would seem too intimate. Yet she longed to do just that, even longed to put her arms around his neck. But now she didn't worry so much about him taking it wrong as she did about making a fool of herself. Besides, her condition was probably playing games with her, making her feel more vulnerable than she would normally feel. "What kind of women are in Lander?" she asked, suddenly self-conscious and wanting to make small talk.

"All kinds. Wives and mothers, women who run their own businesses, like clothing stores and bathhouses and such, and the kind of women who live over the saloons."

Kate hated the thought that he might take up with the saloon women once they settled in Lander for the winter, yet she had no right objecting. She didn't own Luke Bowden, but a small part of her wished she did.

Luke carried her several feet from the cave entrance to a small pine tree and carefully lowered her. "This is a safer spot than by those rocks where I left you last time. This isn't so close to the edge of that hill, and the low-hanging branch on that small tree will be safer to hang on to. Watch that leg." He showed her the branch and handed her the box of tissue paper. "I'm sorry I didn't remember this paper the first time I brought you out here. I was a little upset with you."

"I don't blame you. I was behaving badly."

"You were just being yourself. Fact is, I guess I would have been more surprised if you *hadn't* been a little upset. But I *did* have your best interest in mind. I just need you to understand that." He set her on her feet. "I'll go check on the fire and come back when you give me a yell."

Luke left, and Kate managed to take care of necessities, smiling at how Luke had thought of everything, even tissue papers. The fact that he was so able and efficient made her realize what good husband material he was. *Don't be a fool, Kate Winters*. She called out his name when she finished, and quickly he walked out and lifted her again, carrying her back to the cave. Just as he set her down, they both heard a man let out a loud whistle, followed by shouts somewhere in the distance.

"Luke, someone's coming!"

Kate hardly got the words out before Luke grabbed his rifle and hurried to the cave entrance.

"What is it?" Kate asked anxiously.

Luke watched quietly for a moment. "Six men," he answered. "Headed up here, probably to sleep for tonight. I figure they are on their way someplace else because they have extra horses, a few cattle, and a wagon with them. Looks like it's loaded up with supplies."

"Luke, they could be dangerous!"

"Just like every man out here," he answered, "including me, under the right circumstances."

Including you? Kate remembered the six-gun Luke had left her—the gun she'd killed Buck with. It still lay under the saddle she'd used for a pillow. She reached under the saddle and pulled it out to check the cartridge chamber. It still had four bullets in it. The fifth one had gone through Buck and her leg, and she'd fired the sixth one point-blank into Buck. She shivered at the memory.

"You keep calm," Luke told her. "Let me do the talking. And go along with anything I say, understand?"

"Yes."

"My gun belt is still laying over there near you. Make sure that pistol is fully loaded."

Kate did as she was told, nervously putting two more bullets into the revolver.

Minutes seemed like hours as the men rode closer. "They're checking out that fresh-dug grave," Luke told Kate. "Now they're looking up here." He cocked his rifle and moved farther outside, raising his rifle and taking aim. "You men stay right there!" he shouted, his voice echoing against canyon walls. "One of you can come up, but come up easy, and leave your gun with the others. I have you in my sights!"

There came a pause.

"We're just lookin' for a place to get out of the hot sun," one of them finally yelled in reply.

"They're checking out my horses," Luke told Kate quietly. "I'll be damned if I let my stock be stolen again."

"Looks like you have some fine horses, and a young bull," the man below shouted. "You on your way to a ranch or somethin'?"

"None of your business!" Luke answered. "And if anybody has ideas about my horses, you ought to know I already killed three men in Lander who stole some cattle from me."

Kate swallowed, afraid for Luke, yet a little afraid *of* him at the moment. His whole countenance had changed when he saw the men coming.

"You the one we heard about back in Lander?" one of the men asked.

"Most likely."

"Heard you paired up with Jake Harkner."

"I did."

There was a moment of silence.

"Who is Jake Harkner?" Kate asked.

"I'll explain later," Luke told her. "Seems using his name helps. The man doing the talking down there just handed his gun to the others, and he's coming up here."

Kate pulled a blanket around her shoulders, not wanting to be seen in just a nightgown. She clung to the six-gun, ready to use it if it meant defending Luke. After a few minutes, a shadow loomed into the sunshine at the entrance, and finally a man stepped inside…a big man wearing a floppy, soiled hat and a shirt and leather vest that both looked as though they had seen better days. His eyebrows shot up in surprise when he saw Kate sitting by the fire. He turned his gaze to Luke then. "You didn't say anything about having a woman up here."

"Nobody's business but mine. And she's my wife, so forget about what you're thinking."

The man glanced at Kate again, then back to Luke. "Could it be she's a whore from Lander, and you just don't want to share?"

Luke turned the barrel of his rifle to aim it directly at the man's face. "I told you she's my wife, and men don't usually share their wives. Make another remark like that, and I'll be kicking your dead body down that hill for your friends to bury."

The man studied Luke a moment and stepped back a little. "No offense, mister. Out here a man needs to know for sure, that's all."

"You said you just came from Lander, so I highly doubt you've gone without for long. There are plenty of women there for whatever a man needs."

Kate felt her cheeks flushing at the remark.

The intruder held Luke's gaze and nodded. "You're right. But that over there is a right pretty woman, so you can understand why I asked. Me and the boys down there ain't into abusin' women or messin' with men's wives, so rest easy, mister." He looked around the cave. "It's just that we know about this cave and figured we'd stop here to rest and maybe stash some supplies. Looks to me like you have plenty of your own supplies, so if you don't mind, we'll put a few things in that corner over there and trust you to leave them whenever you and the woman leave."

"You can trust me. I'm no damn thief."

The man grinned. "I can't say as much for me and those men down there, but we only rob banks and steal range cattle. We don't steal from good folks, and I have a feeling you're good folks. I'll stash our supplies, and if you don't mind, we'll take a little siesta in here out of the sun. Leavin' supplies in this cave is kind of an understandin' amongst men in these parts. We never know when we'll need to hole up here like this."

"I figured as much," Luke answered. He cautiously lowered his rifle. "I found just enough things in here when my wife and I first arrived to help keep us alive before I could go into Lander and get what we needed. We were in kind of a bad way when we first got here."

The man nodded. "Me and the boys are headed south to Brown's Park. We have our own spread there and figure on pickin' up a few strays on the way, then herd them all farther south to sell before winter sets in. If we go south, the weather shouldn't be too bad."

Luke nodded. "Fine by me, as long as you leave my bull alone."

The man nodded and put out his hand. "Hank Snyder. I own the Double S down by Brown's Park."

Luke shifted his rifle to his left hand and shook Hank's hand. "Luke Bowden. Got no home right now but I plan on settling in northern California with the little woman over there come spring. Her name is Kate."

Hank nodded to her, then looked back at Luke. "Who's buried down below?"

"Man by the name of Buck," Luke answered. "Don't know his last name. He got the idea he could take advantage of my wife. I wasn't here when it happened, so she set him straight herself. That ought to be more reason for you and your men to mind your manners. She won't hesitate to use her own six-gun."

Hank grinned. "*She* killed that man out there?"

"She did. She'll kill you, too, if you go near her."

Hank noticed rolled-up bandages near Kate's bedroll. "Somebody hurt?"

Luke nodded. "When my wife shot Buck, the bullet went through him and then took a good deal of flesh off the front of her leg. It got infected, but she'll be okay."

Hank frowned. "How can shooting a man in front of you end up sending a bullet down—" He hesitated. "Oh. I reckon I understand." He folded his arms and took a deep breath. "Well, Luke, I can see you two aren't somebody to mess with. My men will respect that. You have a bit of a reputation after what you did back in Lander. I'll make sure my men leave their weapons below with the horses and gear before they come up here to get out of the heat. Soon as the sun goes down, we'll all go back down below to camp for the night. We'll be out of your hair come mornin'."

Luke stepped back a little. "That's fine. Bring your men on up."

Hank turned to Kate and nodded, tipping his hat. "Ma'am. I hope your leg heals all right."

Kate glanced at Luke, then back to Hank. "Thank you."

Hank turned and left.

"Are you really going to let all those men come in here?" Kate asked Luke, alarmed.

"It's just for a while. I read men pretty good, and I believe Hank means what he said. They won't bring any harm. You just lie back and rest easy. I'll keep watch 'til they leave."

"What about later tonight, when they think we are asleep?"

Luke shook his head. "They won't try anything. They know I mean business. Even so, I'll keep watch all night."

"But you need your sleep, too."

"I'll manage. I'm used to sleeping with one eye open. We might have to share some food with them, so don't get upset. Men with full bellies are generally easier to deal with."

"But there are *six* of them."

"And two of us. You're my back-up, good as any man." He winked at her. "You used that gun on Buck, and they know you'll use it again if you have to. Either way, they know I won't hesitate either, and they think you're my wife. Out here, that's usually respected. You'll be okay."

Kate thought how it might not be so bad if she *was* his wife, then shook off the silly thought.

Minutes later, the men began filing in, carrying blankets and canteens. Some brought in gunny sacks full of supplies and laid them against the wall where Luke had promised they would be left behind when he and Kate left. They were decently clean, after having been in Lander just a couple of days earlier. Each man nodded to her and tipped his hat, calling her "Ma'am," and keeping their distance. They were a mixture of sizes and ages, a couple of them dressed better than the others. They put down blankets and stretched out on them, thanking Luke for letting them get out of the sun for a while.

"Won't be long before you're *wishing* for hot sun," Luke answered. "A few days ago, we rode through a snowstorm to get here."

"Strange weather in this country," Hank commented.

Kate wondered how many times she'd already heard that remark.

"Could be snowin' again by tomorrow," another spoke up. "I do a lot of betting at cards, but I would never take the chance of betting on the weather out here."

"Neither would I," Luke told him. He offered coffee to all of them, but they just wanted to sleep for a while. Luke moved to the cave entrance, where he could see all the men from the light that shafted through the opening. He leaned against the wall and laid his rifle across his lap, seemingly unconcerned that six strangers had just walked in, all of questionable character.

Kate felt like a swan in the middle of a pond of alligators. It was a strange code of ethics men like these shared…hang a man for stealing cattle the hangmen had already stolen themselves…shoot a man for cheating at cards…beat a man to death or turn around and back him up in a fight against someone else.

If Luke left her on her own, how in heck was she supposed to determine who could be trusted and who could not? If anyone could have taken advantage of her situation, it was Luke. She felt lost and vulnerable in a world of disreputable men, most of whom were lawless in one way or another, including Luke. Hank had commented about what Luke did in Lander, which reminded her he could be just as ruthless as any of the others when necessary.

And a man was just a man. She and Luke would likely continue to be alone together for some time to come. How long could she trust him not to expect something more from her once she was healed?

She'd never dreamed when she'd left Indiana that she would end up in a cave with a wounded leg from being attacked—that she would kill the man who'd attacked her—and that she'd be surrounded by outlaws, depending on one man she hardly knew to protect her and bring her no harm—all the while hoping he could get her to Oregon. Now she'd have to spend the winter with one Luke Bowden...or they would have to part ways and she'd be on her own somewhere this side of the Rockies...waiting for spring, again...with strangers.

She wrapped herself in the blanket and decided to lie down. Her leg hurt from trying to walk on it earlier. She glanced at Luke, who was looking outside, his rifle still lying across his knees. He turned and met her gaze, then nodded. "Get some sleep," he told her. "You'll be okay."

Will I? It didn't seem right to trust him so much, yet there was a sincerity about him that made her feel safe...maybe *too* safe. His skills and dependability, and his ability to actually care, were creating feelings deep inside that shouldn't be there. She realized her feelings right now could be more dangerous than her situation.

SIXTEEN

Just as promised, Hank and his men picked up their bedrolls once the sun went down and carried them back down the hill, where they built their own campfire. As each man left the cave, he tipped his hat and nodded again to Kate. "Thank you, ma'am, for letting us intrude," Hank told her. "I hope your leg heals up fast."

Kate answered, "You're welcome," thinking how strange and different life was out here as the last man left.

Luke stayed at the cave entrance and kept an eye on all of them as they built their fire and bedded down around it. "I'm going down there and get our horses," he told Kate. "I'll string up a picket line near the cave to the left. There's hardly any grass there, but they'll be fine for the night at least."

"I thought you trusted those men down there."

"I do, as far as not harming us. But Scout is a prime bull, and our riding horses are good stock. I trust Hank, but I'm not so sure about a couple of the other ones when it comes to horses and cattle. It wouldn't be unusual for one of them to get up in the middle of the night and make off with another man's stock." He looked her way. "I trust them as long as I'm around, but I wouldn't go so far as to leave you here with them while I go after what's mine again. You just rest easy there."

Rifle in hand, Luke picked up a length of rope from near his saddle and walked outside. Within five minutes, the sun settled completely behind the western mountain range, and the light outside the cave entrance faded. After a few minutes, Luke ducked inside long enough to tell Kate he'd rigged a picket rope by stretching it between two large rocks and tying each end. "I'm going down to get the horses," he told her before again disappearing.

Kate kept hold of her six-gun and waited, still finding it hard to relax with six men outside whose promises could be fleeting. Now she feared not just for herself, but also for Luke, whose care for her so far had made her trust him more. That trust was beginning to move beyond just leaning on a stranger for help. She realized again that she cared about the *man*, in ways she shouldn't. Maybe once they reached civilization, she would get over these confused emotions.

The crack of a gunshot suddenly pierced the crisp, night air. Kate jumped, fear engulfing her. "Luke!" she muttered. She threw off her blanket and managed to limp to the cave entrance. "Luke!" she called out louder then.

"It's okay," came his shouted voice in reply. "Stay off that leg!"

She heard men's voices but couldn't determine what was going on. She sat down at the cave entrance to wait, her heart pounding. Finally, she saw a shadowy figure walking up the hill and heard the soft trot of horses' hooves. Luke loomed into the light of the cave entrance, pulling his horses and Scout behind him.

"It's all right," he told her when he spotted Kate sitting at the entrance. "One of those men's horses went lame earlier today from a leg that's infected and swollen. We all decided to put her down." He spoke the words casually, as though killing a horse was all in a day's work. He walked past her to tie his horses and the young bull to the picket line. He finally returned to check on Kate again. "Quite a little remuda we've got going for us out there," he said, frowning. "What the hell are you doing clear over here? You could mess up that leg."

"I came over here when I heard the gunshot," Kate answered, looking up at Luke, who looked even taller and broader when she sat on the floor and he stood over her. "I was scared for you."

Luke bent down and scooped her up into his arms. "What do I have to do to make you stay put?" he asked. "And by the way, those men down there can't see anything up here in the dark. Do you need to tend to anything personal before you settle for the night?"

Why did it feel so good to be in his arms? All of Kate's fears and trauma seemed to gather into one sudden, deep sob as she wrapped her arms around Luke's neck. "I thought they'd shot you," she cried, hugging him tightly and burying her face into his shoulder. He smelled of leather and horses and man— comforting smells, an odor that spoke of protection and strength.

"Hell, woman, I told you I know when a man can be trusted. Don't be worrying about me."

"I can't...help it. You're all I've got out here, and after what happened with the wagon train...and Buck..." Kate wept.

Luke carried her to the little pine tree. "Well, we've got a whole string of horses and a bull that's worth a lot," he said, "and a whole bunch of supplies, plus weapons. If something happens to me, you just tie all that together and head north, and in no time, you'll make it to Lander and find help. You don't need me, especially once we get that leg healed up."

"That's not what I mean," she told him.

Luke hung on to her and lowered her beside the tree. "Do what needs doing while I go stoke the fire. I'll be right back."

Kate took care of personal matters, then wiped at tears with the sleeve of her gown as she stepped back. Luke hadn't answered her concerns directly, and now she worried that maybe she'd said something wrong. Maybe somehow she'd either offended him or scared him to death with her crying and her needy words. Did he figure she was beginning to care a bit too much? Was she wrong in thinking he had any kind of feelings for her?

Now she felt embarrassed. Worse, maybe if he thought she cared, he would begin to think he could take privileges. She heard his footsteps then.

"It's me," he told her. He whisked her into his arms again. "Remember that if something happens to me, you head for Lander, like I said," he repeated. "Ask for a woman named Nora Keil. She owns a rooming house. You mention my name, and she'll help you out—keep you safe. She and a woman who owns a clothing store helped me pick out your clothes. They're both expecting me to bring you back there."

Kate felt humiliated at the change in Luke's attitude. His voice sounded a little firmer, his countenance a little cooler. She'd said too much, shown too much emotion toward him. He probably couldn't wait to get her healed up and get rid of her. She felt like a silly, weak fool.

Luke carried her inside and set her down on her bedroll. "Let's re-bandage that leg," he said. "I'll dump some more whiskey on it." He left her to search through his gear for clean bandages.

"I'm sorry," Kate said. "That gunshot just scared me. It made me behave foolishly."

"We all behave foolishly sometimes, depending on what's just happened to us," he told her. "I killed men in the war who probably didn't deserve it. And I almost killed my own brother when the war was over. He'd stolen the woman I intended to marry. They were already married and had one kid and another on the way when I got home." He came over to where she sat and knelt near her foot. "Only thing that kept me from killing my brother was when their little boy looked at me with big ole innocent eyes. I figured he wasn't responsible for any of it, and I didn't want to take away his daddy." He paused and sighed. "I guess a man can't expect a woman to wait forever, not when she knows he could be dead anyway."

He began unwrapping the old bandages from around her leg. Kate watched silently. So, here was something he hadn't told her yet, a little more of a reveal about the real Luke Bowden. He'd ridden off like a war hero, then come home to find the woman he loved, the woman he probably thought about all through the war, married to his own brother.

"Bonnie was young and not the patient type," he continued. "I didn't blame her, but my brother knew I loved her. He's the one who, in my eyes, committed the ultimate betrayal. It would have been bad enough if the man she married had just been a friend or acquaintance, but being my own brother, that cut like a knife. I did a lot of drinking after that. A *lot* of drinking."

Luke didn't look at her the whole time. He reached for a flask of whiskey and poured some over the wound. Kate flinched and jerked her leg.

"Sorry," Luke told her. "By the firelight, your leg doesn't look too bad. I think it's healing okay." He slugged down some of the whiskey himself, then began wrapping fresh gauze around her leg, his touch gentle, and the feel of his big hands on her leg and foot disturbingly erotic. Kate considered the strange relationship they had. They were strangers, acquaintances, friends, rescuers of each other, dependent on each other in many ways, yet each probably capable of going on without the other.

"I'm sorry about what happened with Bonnie," Kate told him. *Now I know why you try to remain distant. You've decided never to love or trust a woman again.*

Luke shrugged as he tied off the fresh gauze. "Just explaining that I understand foolish," he said. "Foolish is trusting your heart to someone else. It's okay to trust me to watch out for you and get you where you're going, Kate. Just don't trust me any more than that. It's easy to turn to a stranger when you're feeling scared and alone. You'll feel better when I get you to Lander, and you can be around other people."

Don't even think about having feelings for me. Kate knew that's what he really meant. What happened with Bonnie had turned him against bothering to care about someone else too much. He finished bandaging her foot, then sat down beside her and lit a cigarette. Kate waited. She'd struck a nerve and sensed she shouldn't say anything.

"I left home and headed west because this is where a lot of men were heading after the war," he told her before taking a deep drag on the cigarette. "I landed in these parts and kind of liked the fact that a man can be himself out here and not answer to another man or even the law. When I first got here, I wasn't feeling very law-abiding, if you know what I mean, so I stayed, got in a few fights out of my own deep-seated anger, narrowly missed getting myself shot dead in a gunfight, worked for different men, learned who could and couldn't be trusted. When you found me, I'd cured myself of drinking and fighting. I was meaning to go on west and settle…try to live like a normal man ought to live, but I'm not sure I'm capable of ever living that way again."

Kate fingered a button on her flannel nightgown. "You're saying that after my own bad experiences and all that's happened to me out here, I shouldn't trust my feelings."

"Something like that."

Don't make a fool of yourself, Kate Winters. Kate pretended a smile. "Well, I don't know where in God's name this place is or if I'll live through the winter, but maybe by spring, I'll have my senses back. Right now, I feel like I'm not living in the real world anymore." She wiped at the remaining tears on her cheeks.

Luke touched her arm. "I'll get you to Oregon like I promised, Kate. We just have to wait out the winter first, probably in Lander. I told you that you could trust me to get you where you need to go, and you can."

But by then I could depend on you—maybe love you— too much to part ways, Kate thought. "I know, and I appreciate that." *And I'm older than the kind of woman you will want if and when you decide to settle again.* Kate sensed he was thinking the same but didn't want to hurt her feelings by telling her. A younger woman could give him the children he wanted. She wasn't even sure she could have children. After almost two years with Rodney before he left for the war, she'd never conceived. Now she was older.

She laid down, pulling a blanket over herself. "I'm sorry I acted like such a child earlier," she told him. "I think I'll try to sleep. I'm not really hungry."

"You mean you don't want me to cook that rabbit I shot earlier?" Luke asked, rising.

"Not really. If those men are cooking something down there, it's okay with me if you want to go and share some of it. Just be careful, Luke. I'm not so sure I'd be all that safe if something happened to you. That's why I got so upset when I heard that gunshot." She was not about to tell him it was because she feared she was falling in love with him and would be devastated if she lost him.

"Well, as long as you don't mind, I think I *will* go on down there," he told her. "It's a warm night, nice for sitting out under the stars sharing man talk—things your ears shouldn't hear."

"I'm sure I shouldn't."

Luke chuckled and proceeded to clean up the old bandages. He threw them onto the fire, then repacked the rest of the clean gauze. He built up the fire yet again and picked up his rifle. "You sure you'll be okay?" he asked Kate.

"Yes," she said. "You deserve a break from constantly caring for me, and from that very hard trip to Lander and back. Just be careful of those men."

Luke nodded. "You need to stop worrying about me. I've been taking care of myself out here for a long time."

He left, and Kate noticed he took the flask of whiskey with him. *Probably to forget about Bonnie,* she thought. She figured he was a good man, meaning to settle and provide for a family before the war. How many men returned home to heartbreak when the war ended? And how could that woman betray Luke like she had? It had left him unable to trust *any* woman. She would not again make the mistake of letting Luke Bowden know she was developing feelings for him.

SEVENTEEN

Luke stayed with Hank and his men at their campfire all night. Kate heard plenty of laughter and hooting and whistles, and she wondered just how different Luke was from the rest of them. Maybe he'd chosen to stay with them to keep a better eye on them. But Kate didn't doubt he'd also enjoyed it and had drunk plenty of whiskey. She awoke to sunlight and the sound of several horses riding off.

So, they left with no trouble, as promised. A few minutes later, Luke came inside the cave carrying something wooden in his hand. Kate met his gaze and noticed his eyes were bloodshot. "Too much whiskey?"

Luke smiled sheepishly. "You might say that. I won some money playing cards, though." He stepped closer, setting what looked like a saw horse beside Kate. It wasn't the normal size of a saw horse, but rather only about eighteen inches long and roughly the height of her waist, from what she could tell.

"What's that?" Kate asked.

"Hank had a whole wagon full of supplies, including some lumber for framing a couple of his cabin windows. I talked him into selling me three long boards, and I made this for you, using Hank's tools and nails."

Kate frowned. "Whatever for?"

"You can use it to walk." He reached out. "Let me help you up, and I'll show you."

Still confused, Kate reached up and took his hands with hers, secretly enjoying their warmth and strength.

"Just use your right leg to push yourself up," he warned. He pulled her up as though she were as light as a two-year-old. "Now, hang on to the middle of the saw horse."

Kate grasped the saw horse, and Luke stood back. "See? You can lean on that. Move it forward with each step and use it to support yourself when you need to walk outside. Just step real light on that left leg. This way, you can go out and do what you need to do for yourself. You can even use this thing when you need something to hang on to in order to squat down. It will help you get some exercise, too, and that will help build up the strength in that leg."

Kate lifted the saw horse and moved it slightly forward, then took a step. "Luke, however did you think of this?"

Luke shrugged. "The boys and I talked about how if you just had something to hang on to, you could start walking on your own. Of course, they all said there was nothing wrong with me having to haul you around in my arms."

Kate met his gaze, embarrassed by the remark. Was he afraid to keep holding her in his arms? Afraid they might get too close? She watched him lovingly, without even realizing at first that he probably saw the admiration in her eyes. "Thank you, Luke," she said softly. "It was kind of you to think of this."

Their gazes held for a moment, words unspoken. Luke suddenly turned away and walked around her. He knelt to stir the fire and pulled a sack of fresh coffee grounds from his stash of supplies. "Don't be thinking I'm all that kind and respectful," he said defensively. "I deliberately stayed down with those men last night because I did drink too much, and I was afraid I'd get wrong thoughts if I came up here and saw you sleeping…that pretty red hair spilling over that saddle. I might have done something to offend you, and that would have made the rest of our trip pretty damn uncomfortable. A man sometimes gets wild ideas when he drinks. I didn't think it would be fair to you to hear my whiskey talk, and that's all it would have been—whiskey talk."

Heaven forbid you should say something you would regret in the morning, Kate thought, *because the whiskey words wouldn't be truthful…and the truth is, you have no particularly romantic feelings for me. I don't blame you.*

She had to respect the fact that he'd realized whiskey might have made him do or say something offensive. At least he cared enough to avoid hurting her, either physically or emotionally. And maybe what they'd talked about last night had caused Luke to start thinking about the very things he'd vowed never to feel again.

"Perhaps when we begin the next step of our journey, you should leave the whiskey in your saddlebags," she warned. "After all we've been through, I wouldn't want to have to turn around and shoot you."

"And I don't aim to get shot," Luke answered, grinning. He walked outside and dumped out the old coffee, then came back in and filled the rusting porcelain coffee pot with water. "Why don't you practice with that thing and see if you can walk outside with it and take care of personals," he told Kate. "I'll heat you a pan of water and then turn the horses out to graze and take care of my own business—give you time to put on a real dress and underthings. I'm sure you'll feel better if you can do that much. Is that leg good enough to step on lightly?"

"I think so." It almost irritated Kate that he always seemed to think of the right things—that he knew what a woman needed. He was being too good to her, and that didn't help her erase fond feelings for him. She slowly limped out of the cave and into the warm morning light, wondering when the weather might suddenly turn wicked again. She took care of business, as Luke had put it, and went back inside to smell coffee brewing. Luke stood up and took some things from his supplies, carrying them over to her. He laid a package wrapped in brown paper beside her bedroll, then stood near her.

"There are two dresses there. I hope they fit. I didn't bother with slips—figured they would just be in the way on our trip to Lander." He shrugged. "Anyway, you have two dresses to choose from. Personally, I think the blue one would look best with that red hair."

Kate looked up at him…so tall, rugged, and sure… but she smelled whiskey on his breath, and that made her wary. How often did he still drink in an ordinary day? And what did whiskey do to him? He'd kept away from it in the short time they had been together, but apparently last night he'd given in to his demons.

She turned away. Why couldn't she fight this attraction, especially since he didn't feel the same about her? And if he didn't care about her all that much, why had he mentioned that the blue dress would look good with her red hair? He'd called her a handsome woman, and he'd seen things he shouldn't. His touch and his compliments left her totally confused.

"I very much appreciate the dresses." Kate noticed he'd set a pan of warm water beside her things, as well as a towel. So thoughtful, yet still so unpredictable and difficult to understand.

"I'll go tend the horses," he told her. He picked up his rifle and gunny sack of his own supplies and left. Kate quickly washed, enjoying the feel of being clean, especially in private places. She hurriedly pulled on bloomers and hooked a camisole around her middle. It was a little big, but it worked well enough. She'd always thought her breasts were too small, and she wondered if Luke had looked at them and thought the same thing, since he'd bought a camisole with small cups.

Dear God. She cringed at the thought and wondered if she would ever get over the constant humiliation of knowing what Luke Bowden had seen. She chose the blue dress and slipped it over her head, deciding she just had to stop letting her embarrassment get in the way of common sense. She buttoned the front of the dress, then wondered if she'd subconsciously chosen the blue one because Luke said he preferred that one.

She finished buttoning it almost angrily. *Don't be a fool!* she told herself. She folded the other dress—a soft green one with a yellow flowered print.

"I'm coming in," Luke yelled from outside a good half hour later. "Is it okay?"

"I have little left to hide from you," Kate answered.

Luke ducked inside, then paused, looking her over appreciatively. "I was right," he said. "Blue looks good on you."

"Thank you. I'll find a way to pay you back for all these clothes."

"I already told you it's not necessary. You saved me from a hanging, remember?"

"Well, not exactly saved you from a hanging. You'd already been hanged. I just made sure it didn't kill you."

Luke laughed softly as he placed a black frypan on the fire. He brought a small wooden barrel closer and used a wooden spoon to dig through the lard inside of it, then began pulling out strips of bacon. He laid them into the frypan. "I guess you're right," he told her. "The hanging still took place. You just made sure its purpose wasn't realized."

Kate began twisting her hair around her head, securing it with the combs Luke had bought for her. "How did you think of all these things?" she asked him. "Combs, skin cream, soap. You even got me cheek rouge."

Luke answered sheepishly. "The same women who helped me pick out the right size clothes suggested the other things. And if something happens and you end up going to Lander alone, remember the woman who runs that rooming house is named Nora Keil. She'll let you stay out the winter there. You mention my name and she'll find some reputable men to get you to Oregon. She knows everybody in town."

Did you sleep with her? Kate wanted to ask. She hated to realize that her thoughts brought feelings of tremendous jealousy.

"And no, I didn't sleep with her," Luke said, as though to read her mind. He turned the bacon.

"I… I never asked—"

"I know what you were wondering." Luke met her gaze. "Kate, I was worried about you. I got back here as fast as I could, which means I didn't have time for the pleasures of life. I got those men and my money. I hurried up and bought all these supplies, and got the extra horses from the stables. I cleaned up and slept a little, in those same stables, and I left before dawn to get back here. That's the God's truth."

Kate looked away. "It's really none of my business." He was clean-shaven and looked wonderful. She turned to watch him set some biscuits near the fire to warm them.

"I just want you to know I'm not the kind of man who thinks he has a right to expect some kind of payment from a woman he's helped," he said. "I want you to feel safe around me." He sat down on his bedroll and lit a cigarette. "We should leave soon as we can. We can decide our next step when we get to Lander. You need a real room under a roof and a real bed to sleep in. There might even be a doctor in Lander who can look at that leg." He poured Kate a cup of coffee and handed it out.

Kate sat down on her bedroll and took the coffee. "What really happened in Lander, Luke, when you went after those men who hanged you?"

Luke took a deep drag on the cigarette. "I got lucky, that's what. I found my cattle in the stockyards and figured the men who hanged me were most likely in one of the saloons with the women who ply their trade upstairs." He exhaled completely. "I found them, all right, and if not for a wanted man named Jake Harkner, I'd be dead. He was sitting right there at one of the card tables when I shot one of those men who'd been sitting at the same table. Almost the same time my shot went off, Harkner fired his .44, and a second man fell from the balcony. The son of a bitch was fixing to shoot me in the back, but Harkner stopped him."

"Why did he help you?"

Luke shook his head. "I don't even know. He believed my story, I guess—didn't like the fact that those men tried to hang me. He's an outlaw through and through, but he's also a fair man. He even has a family waiting for him in California. Can you believe that?"

"Out here I'd believe anything."

Luke drank down some coffee while the bacon cooked. "We'll run into plenty more strangers out here, Kate, men you meet one day and then never see again. Harkner and a friend of his helped me raid another saloon and find the other two men. I killed both of them myself, dug through their pockets and got my money back. I sold my cattle to a butcher who said the people in Lander could use the meat for the winter. But I kept Scout." He drew on his cigarette before continuing. "I'm still real sorry about what you went through with Buck."

Kate sipped her coffee. "You couldn't have known." She studied him a moment. "It didn't bother you? Killing those men?"

"No. I hate thieves. I guess there was a time when it would have bothered me, but not anymore. They didn't care what happened to me, so I didn't care what happened to them. Others in town just dragged them outside and went on about their business. That's how it is out here. I'll never see Harkner again, but I hope he can get his family back and live in peace. He was headed for Colorado to look for work. We'll never see Hank and his men again either. Nothing lasts in this part of the country. There are a few true settlers out here, but most men here are on their way someplace else, or just hiding out for a while. I'm one of them."

Hiding from your feelings, Kate thought. Part of her wanted to reach out and hold him, to tell him not all women were like his Bonnie. And not all men were out to betray him.

"I think I might be able to ride tomorrow," she said aloud. "I need to get to civilized places and find a way to write my brother-in-law and tell him what happened, and that I won't get to Oregon until next spring."

Luke kept the cigarette between his lips and stirred the bacon again. "Too soon for you to ride. You need a couple more days of walking around using that contraption I made for you. Once we do start, I'll have to lift you onto your horse. You can't be using that leg to mount up. Too much pressure on it."

"I'm sorry to be such a burden."

Luke glanced at her, then took another drag on the cigarette and took it from his lips. "That wound you suffered is from something that happened because I wasn't here. You aren't a burden, and I feel responsible for your pain. You just remember what I told you to do if something happens to me. Everything I have is yours." He put some bacon and a biscuit on a plate. "Lord knows I've got no one else to leave it to." He handed her the plate, and their gazes met. "That includes my money," he told her. "Don't go trying to find my brother to give anything of mine back to him. The son of a bitch doesn't deserve it."

Kate took the plate.

"Matt paid me off for my share of the family farm before I left," Luke explained. "More of a guilt payment than anything legal." He dished up his own bacon and biscuit.

"I'm so sorry, Luke."

He shrugged and took another drag before rubbing the cigarette out against the stone floor. "Water over the dam."

And you're still hurting.

"My only concern now is getting you through the winter safely and helping you get where you need to go come spring." He started eating.

"Well, thank you for offering your things to me if something happens to you, but I'd prefer it if you stayed alive, Luke Bowden. I will feel much safer out here with someone who knows his way around."

"I'll do my best not to die," he said jokingly. "If not for you, I wouldn't be here. And with those men who tried to hang me being dead now, maybe we'll be okay."

Kate wondered if he was thinking the same thing she was. How and where would they get through the long, cold winter together? And would they really want to part ways come spring? She'd known Luke Bowden only six days, yet somehow, she couldn't imagine letting him ride out of her life, never to be seen again. *Someone has to love you, Luke. Someone has to take care of you.*

It was going to be a long, cold, lonely winter, wherever they landed to wait it out. She concentrated on eating, refusing to meet Luke's gaze, afraid he would read her thoughts again.

EIGHTEEN

Kate spent the next two days walking outside the cave, using the sawhorse Luke had made for her. She was still impressed by Luke having invented the little walking aid. Perhaps it was more because he was tired of carrying her around than it was out of concern, but either way, it turned out to be a wonderful idea.

She otherwise spent a good deal of time making bread, kneading it and keeping the dough in pans in the warm sun to rise. She baked the bread in the Dutch oven Luke had brought from Lander. She wanted to make extra for their journey, in case they should get stranded again on the way. She'd learned the hard way that in country like this, a person had to always be prepared. She also mended some of Luke's shirts and socks with needles and thread the women in Lander had advised Luke to add to his supplies.

Luke kept himself occupied with tending the horses and taking care of gear and tack. A couple of halters and cinches had to be repaired, stones had to be dug out of hooves, new straps had to be cut for a latigo because the leather strap holding the cinch had worn through. He hobbled or picketed the horses every night and rearranged the packed supplies.

Luke seemed to be deliberately staying busier than necessary. Kate suspected it was because he was becoming as uneasy as she was over being alone together all day long. Up to now, each of them had been injured and in need of help in one way or another. Now things were peaceful, at least for the moment, and as soon as Kate's leg was healed enough, they could be on their way...away from thoughts and feelings that were becoming more intense, yet unspoken.

Everything began to feel familiar between them. They'd become more like old friends, even at times like husband and wife. Kate suspected Luke wanted to get her to civilization so they both could get back to reality and stop depending on each other. He'd shown her how to cut weak harness leather into strips and braid it to make it thicker and stronger again, how to tie the pack horses to each other, and he'd told her how much each animal was worth if she should have to sell them. He had a vast knowledge of survival and a take-charge attitude, something Kate guessed was left over from a hard farm life and then the trials of survival and ordering men around in the war.

The stronger they both became, the more they admired each other's skills and abilities. For Kate, Luke Bowden was becoming more and more attractive as a man who knew what he was about and one who could handle animals and guns...and probably women. She told herself to ignore the feelings she had for him that continued to grow to dangerous proportions—dangerous because she was certain he saw her only as a friend in need, a woman who, once they reached Lander, would be left to fend for herself until spring.

Fending for herself was probably best. She'd gone this long without a man, and she didn't need another, nor did she want to risk the heartache of loving a man and then losing him to death as she'd lost Rodney. Letting herself feel too deeply for Luke would be to toy with the heart, and both of them had hearts that had already been broken by the war. She'd simply lost too much herself, and Luke Bowden was a man determined never to trust or care again.

It was nearly dusk when Luke came inside the cave. Kate was just taking warm bread out of the Dutch oven.

"Damn, that smells good," Luke told her. He removed his hat and brushed dust from his hair and off the shoulders of his shirt.

"And men seem to know exactly the right time to come in from working," Kate replied. "My father used to come in from the fields just as my mother was setting the table for supper."

Luke paused to light a cigarette. "Well, you can't exactly call what's outside this cave fields, but I've been working just the same."

"I know you have. We can pack this Dutch oven as soon as the pan cools." She set the bread aside on a towel. "You still plan on heading for Lander in the morning, right?"

"Yes, ma'am. Everything is ready. You think you can use that leg to balance yourself once you put your foot in a stirrup?"

"I'll manage." Kate took out some jam.

"I plan to help you the first day or two. I'll lift you onto your horse myself."

Kate wasn't sure her feelings were safe if she found herself in his arms again. "I wish we had butter," she said, trying to change the subject.

"We'll have butter when we get to Lander. You can bathe in a real bathtub there—sleep in a real bed, and we'll both eat full meals."

"Sounds wonderful." Kate sat down on her bedroll and glanced at Luke. Here they sat, planning their trip to Lander together, fresh-baked bread sitting nearby. This was almost like sitting at the supper table with her husband. "My journey west certainly took some unexpected turns," she commented.

Luke also sat down. He smoked quietly for a moment, staring at the flames of the fire. "Things haven't worked out exactly like I planned either," he said. He exhaled with his next words. "I didn't figure on getting hanged, or on traveling with a woman I don't even know. 'Course I'm not saying that part has been all bad."

"Well, I appreciate your trustworthiness, Mister Bowden," Kate answered facetiously.

Luke nodded. "Looking after you was only the right thing to do, after what you did for me. You have actually been a bit of a bright spot in some lonely times, Kate, in spite of all the care you needed at first."

So, that's all there is to it, Kate thought. *Something to take care of and talk to.* She'd come to see Luke Bowden as a solid, able man who was nothing short of handsome. She wondered if, when he called her a "handsome woman," he only meant it as a compliment to someone he liked but could never love or settle with. Maybe that was why it was so easy for him to see her naked without making advances or allowing the man in him to be attracted to her. Maybe it was because he didn't find her attractive at all. And, of course, his heart still seemed to yearn for the woman he'd lost to his brother.

"I'm glad you consider me a bright spot and not a burden," she told Luke. She sliced bread for them, and they put jam on it and drank coffee. There was so much Kate wanted to say, but it was best left unsaid. "I suppose we should retire early," she finally said. "Tomorrow will be a long day."

Luke finished his bread. "It will, so yes. Get some rest. I'm going out to check on the animals once more. Thanks for the bread."

Kate watched him leave. Since they were both better, sleeping together in the cave was beginning to feel awkward—another reason to head for Lander. But she hated that her heart was beginning to ache at the thought of Luke Bowden riding out of her life, perhaps sooner than later. She cleaned up from cooking, then lay down on her bedroll, leaving her dress on, as she'd done the last two nights.

She pulled her blankets around her. Did Luke ever think about what he'd seen? Had he even once wanted her in the way most men wanted a woman when they were alone together for so long?

She drifted off, not sure how long she'd slept when she vaguely sensed Luke coming back inside. There was the smell of cigarette smoke, the smell of man. Was he kneeling close to her, or was this just an odd dream? Was there something he wanted to say? To do?

"Kate."

She thought she heard someone say her name softly. She stirred awake. Opened her eyes. Someone leaned close, and she knew it was Luke because of his familiar scent. In the next moment, his lips were on hers, so gentle that she wasn't sure if this was real or a dream. Shouldn't she resist? Was that whiskey she smelled on his breath? She felt him gently put his hands to either side of her face. "I'll miss you," he told her.

She could see his face very dimly lit by a dying fire. "I'll miss you, too," she answered. "You aren't leaving me, are you?"

"No." His voice was so close. One more kiss. "I just wanted you to know that once we reach Lander, it can't be like this."

The quick sprout of a bright flame flickered in his eyes. "I know," she told him. "But I won't forget you, Luke. Ever."

He just held her face and stared at her a moment longer, then suddenly stood up. "Jesus, I'm sorry," he said. "I've been drinking." He walked out.

Kate watched after him. She licked her lips and noted a lingering taste of whiskey, which told her she hadn't just dreamed the moment. It had really happened, and for some reason, she wasn't the least bit alarmed by it.

She curled up on her side and fell right back into a deep sleep, then awoke later to see Luke sleeping across the fire from her. The fire was bigger again, so he'd stoked it sometime after their encounter. She heard soft snoring, and his back was to her.

Kate sat up, rubbing her temples. Never had she

been so confused. What did it all mean? Tomorrow they would head for Lander, possibly getting there the same day. Would that be the end of them? She looked around the cave, the flickering flames creating odd shadows. She couldn't help breaking into tears over the barrage of feelings that overwhelmed her. She didn't want to leave, but there would be no stopping it. Come morning, the past few days spent here would be only a memory.

NINETEEN

After a breakfast of more bacon and biscuits, Kate helped with the final packing, tying on the coffeepot and the little barrel that held the bacon packed in lard. As promised, they left behind the supplies Hank and his men had stored in the cave.

They moved methodically, adjusting bits and bridles and chokers and cinches on Red and on the horse Luke had brought for Kate to ride. They used Buck's horse as an extra pack horse, securing the man's saddle and some supplies on the mare and on the other two pack horses. Kate packed her own things while Luke did the heavier work of lifting saddles and tying on supplies.

It was surprisingly warm, considering that winter was right around the corner and a snowstorm had caused them to hole up in the cave in the first place. Luke wore only a red calico shirt, and Kate tried her best to ignore the sight of him loading gear and supplies and tightening cinches. His sleeves were rolled up, and his solid arms tensed and showed distinct, hard muscle with every move. The way the shirt fit, she could even see the movement of some of his shoulder and back muscles. Literally living with the man and being aware of his kind care and his respect for her personally…remembering how it felt when he carried her in those arms…it all was beginning to affect everything that was woman in her. Combined with the fact that they were leaving this place and possibly headed for an eventual parting, her feelings for Luke Bowden were getting the better of her.

She didn't know what to think of last night. Luke had said next to nothing to her this morning as they drank some coffee and ate. Maybe she really did dream his kiss. If she didn't, Luke apparently didn't want to talk about it, and she figured maybe he was embarrassed and angry with himself for what he'd done. Heaven forbid he should give her the idea he actually cared about her romantically. After all, he did say *I'll miss you*, which meant he did intend to leave her in Lander, at least until spring. He'd said he always kept his promises, which meant he had to come back in the spring and take her to Oregon, or at least arrange for someone trustworthy to take her. Either way, it seemed he intended to ignore any feelings he had for her.

Ending this short and moving relationship, and leaving the cave where it all happened, upset Kate so much that she kept wanting to cry. She fought the feeling, not wanting to look like a silly, blubbering idiot…and not wanting Luke to have any idea she had these sentimental feelings.

"You're walking around too much on that leg," Luke told her as she checked her saddle again. He walked up to her and helped her finish cinching the saddle strap, slapping at her horse's belly and forcing the animal to pull it in a little before he jerked the cinch much tighter than Kate was able to. "All we need is for this damn thing to slip sideways and throw you off," he said. "You could land on that leg and make things worse again."

Kate sensed he was in more of a hurry than necessary. Was he anxious now to get rid of her? "My leg feels pretty good today, but it wouldn't hurt to keep my little sawhorse and load it onto one of the pack animals," she said. Why did she want to beg him not to leave her once they reached Lander? Why did she want to tell him she no longer wanted to go to Oregon?

She reminded herself that Luke was nothing more than a stranger she'd come across who'd ended up helping her, just like she'd helped him. That's all they were to each other. Lucky for her, Luke ended up not being as bad as most men out here. He'd been kind and helpful, and he'd been through his own dangers and heartbreak. Now he had goals and dreams, and a life of his own to get back to. He was probably anxious to reach Lander, not just to end their relationship, but so he could take out his manly needs on the loose women he could find there and do other "manly" things he missed, like drink and gamble. He was probably glad to get away from the cave and having to constantly care for her.

She started to mount up when he took hold of her arm. "Kate." He turned her to face him. "I'm sorry about last night. I took to drink after you fell asleep, and I took privileges I shouldn't have. I was just thinking about having to part ways when we reach Lander, and I want you to know I can't pay you back enough for saving my life the day you found me hanging from that tree. You had no idea you could even trust me, and maybe you still can't. I just want you to know I really will miss you when the time comes to go our separate ways."

It took all of Kate's courage to meet his gaze. Looking at him made her want to throw her arms around him. "It's all right. Somehow, I understood," she said. "It's hard to explain or understand the kind of friendship we have, Luke. I wasn't scared, and I wasn't offended." She managed a smile. "In fact, I was actually wondering this morning if it really happened. I was in a pretty deep sleep when you woke me."

Luke smiled softly, looking her over in a way that disturbed her baser needs. "You're a good woman, Kate Winters. I'll make sure you are well taken care of in Lander." He took a blanket he'd thrown over his shoulder and laid it over the saddle of her brown-and-white pinto. "I bought this mare for you because it's a bit smaller than the rest of the horses. I figured it would be easier for you to get on and off her," he said. "Her legs are shorter than the other horses, and the man who sold her to me said she's real gentle. I guess I should have seen if the store in Lander had women's riding pants, but I didn't, so you should have a blanket under you. Your legs are bare under that dress, and you don't want bare skin against leather all day. You'll have blisters in unmentionable places."

Kate felt the color come to her cheeks as she grasped the saddle horn while Luke put his hands at her waist and lifted her, setting her into the saddle.

"Thanks for the blanket," she said.

Without a reply, Luke adjusted the stirrups to fit. She realized her left leg was completely bare, so she raised up a little and adjusted her full skirt so it would cover her legs. Luke checked all the straps again, and Kate watched his hands as he did so. They were strong and solid, with stubborn dirt stains in creases that refused to come clean. They were the hands of a man used to hard work and the elements—the hands of a man who was able in all the ways a man should be.

"I can't begin to thank you enough for the clothes you bought me," she told him, "and for all your care and all these supplies."

Luke shrugged. "It's the least I could do for the person who saved me from a slow death by choking." He looked up at her. "I still don't like you putting all your weight on that leg to mount up, so let me lift you into and out of your saddle the rest of today. This mare is not a tall horse, so it won't be any trouble."

Kate shook her head. "You've done enough of hauling me around," she told him. *And I'm not sure I could stand the feel of your hands around my waist or the attraction of how easily you lift me.*

"Nonsense," he answered, grinning again. "Do you really think I mind it?"

Kate looked away from his easy smile. "At least let me try to get on and off on my own," she answered.

"We'll see how it goes," Luke said. He walked away to mount his horse.

"Does this horse have a name?" Kate called out to him.

"No idea."

"Well, I can't ride a horse without a name. I'll have to talk to her once in a while."

The mare snickered and nodded her head, as though she understood what Kate had said. Kate patted the horse's neck and smiled. "I think I will call her Jenny," she told Luke. "That's the name of a neighbor of ours back in Indiana who was the sweetest old lady—gentle and kind and always baking and bringing me pies and cookies. I truly mourned her when she died." She wiggled more comfortably into her saddle. "I know it sounds silly to a man to fuss over naming a horse, but that's just how I am."

"Yeah, well, I've never known a woman who wasn't sentimental about things," he told her.

And how many women have you known? How many had he turned to after being so hurt by Bonnie? Had there been anyone else who'd interested him enough to consider settling with her? Or had his heart and trust been broken for life?

Luke moved his horse closer beside her. "You really ready for this?" he asked for the hundredth time. "We can wait a couple more days if you aren't. I don't want that leg to flare up from too much exertion."

"I wouldn't dream of changing my mind now," Kate answered. "Not after all the work we've gone to in order to get everything ready. Besides, the sooner we get to civilization, the better. The thought of sleeping in a real, soft bed is like a wonderful dream."

Luke nodded. "Can't argue that one." He looked back at the three pack horses tied to Red, then gently kicked Red into motion. "Let's go," he told Kate. He headed down the steep hill, and Kate followed.

Wait! She wanted to shout. She wanted to look around inside the cave once more, as though she were leaving a fine home where she'd lived for years, never to see it again. She knew it was silly and sentimental, but she wanted to burst out crying at the thought of leaving. Too many things had happened in too short a time. Her world and her plans had been turned upside down. Her parents were gone. Her farm and Rodney's store were gone. Rodney himself was gone. She didn't even have a child she could love and through whom she could remember her husband. The people she'd traveled west with were gone, their bodies lying out there somewhere amid burned wagons, probably devoured by wolves and buzzards. And in the not-so-distant future, Luke Bowden would also ride out of her life. If he found someone trustworthy in Lander who could take her on to Oregon in the spring, he might move on by himself to get a little farther west before winter set in.

Never had she struggled harder not to cry. Why on earth *wouldn't* the man keep going a bit farther? He had no more obligation to stay with her, even though he'd declared he probably would see her to Oregon himself. Maybe he'd decided that wasn't such a good idea after all. Or maybe if he stayed the winter in Lander, he'd find some young woman who interested him.

All these changes were such a burden to her heart. She glanced back at the cave once they were down below and heading north. As men came and went, using the cave for whatever reason, none would know that Luke Bowden and Kate Winters had stayed there, two strangers who'd been brought together by fate in

this wild, lawless land. She couldn't even see where
Buck was buried, the dirt over his grave now just a
part of the landscape. There was no marker.

She'd killed a man, and now he was just another
part of the elements out here, a body disappeared into
the dust and rocks, missed by no one. Despite what
he'd done, she felt bad for him.

Luke, I want to go back, she felt like screaming.
Leaving meant she would never have Luke Bowden all
to herself again. He would move on, and she needed
to realize that and consider moving on herself. It was
time to finish what she'd started out to do—go to
Oregon. There she would join her brother-in-law
and his family. There, she would get over what had
happened to her and maybe, just maybe, find a man
to marry. There, she would be a woman again and
somehow find a life that somewhat resembled what
she'd lost back in Indiana.

She stayed far behind Luke for a while, so he
wouldn't hear her soft sobbing or see her tears.

TWENTY

Luke noticed details of the landscape that he'd paid no attention to when he first rode to Lander to hunt down his hangmen. He'd been to Lander before, but never through this area until his hard ride there and back a few days ago. He'd headed this way with a raw scar around his neck and hardly able to use his voice. Now the scar was healing, his voice just a little scratchy, and his throat no longer sore—all thanks to Kate Winters.

He owed her so much. Too much, he figured, to ever truly repay her. That left him with these crazy, mixed-up feelings that were keeping him awake at night. Sometimes he saw something in her eyes that made him wonder if she wanted him the way a woman wanted a man for more than just help and protection. He figured she was mostly feeling scared and alone, which caused her to feel dependent on him. It could have been left at that if he'd not been a damn fool and drank last night.

He should have known better. He drank because something inside made him realize he didn't really want to leave Kate behind in Lander at all. And he drank just enough to stir up neglected manly needs that made her even more desirable than she was when he was sober. Thank God he'd had sense enough to get the hell out of that cave for a while after he'd kissed her.

Trouble was, she hadn't reacted the way she could and should have. She didn't push him away. She didn't seem shocked. In fact, he wondered now that if he'd done more, maybe she would have accepted him. But then that would have meant commitment—and trust. Trust was the hardest of all for him to accept, because he'd vowed never to trust a woman again. And he didn't even know Kate Winters well enough to know for sure if she could be trusted at all. Her situation only meant that once she was safe and settled, she might regret giving herself to him and look for some other man, or maybe no man at all.

He told himself that it wasn't right for either of them to trust their emotions in a situation like this. Man or woman, it didn't matter. Kate Winters was growing too accustomed to having him around for protection and as a provider. He, in turn, was getting too used to the sound of her very soothing voice… too used to the smell of soap on her…the way she felt in his arms…the memory of how she looked naked.

Damned if she didn't have a beautiful body. She had white teeth, full lips, a slim waist, and pretty legs. And he loved her thick, red hair. And those eyes…blue as a summer sky. She had a lovely shape and small breasts. He'd always liked smaller breasts.

Stop thinking about her that way, he told himself. *It's easy now, but a man shouldn't care about a woman just because she saved his life. And she shouldn't care about him just because he happened along when she needed his help the most. People make bad decisions under these conditions.*

What if he accepted her into his life and into his heart, and after a time regretted it because he learned something about her he didn't like? Or there was the very real possibility he could end up a heavy drinker again. She would hate that. And what if these feelings he had were just the result of missing Bonnie...aching for Bonnie...being angry with Bonnie?

No. He wasn't ready to care about another woman. Maybe he never would be. Kate Winters was just a companion, a woman who'd come along needing help and helped him in return. Seeing her naked had damn well scrambled his reasoning about the whole thing. Holding her in his arms didn't help either. Last night...watching her sleep...kneeling close and wanting her in every way for their one last night together, that was all due to whiskey. Good God, what a disastrous decision it would have been to act on his desires! Kate would have either knocked him on his ass or demanded marriage. Either one would have mortified him, and the rest of this journey would have been uncomfortable as hell.

Maybe once they reached Lander, he could find someone who'd promise to get her to Oregon next spring. He could pay them and move on...get away from the woman altogether and put her out of his mind.

He looked back at her. Why was she staying clear at the back of the string of horses? "Come on up here where I can keep an eye on you!" he called to her.

Kate continued to lag behind a few more minutes

before finally catching up. "I was just enjoying the scenery," she told him. "I've never seen such big country. In a way, a place like this seems to epitomize the meaning of lonesome."

Luke wrapped Red's reins around his saddle horn and pulled a cigarette from his shirt pocket as the horse kept up its casual pace. "That it does," he answered before lighting the smoke. He squeezed the end of the match to make sure it was fully out, then tossed it. "I guess that's why I liked it out here when I first arrived two years ago. The land seemed to fit how I was feeling. And country like this makes a man feel small, which in turn makes his troubles seem small, too." *Damn!* The drift of the wind brought her sweet smell to his nostrils. He should have left her where she was.

"I hope you can get over all those troubles and get on with life, Luke."

He shrugged, afraid to look at her. Afraid she'd see something in his eyes that she shouldn't see. "I wish the same for you," he said. "It will be good for you to be around other women when we reach Lander. There are some good women there, wives and business owners and such. Some are widows like you, so they'll understand your situation. And don't be intimidated by the, uh, the kind who live above the saloons. Some of them can be pretty nice and even help you with advice on who to trust. They know the good men from the bad ones." He looked around, suddenly uncomfortable being so close to her, which was pretty ridiculous, considering he'd been around her for days and had even seen everything there was to see. It seemed as though the closer they got to civilization, the more he realized things would have to change between them. "You might even be able to find a job cooking or baking or something like that for the winter."

"Maybe. I certainly can't keep depending on you, and if I stay at a rooming house, I will have to find a way to pay for it."

Small talk. "There are a lot of men who will need shirts and socks mended, clothes scrubbed. That's something else that could keep you busy. Just be damn careful, Kate. Most of the men out here can be trusted because there's kind of a code among them. A man doesn't abuse a woman, not even the pros—Err, not even the looser ones. Women are rare, and any man who abuses one has to answer to the outlaw code of ethics. These men will rob you blind or kill a man at the drop of a hat, as one barkeep put it to me a few days ago. But abusing the women is punishable any way they choose to make a man pay. There might not be any real law out here, but most men have that basic instinct of what's right and wrong. Just remember that there will always be those who think a woman is good for only one thing, no matter if she lives over a saloon or is a married lady with kids."

"I understand. "

"I won't always be around to look out for you."

"I understand that, too. Speaking of which, you talked about ways for me to stay busy. How about you? How will *you* stay busy?" Kate asked.

Luke smoked quietly for several seconds, thinking. "I don't know," he answered. "I still have plenty of money. Maybe I'll be able to work at the stables or tend bar…whatever I can do for a buck here and there. And I'll still watch out for you, check on you." *God, it's going to be a long, cold winter.*

"I'll try my best not to be a burden," Kate told him.

"You're no burden," Luke answered. "You keep forgetting I owe you. I'll always owe you."

"It's okay, Luke. And just remember that I can keep doing *your* mending and such if you need anything like that." She pointed to mountains on the western horizon. "Are those the Sierras?"

"Rockies. The Sierras are beyond that, and believe me, you don't want to be caught in *any* of those mountains in winter. If we stay to the north and go to Oregon next spring, we'll have to get over the Bitterroots and then the Cascades. If we were to go to California, then we would go through the Sierras after getting over the Rockies. Either way, there will be a lot of mountains to get through when we head farther west." He drew on his cigarette. "If it's not me that takes you, I'll make sure it's someone who damn well knows what he's about when it comes to getting through the mountains."

"Is it possible for us to winter in another town besides Lander? One that's closer so we have less distance ahead of us come spring?"

"It might be possible. I'll talk to some of the men in Lander and get their advice, but the safest thing might be for us, or at least you, to stay in Lander."

Luke noticed Kate didn't answer right away. He glanced sidelong at her and was surprised to see she was quickly wiping at her eyes.

"Yes, I suppose you're right," she said, her voice sounding strained.

"You okay? I didn't mean to upset you. I mean, if somebody else takes you to Oregon, I'd make damn sure they would be trustworthy and capable."

Kate sniffed. "I know you would."

She's grown too dependent on me. Damn! Luke noticed a prairie hen trotting across their path. "Look there," he said, glad for the interruption in their conversation. "Supper." He quickly drew his six-gun from its holster and took aim. He fired, and half the hen's head flew off. The bird jumped into the air, then flopped to the ground. Luke charged up to it and dismounted. He picked up the hen and carried it over to the first pack horse, tying it to the horse by its feet. He took out his knife and whacked off the rest of its head.

"Letting the blood drain will help keep this thing from spoiling before we make camp tonight," he told Kate. "I decided to make this an easy trip for you and not ride too hard—figured we'd spend one night out here before reaching Lander tomorrow. I want you to be rested up when we get there, and I want you to be able to put that leg up for a while." He headed back to Red, then stopped. "Shit," he swore. "There are men out there watching us."

Kate looked in the direction Luke did. "Oh my God!"

"Stay calm," he told her. "They're probably just friendly passersby."

Luke walked back to his horse and mounted as five very rough-looking men approached them. "Once they reach us, let me do the talking," Luke told Kate.

"Be careful, Luke. I'd hate to see something happen to you after all we've already been through."

Luke caught the terror in her voice. "It's likely they're after our horses and supplies without killing anybody," he told her.

"I hope that's *all* they want," Kate answered.

"Just be casual and friendly. And it's best they think you're my wife, just like back at the cave when Hank and his men came along. Just go along with whatever I say."

"If you say so." Luke carefully cocked his rifle and laid it back across his lap. "Move Jenny closer to my horse."

"Gladly." Kate urged her horse closer to Red. "Should I take out my pistol?"

"Wouldn't hurt," Luke told her. "Keep it hidden in the folds of your skirt."

Kate obeyed.

Luke glanced her way. Why would it feel so natural to call her his wife if he had to? Hell, they'd been living practically like husband and wife already.

"Luke," she said softly.

"What?"

"If this doesn't go well, it's been nice knowing you."

Luke grinned a little, but his heart went out to her. She'd been through so much already. "Same here," he answered. "I sure do seem to have trouble holding on to any stock I have, don't I?" he told Kate in an effort to jokingly keep her spirits up. "First all my cattle, now maybe my horses. I must be in the wrong business."

"How can you joke at a time like this?"

"What's left?" Luke steadied his horse as the five men caught up to them. "Might as well go out with a smile."

"I can think of a lot of reasons *not* to smile." Kate took a deep breath and faced the men, all of them intimidating in their appearance, and all well-armed. Poor Luke wouldn't have a chance if they decided to kill him and take everything—including her.

TWENTY-ONE

"GOOD-LOOKING BUNCH OF HORSES YOU HAVE THERE," the apparent leader of the formidable gang of men told Luke. His eyes were on Luke, but the rest of the men were gawking at Kate. Their leader was a burly man with a big belly, a thick beard, and long, uncombed hair. He wore a buffalo-skin coat, even though it was quite warm today.

Luke nodded, keeping hold of his rifle. "I just bought these horses in Lander a few days ago," he answered, "and the wife and I are headed back there now."

"That so?" The big man turned to Kate and tipped his hat. "Mornin', ma'am."

Kate nodded in reply, while inside she felt faint at the thought that these men could kill Luke and ride off with her. She didn't even want to think about what that could mean.

The leader turned his attention back to Luke. "Name's Nate Bartley." He turned to the man beside him. "This here is Billy." He then indicated each man beside the one introduced. "Cal, Red Horse, and Tully."

Each man nodded at Luke and Kate both.

"We hunt buffalo and other wild game—sell it in the different towns out here," Nate explained. He turned and pointed. "Our camp is back there a ways, wagons for hauling our meat and skins. We're headed south." He turned back to Luke. "Heard your gunshot and figured we'd come and make sure you weren't in some kind of trouble. Lord knows trouble is easy to come by in this country."

Luke studied him closely, gauging the man's honesty. "That's friendly of you. We appreciate it."

"She's awful perty, Nate," Billy spoke up, ogling Kate more.

Without warning, Nate swung his rifle around and knocked Billy off his horse. Kate gasped at the sudden movement and backed up her horse, and Luke started to raise his rifle, until realizing Nate's move was to defend Kate. The man turned his horse and looked down at Billy.

"Don't you know a lady when you see one?" he barked. "Get back on your horse and ride back to camp!"

The side of his face already starting to show a bruise, Billy scowled as he got to his feet and remounted his horse. "I didn't mean nothin' bad," he grumbled before riding away.

Kate glanced at Luke, who kept watching Nate and the rest of them without a flinch. "You'll understand me when I tell all of you to ride on," Luke told Nate. "Like you said, this is dangerous country. A man doesn't know who to trust. When we saw you riding this way, it scared my wife. I appreciate you defending her like you just did, and I'm thankful for your concern that we might be in trouble, but we're fine. I killed a prairie hen for our supper. That's the gunshot you heard."

Nate nodded. "I know we're a sorry-lookin' bunch. It's hard not to be with what we do, but we clean up good." He looked around the vast landscape surrounding them. "I heard there's another bunch of outlaws been sneakin' around these parts stealin' horses and cattle. They've got no respect for women, if you know what I mean, so if I was you, I'd keep a good lookout till you get to Lander."

Luke tipped his hat. "We'll do that."

Nate glanced at Luke's rifle. "You good at handlin' that thing?"

"Good enough to kill the first man who threatens me or my wife. I can generally get off two or three good shots before the average man can pull a handgun and fire it."

Luke's answer was straightforward and firm. Kate waited with baited breath while Luke and Nate glared at each other for a moment.

"My wife is not incapable of killing a man either," Luke added. "In fact, she *did* kill one who had the wrong idea just a few days ago, and right now she's holding a six-gun on you. It's like I said, I appreciate your offer of help, and I don't mean to offend, but I'm also a man who understands other men out here. The wife and I would rest easier if all of you went on your way south."

Nate grinned, showing brown teeth from too much chewing tobacco. "Maybe you could spare some tobacco?" he asked. "You've got my word we'll be on our way after that. I won't ask anything more of you." He shifted in his saddle and sobered, but the other three men grinned eagerly.

"Hell, you wouldn't kill a man over some lousy tobacco, would you?" Nate added.

Kate felt a heavy thickness in the air. She swallowed nervously, her ready gun hand starting to ache. Luke slowly pulled back the hammer on his rifle.

"Not over tobacco," Luke answered. "But I'd kill a man over a horse and supplies, and I'd kill every man in sight over my wife. Over *any* woman, for that matter."

Nate finally broke into another grin and chuckled. "I expect you would." He turned to the others. "Go on back to camp. We need to be on our way."

"Ain't you gonna' at least get some of his other supplies, Nate?" The question came from Tully.

Nate kept his eyes on Luke. "This man ain't one to mess with, even when he's outnumbered," Nate answered. "Anybody in this bunch left alive if we try to take this man can have what they want, but I don't aim to die today. I expect I'm the first one he aims to shoot, so we'll be on our way. We're set for supplies anyway, except for tobacco. Go on, now. You don't want to die today either, do ya?"

"Shit," Tully grumbled. "That's one good-lookin' woman."

"And she belongs to this man here, so get goin'," Nate ordered.

The other three men turned their horses and rode off to catch up with Billy, who'd stopped in the distance.

"How about that tobacco?" Nate asked Luke.

Luke backed Red a little. "I just smoke it. I don't chew it," he answered. "But out here, a man is crazy if he doesn't have chewing tobacco along for trading."

Nate laughed and nodded. "You're a smart man, mister. What's your name anyway?."

"Luke Bowden, and I'm not so smart as I am just careful." Luke never once took his eyes off Nate. "Get a couple cans of tobacco out of that third pack horse, Kate," he ordered. "They're in that smaller saddlebag hanging over the big one."

Kate backed Jenny, afraid to turn the horse and have her back to Nate Bartley. She found the saddlebag Luke mentioned and fished around inside, pulling out two cans of Beech Nut chewing tobacco. She rode up beside Luke.

"Take them on up and hand them to Nate," he told her, not wanting to take his hand away from his rifle.

Kate hesitated.

"Go ahead," Luke told her. "It's okay."

Kate nudged Jenny forward and handed out the tobacco to Nate, feeling sick at the thought of the slovenly man touching her. Even having to touch his fingers when he took the tobacco made her shiver.

"Thank you, ma'am," he told her, grinning. He turned his gaze back to Luke as Kate backed her horse up again. "I thank you, Luke," he said. "And I expect you know the code out here. I promised this is all I'd take, and I live by the code for women, too, so you two can go on about your business and not worry about us. We'll be on our way. We've got meat and furs to deliver."

Luke nodded in reply. "I'll expect you to keep your promise."

"Yes, sir. Out here, a man knows when he can take what he wants, and when he can't. When I go up against a man, it's for a proud reason, not to pick on one who's weakened on account of he's outnumbered, and not to disrespect a good woman. In your case, though, I have a feelin' bein' outnumbered don't make you any weaker."

Luke actually smiled. "It's best you don't test me out."

Nate laughed hardily, his belly shaking. He held up the cans of tobacco and rode off, joining the other four, who then kept riding back with him to their camp. It was so far away that they actually disappeared into the horizon as they kept riding.

Kate let out a sign of relief and shoved her pistol back into the gun belt that hung around her saddle horn. Luke gently released the hammer of his rifle and shoved the long gun back into its boot. "You okay?" he asked Kate.

Unable to stop tears of relief, Kate took a moment to answer. She took a deep breath and pulled a handkerchief from a pocket on the skirt of her dress. "I think so." She blew her nose and wiped at her eyes. "I was so scared for you. I thought I was going to watch you die all over again. All I could think of was how I saved you from that hanging, only to watch you be killed some other way." She wiped at her eyes again. "I care enough about you that I would truly mourn you, Luke. And the thought of being out here alone again, and at the hands of men like that—"

Luke smiled and reached out his arm. "Come here."

Kate met his gaze. "What?" she asked.

"Come on over here," he repeated. He moved Red closer and put an arm around her waist. He pulled her off her horse and onto Red, plopping her in front of him. "You are one hell of a woman, Kate Winters. You did a good job of bravely facing those bastards."

Kate withered against his shoulder. "I don't feel brave at all. I just wanted to back you up." She moved her arms around Luke. "Do you think we can trust that man to ride off like he said?"

"Yes. That's the code out here. I can generally read a man pretty good. That bunch is capable of God knows what, but their word is their word, and he knew I meant business. He also knew he'd be the first to be shot if he tried anything. Most men like that can sniff out weakness like a wolf prowling after a wounded deer."

Still shaken, Kate relished the feel of his arms around her, reveling in his strength and sureness. "I thought they were going to fill you with bullet holes and do awful things to me!"

Luke's arms tightened around her. "Hell, I would have gotten at least three of them first," he told her, trying to reassure her. "And you would have got the other two."

Kate couldn't help smiling. "I'm not so sure about that. I just know I need you a while longer, until we get to civilization," she said, her head still on his shoulder. "Sometimes I feel like a little mouse surrounded by foxes and coyotes."

Luke kissed her hair.

What is happening? Kate wondered. Something had changed, but she couldn't put her finger on it. Luke was so damn close. Too close. She was afraid to look directly into his eyes.

"Which one am I?" he asked her. "A fox, or a coyote?"

They sat very still, Kate still in his arms. "I'm not sure," she answered. "I am thinking neither one. You're just a man I've grown to trust and care about."

"Yeah, well, sometimes just being a man is a problem in itself," he told her. She felt him move, looked down to see him take a spyglass from a loop on his gear. "Just sit still," he said. He raised the telescope and looked through it toward where the buffalo hunters had ridden.

"They kept their promise," he said after a few seconds. "The wagon is moving, and they are headed south. We should be safe." While she was still sitting in front of him, he turned Red slightly in all directions and scanned the entire horizon before closing the spyglass and putting it back in place. "We're alone."

An unexpected wave of desire suddenly swept through Kate at those two words...*we're alone*. Why had he checked to be sure? Why did this closeness disturb her in all the right places? She told herself to be careful, wondered what Luke had meant by telling her that sometimes just being a man can be a problem.

"Look at me, Kate," he told her, leaning back a little and putting a gentle hand under her chin.

Kate finally met his eyes. A soft breeze ruffled strands of his thick, brown hair that stuck out from under his hat, and she was again struck by his good looks.

"I don't know how to explain this," he said, nothing short of adoration in his dark eyes. "It just feels like we need to seal this friendship before we reach Lander. Once we get there, I won't see you often, because I don't want to soil your reputation. I know you to be an honorable woman, Kate Winters, and that's how I want folks there to see you. Am I making any sense?"

It took all of Kate's courage to admit the truth. "Yes, because I feel the same way—that is, if you're saying what I think you're saying." She closed her eyes and rested her forehead against his lips. "Last night, when you kissed me, you said you'd miss me. I'm sure you meant that things will all be different when we reach Lander." She met his gaze again. "I'll miss you, too. I mean, we won't be together like this after we get there. People wouldn't understand."

"And out here, men need to be damn straight about a woman's honor. You're a pretty woman and a widow alone. Some will see that as an opportunity, so I want your honor and reputation to be unquestioned."

"What about you? What will *you* think of me?"

"I'll think you're the finest woman I've ever known, but I'm guessing you're needing a man right now as bad as I need a woman, and whatever happens, it will never change my opinion of you."

"I need your promise on that. We've been through so much together in these few short days, and—"

Luke cut off her words with a deep, hungry kiss, and Kate decided that Luke Bowden damn well knew how to kiss. It was the best kiss she'd ever enjoyed, even from her own husband. He left her mouth and continued kissing her across the cheek, down to her neck, sending shivers through her.

"It just seems like this is necessary," Luke told her. "I can't explain it any more than that."

"I know."

Luke moved his lips to her mouth again, tasting, searching. He put his hands to either side of her face and kissed her eyes. "Damn it, woman, say no now if you aren't sure, because I've had all I can take. You're the one who said a woman is vulnerable out here, and I'm about to take advantage of that."

"Maybe I'm the one taking advantage of *you*," Kate answered softly.

Luke found her lips again, and Kate didn't pull away. She moved her arms around his neck, and he wrapped her in his arms and pulled her tight against him again. He kissed her deeper, harder, with more hunger. She answered the same way.

"Hang on," he finally told her when he was able to bring himself to leave her mouth again. He dismounted, pulling her off the horse with him and falling with her into the deep grass.

TWENTY-TWO

ALL REASONABLE THINKING LEFT KATE AS SHE allowed herself to relish the feel of a man's arms around her, the taste of his full lips, the utter ecstasy of letting his hands feel her breasts, the deep satisfaction of a broad, powerful chest hovering over her. She was tired of being alone. Out here in this big, lonesome, untamed land, what did it matter if this was right or wrong?

Luke ran a hand up her side, against her breast, then over her breast again, squeezing gently as his kiss deepened. She whimpered at his touch. He moved his lips from her mouth to her neck.

"Jesus, this is wrong, Kate."

"I know."

He moved his hand to the side of her face and kissed her eyes. "I'm so goddamn lonely," he told her.

"So am I," she said softly.

Luke's kisses grew wild and demanding, over her eyes, her hair, her cheeks, her neck, her throat. "I want to be inside of you," he said gruffly.

"I want to *feel* you inside of me. I need a man,

Luke, and I can't think of a better man to remind me I'm still a woman."

More kisses.

"You're beautiful," Luke whispered.

Beautiful. How long since she'd heard those words? "I've had no one for so long, Luke. Just myself, and I'm scared all the time. It feels so good to be held and protected."

She'd worn her hair loose, and Luke wrapped a hand into it, grasping tightly. He paused, looking into her eyes. "I can't make any promises, Kate."

"It doesn't matter." Kate hugged him around the neck and kissed the side of his face, not minding the stubble. "Out here *nothing* matters anymore…nothing but giving each other what's needed." She lay back again, and Luke traced a finger over her lips.

"Last night when I came back into that cave and you were sleeping," he told her, "I knelt beside you, and it took all my strength not to wake you up and ask to take you then and there."

"I probably would have let you," Kate told him.

"I wasn't sure. And I'd been drinking. I'm not as gentle when I drink. You might have ended up regretting it."

"I won't now," Kate answered.

Their lips met again, desperate, lonely, needy, on fire. Were they in love or just good friends? Kate could hardly believe she was being so brazen. Luke's hand was still tangled in her hair. "God, Kate, I don't want to just use you."

"If I thought that, or if I didn't want this, I'd tell you to stop."

Their bodies flattened out the grass underneath them as Luke pulled up her dress. Kate was instantly lost in him, not caring what he did with her. She felt a hand on her leg, felt his fingers move up over her belly and inside her bloomers and into the folds of her most private place. She cried out when he gently slid his fingers inside of her, drawing out the juices waiting to invite him inside.

How long had it been since a man commanded her this way? How long since she'd cried out from want and need? How long since her insides exploded in erotic, shameful, wonderful, glorious, desperate need?

Luke removed her bloomers, then he kissed her thighs and the hairs that hid that throbbing place that begged for more. He pushed her legs apart and licked at her folds, making her cry out. When he moved between her legs, he began kissing her neck, her eyes, her mouth. She could taste her own juices on his lips.

When had he removed his gun belt? When had he managed to release what she felt against her thigh now...hard and hot? She didn't even remember him pausing for any of that. She was only aware that he was on top of her. She cried out when he entered her almost roughly. After so long without a man, his shaft felt huge and hot, bringing a strangely enjoyable and erotic pain that made her arch against him in the deepest satisfaction she'd ever known.

This was Luke...handsome, strong, brave, able Luke Bowden. She'd saved his life and he'd saved hers. How many days ago was that? She still didn't know the whole man, yet it didn't matter. They moved together in sweet rhythm as though they'd been doing this forever. It all seemed right and natural.

I can't make any promises, he'd told her. Kate didn't care. She cried out with almost every thrust, and his own groans of pleasure told her she was indeed still able to please a man. He gently squeezed her breasts and nuzzled her neck, his broad shoulders hovering over her as he took her and took her. Their kisses deepened, and he moved his tongue into her mouth as though he wanted to take her in every way possible. Neither one of them was fully undressed, and Kate longed to be naked against him...to see him naked, too.

He shoved hard, over and over, as though he couldn't get enough of her, and through it all, they said nothing. They needed only this...to touch, to taste, to invade each other and release pent-up needs and loneliness. Kate gloried in his last thrusts...they were a pair who in ways were still strangers...mating in the middle of outlaw country...no one around... no life other than their horses, who grazed quietly, paying no attention to the man and woman who were writhing together in the tall grass.

Luke raised up, grasping her hips and pounding into her until Kate felt his life surge into her. She looked up at the sky...such a big sky...such a big lonesome.

TWENTY-THREE

LUKE SIGHED, LEANING DOWN TO KISS KATE LIGHTLY before adjusting his long johns and pants. He straightened Kate's dress, then lay down beside her, pulling her close.

Kate rested her head on his shoulder and reached one arm across his chest, unsure what he must think of her now. She'd been brazen and wanting, and now here she lay with a man who'd been a stranger just days ago. She breathed in his scent—a scent unique to Luke Bowden, a scent she would never forget.

"Are you all right?" Luke asked.

"I'm fine. I just wish I knew what you are thinking."

Luke faced her and smoothed some of the damp hairs away from her face. "I'm thinking that you're a good woman who needed a man, and I took advantage of that."

"I didn't stop you. You've been lonely long enough, Luke Bowden, and you're one of the finest men I've known. You need to be loved, and you need the kind of taking care of that only a woman can give you."

Luke kept a hand at the side of her face, gently

stroking her cheek with his thumb. "I just realized your burns are almost healed."

Their gazes held, and a deep sadness came into Luke's gaze. He closed his eyes and laid his head back down. "I can't tell you I love you, Kate, because I don't know if I do. I'm sorry."

"I didn't expect you to say it. I didn't expect anything at all other than to be a woman, and you know how to make a woman be just that. I *do* love you, Luke Bowden, but I didn't ask for anything more from you than this. I know what men want in women they love and marry. I'm past some of that. I know I'm not—"

He put fingers to her lips. "Don't say it. You underestimate yourself. You're beautiful and strong and brave."

"But I'm not—"

"What did I just tell you? You're more woman than most men are lucky enough to find even once in a lifetime."

Kate took his hand and kissed his palm. She couldn't help the tears that formed in her eyes. "What do we do now?"

"We wash up and ride on, and we make camp someplace a little more private than the middle of outlaw country grassland." He leaned closer and kissed her gently. "And we do this again." He grinned.

Kate couldn't help laughing through her tears at the remark. She turned sideways and threw her arms around him. "Just tell me you still respect me."

"I still respect you. And if you don't mind, I want you undressed the next time. I got a little tired of looking at this beautiful body back at that cave and not being able to touch it. That's damn hard on a man."

Kate laughed again and kissed his cheek, his disheveled dark hair, his lips. "Do you really think I'm beautiful?"

"Yes, ma'am, I do."

"Maybe out here anything looks beautiful to a man."

Luke chuckled. "I guess in some cases you're right." He rolled on top of her again, running a hand over her breasts and kissing her again. "But not in this case. You truly are beautiful."

Kate traced her fingers over the lines at the sides of his eyes—lines put there by living in wide-open country, most of the time with only the sky for a roof and the ground for a bed. The elements had beat up his youth, and the woman called Bonnie had beat up his heart. How could that woman not appreciate this man? How could she not wait for him? "If you went off to war again right now, Luke Bowden, I'd wait for you...faithfully...for years if it came to that."

He squinted, studying her eyes. "By God, I believe you would."

One of the horses whinnied.

"Shit!" Luke instantly was on his feet, buttoning his pants but leaving his shirt hanging out. He yanked his rifle from its boot again and looked around. "A couple of men...way off in the distance," he told Kate. "Looks like they're heading away from us, thank God." He looked down at Kate and grinned. "And here I thought we were completely alone. Some things get in the way of thinking straight, I guess."

Kate sat up. "Oh, for heaven's sake, those men you just spotted could have ridden right up on us!"

"And they would have gotten an eyeful, wouldn't they?" Both of them grinned. "Sit still and I'll get you a towel and a canteen so you can wash yourself," Luke told her, looking her over with a very satisfied gaze. He turned back to watch the men. "You have time. They are even farther away now." He put his rifle back in its boot and retrieved a canteen and a towel, handing them down to her. "I won't look," he teased.

Kate couldn't help the chagrin written all over her face. "What's left that you *haven't* seen?"

Luke folded his arms. "Nothing. But there are still some things I haven't touched...or tasted."

Kate frowned. "*Now* you're being rude. Turn around, Mister Bowden."

Luke turned away and leaned down to pick up his hat, which he'd lost when he was kissing her wildly and they'd practically fallen off of Red. He put it on and began tucking in his shirt.

"For crying out loud," Kate said as she washed herself. "We're out here in a land so big it makes a person wonder if it ever ends—a land where most people wouldn't think of settling, yet I've been attacked, you were hanged, another man came along and attacked me while you were gone, those buffalo hunters found us, and now you've seen two *more* men riding out there somewhere. How on earth can a person run into so many people out here in the middle of nowhere?"

Luke leaned across Red, still watching to be sure the men he'd seen were headed away from them. "The fact remains that if we stayed out here longer it might be days or weeks before we see life again. We just happened to be in the right places at the right times, or maybe the *wrong* times. Fact is, I have a feeling the men I'm watching are headed for our cave."

Our cave. Kate pulled on her bloomers and let her skirt fall. She liked that he'd called it "our cave." She would always think of it that way herself and remembering all that had happened there made her feel like crying again. She realized that ever since Rodney was killed in the war, she'd hardly shed a tear once she stopped crying over losing her husband. She'd refused to let it get her down, told herself she had to be strong and go on with life.

A wagon train attack and Luke Bowden had changed all of that...or had it? She'd certainly met a man again, and she'd even fallen in love again. But he'd said he couldn't be sure he loved her in return. She'd accepted that, yet she'd let him bed her, and she would let him take her again before they reached Lander and civilization...and the world of reality, where Luke might realize he'd been foolish to even consider he might love her or *any* woman.

She studied his back, his broad shoulders. The fact remained that she'd known him only seven or eight days. She'd lost track of time...and she'd lost her own good sense. Truth was, if Luke Bowden chose to ride out of her life, she wouldn't stop him because he wasn't a man to be forced into anything. But he would take her heart with him wherever he went. She would never find it again.

TWENTY-FOUR

As they headed north, Kate thought how, from above, they must look like tiny insects making their way through the high, yellow grass. She continued to stay behind a little, figuring Luke needed time to think about what they had done. So did she.

Here they were, two strangers who had mated, not so different from the wild animals who came together at mating time, made their babies, then parted ways, never to meet again. Was that how it would be for her and Luke?

Looking ahead, one would never know there was any kind of town even remotely close. The incredibly vast valley stretched on and on, a sea of yellow, dotted here and there with a green tree that didn't look like it belonged there at all. On both sides, the brown and red and yellow rock walls that supported vast mesas blocked them from the rest of the world, and always in the distance were the mountain ranges, threatening barriers to the sun and green and warmth of California and Oregon.

Would they truly go their separate ways come

spring? The thought brought a painful loneliness to Kate's heart worse than when she'd lost Rodney. How could that be, when she'd known Luke Bowden such a short time? She could still feel him inside her, still sense the hard muscle of his arms, feel his lips, taste his kisses. She could feel his fingers touching secret places, feel his warm breath against her most private part. Had she really allowed him to touch her there? Taste her there? She could see the way his dark eyes danced when he laughed. She loved his laugh.

She'd invited all of it, and when she did so, she'd invited heartbreak and loneliness. He was a man torn by indecision, reacting to his own broken heart, a man who'd needed to be with a woman and needed to feel what it was like for that woman to want and accept him…needed to know how it felt to trust.

But was that enough? When they reached Lander, he would change, she was sure. They would both come to their senses and go their separate ways to wait out the winter.

They ambled along for three more hours, taking an easy gait for the sake of the horses. Scout trudged behind the little procession, and off and on Luke smoked quietly. They stopped a few times to rest and water the horses and eat, but conversation was only about when they should stop for the night and how and when they should rest the horses or change their gait or shift some of the load between horses so that the animals weren't overstressed. They talked about where she should stay when they reached Lander, what they could do to while away the winter there. Luke warned her about the kind of men who lived there, some just regular businessmen with wives and children, some suffering from war losses or from bad memories. Most were out-and-out outlaws who lived off stolen cattle and money. Some respected women. Some did not. She would have to learn to read their eyes and know the difference.

I can't tell you that I love you, Kate. She told herself it didn't matter. It wouldn't stop her from letting him take his pleasure again, because she would enjoy it just as much as he did. If this was all she would have of him, then so be it. It was better than never having him at all. He was a good man—caring and protective. If he had to die protecting her, he would. She knew instinctively that he'd not just used her for his own selfish pleasure. There had been more to it than that. And the pleasure was not just his. She'd welcomed him inside her body, inside her heart and soul.

They kept going, heading for a log cabin Luke had spotted with his spyglass. It was just a dot on the endless horizon at first. *Another place used by men traveling between Miles City and Robber's Roost*, Luke told her. *If we're lucky, no one will be using it tonight.*

The wind picked up. All afternoon they had watched dark clouds roil over the distant mountains and make their way over plains and mesas and valleys and canyons, over yellow flatland and dry creek beds. As the edge of the oncoming storm approached, the temperature dropped, just like the day they were caught in the snowstorm that forced them to hole up in the cave.

Kate still couldn't quite get over wondering what she was doing out here. She felt like a woman forgotten in time. Somewhere, far, far behind her lay a burned-out wagon train, the dead bodies of those men who'd fought hard to save it all, including the tough old guide who'd told her how to listen for thundering horses. She would never be able to find them again if she had to. They would all disappear into the earth, never to be heard from again. How sad. The thought made her chest hurt.

And somewhere back there was a gnarly old, half-dead tree where she'd cut a man down from a hanging, an act that had changed her life. She'd had no inkling that only a week or so later she'd be lying beneath that man, giving up her most secret places, taking him like a wanton woman.

The wind began to blow harder. Tiny droplets of sleet stung her face.

"Ride a little faster," Luke called back to her. "Let's get to that cabin!"

His words seem to fall away with the wind as it blew past her. She ducked her head and kicked Jenny into a faster trot, staying alongside the second pack horse and making sure the string of horses followed fast enough and didn't drag down Luke's pace. She took a rope from her horse and rode back and forth, from the lead pack horse to the bull, slapping their rumps and urging them into a faster pace.

"Hah! Hah!" she shouted. "Get up there!"

The sleet grew heavier. The wind grew colder. It didn't snow, but it felt like it could start at any moment. There was no time to stop and put on coats. It seemed the wind penetrated everything she wore and she was naked against it. It took a good half hour of hard riding to make it to the cabin. Luke ordered her to help him get all the horses and the bull into a corral and into a lean-to built to protect animals from the west wind that howled down from the mountains and across the vast plains, picking up speed and moisture along the way.

Without saying much, they both spread out some feed grass someone had stacked in a corner. Luke took a small barrel of water from one of the pack horses and poured it into a trough that ran along the back wall of the shed below the feed trough. "That should keep them for the night," he yelled above the wind. "If we can't get back out here to unload everything, they will be okay until we reach Lander tomorrow. They rent good stables there with plenty of food and shelter." He untied a gunny sack of his own things and one that held the necessities for coffee and one small meal. "Grab some blankets and what you'll need for the night," he told Kate. "I'll get my weapons and supplies off Red."

Kate did as she was told, untying blankets, a leather sack that held some of her homemade bread and some honey and hard tack. She walked to one of the other horses to untie the rope that held her heavier coat. She ran toward the cabin, leaning into the wind and putting some of her supplies in front of her face to shield it from the stinging sleet. Luke unloaded the rest of what he needed and followed, closing the gates across the opening of the lean-to so the horses couldn't wander off. He and Kate both felt a sudden and welcome relief from the weather when they barged into the cabin and slammed the door shut.

"I'll get a fire going and warm it up in here," Luke told her. He stood his rifle against the wall near the door and dropped the things he was carrying onto the wood plank floor. The walls creaked against the wind while Kate sorted through their supplies and spread out their bedrolls and some blankets. Luke got a fire going with wood someone had left behind, and soon flames snapped and spit inside the stone fireplace. The warmth created fought with the cold air that insisted on making its way through cracks in the broken chinking between the cabin's log walls.

Kate poured water into the porcelain-lined coffeepot and added grounds wrapped in cheesecloth, then set the pot on a grate near the fire. "Right now, the flames are too high to set the coffee any closer," she told Luke. She thought how she and Luke had worked out a routine over the last few days where each knew his and her jobs. There was no need to ask or to tell the other what to do next. *Like an old married couple.* She sat down on her bedroll near the fire and waited for the tiny cabin to warm up, if that was possible.

"This sudden change in weather could be gone again by morning," Luke said, adding one more log to the fire.

"I hope so," Kate replied. She rubbed at the backs of her arms. "I've never seen the weather change so fast as it does out here."

"*Nothing* out here is normal," Luke commented. "But being out of the wind makes things feel warmer even *without* a fire." He came to sit down beside her and moved an arm around her shoulders. "You okay?

You've been walking around on that leg like it was never injured."

Kate winced as she unbuttoned her left boot and opened it to pull it off. "I'm fine. There are times when you just do what needs doing and hope you don't pay for it later." She removed her other boot.

Luke told her to turn sideways and put her feet in his lap. "I'd better make sure nothing is bleeding."

Kate lay down on her bedroll and offered her feet. Luke reached under her dress and carefully removed her knee-high stockings.

"I should have carried you in here."

"In that awful sleet and wind? And with the supplies we had to carry in? Nonsense." Kate thought how odd it was that only days ago she'd been mortified this man had seen her wearing nothing but a man's shirt when she'd let him take care of her leg. Now she relished his touch.

He examined the bandages wrapped around her leg. "Things look pretty good," he told her. "I don't see any blood on the bandages." He gently squeezed the area around the wound. "Does any of this hurt?"

"No. Just a surface sting from the healing."

"It's going to be that way for a while yet." Luke removed his hat and tossed it aside, then removed his leather vest and unbuckled his gun belt. He gently set her feet aside and removed his boots.

Kate waited, her heart beating faster as he straddled her and reached under her dress, taking hold of her bloomers and pulling them off slowly, as though waiting for her to object.

She didn't.

They were close enough to the fire to feel its warmth now. Luke got to his knees and removed his shirt, revealing man and muscle, a flat stomach and hairs on his chest that led downward and into a straight line toward that part of him she already wanted to feel inside of her.

Luke Bowden had a commanding way about him that made Kate simply lie there and allow him whatever he wanted. Just like out on the plains earlier, all that happened next took place as though it was not just normal and right, but absolutely necessary. Luke leaned down and met her mouth in another delicious kiss, and Kate trembled at the knowledge he was unbuttoning the front of her dress. Without his asking, she sat up and let him pull the dress off her shoulders and down her arms.

Just as the room warmed, so did the heat build between them, overcoming the still-cold outer room. Their gazes held through every move they made. Luke unlaced her camisole and pulled it open, then moved the straps down and off her shoulders. He tossed it aside. Kate braced her arms behind her and raised up, letting him pull her dress all the way off. She sat there naked before him, and his eyes moved over her almost reverently. Brazenly, she lay back, her body fully exposed to his gaze.

Luke got up and walked over to pull down the locking bar across the cabin door. He came back and removed his pants and long johns. Kate couldn't help noticing all that was man about him, huge and hard and eager for a woman. She thought him a beautiful specimen of man as he stood there naked before her.

Luke dropped to his knees, then leaned down to kiss her thighs, then the hairs between her legs. What made this all the more enticing was knowing without a doubt that she could tell him "no" right now and he would stop. She loved him all the more for feeling so completely safe with him, as well as respected, in spite of what she was allowing. Even in making love to her, he was a gentleman. She could think of no other way to put it.

She closed her eyes and breathed deeply when she felt the warmth of his tongue stroking her. She moaned, grasping his thick hair and pressing his lips against secret places, offering herself to him like a wanton woman.

Perhaps she'd *become* a wanton woman. Luke Bowden had done this to her. He'd flaunted his manliness like a rooster strutting for hens.

He moved his lips over her belly and to her breasts, relishing each one as though a delicious dessert— tasting them, fondling them, arousing her nipples until they ached to be taken fully into his mouth. He moved inside of her with a soft groan.

"I love your breasts," he said close to her ear amid rhythmic thrusts.

Kate cried out as he filled her hard and deep, his own groans of satisfaction telling her how pleasing she was to him. Kate kissed his chest, his chin, his lips. She ran her hands over the hard muscle of his arms, his shoulders, into his thick hair, opening herself to him in utter abandon. She told herself this might be all she had, and she was damn well going to take it. It felt so good to be a whole woman again.

She cried out his name. This was Luke, a good man who'd been wronged, a good man who'd respected her in every way when he could have taken advantage, a good man who'd made no promises so she would know this might be all they would ever have together.

"You have no idea how much…I've wanted this," he told her. His words came in bits and pieces as he rocked into her over and over until he could no longer hold back his ecstasy at being inside of her. Again, she felt the power of his life pouring into her.

In moments he relaxed beside her, pulling blankets over both of them. "You're one hell of a woman, Kate Winters," he said close to her ear.

"And you are one hell of a man," she answered.

Luke pulled her close. "Thanks for helping herd those pack horses like you did. I swear you have cowboy blood in you."

"I grew up on a farm. I'm used to hard work and used to animals." Kate could feel his smile without looking at him.

"I want to do this again."

"Do what you want," Kate said softly. "It's been too long since I felt like a real woman, and you know how to make me feel that way."

He fondled a breast as he moved on top of her again and met her gaze. "And you make me feel like a man who is appreciated and respected. Bonnie took that away from me. Coming home to find her married to my own brother was like taking a sword to my pride."

Kate ran a hand through his hair. "I would never do that to any man."

Luke kissed her eyes. "I know you wouldn't, and

I respect all that's good about you. No one in Lander will know about this. That's a promise."

His eyes spoke only admiration and respect, and Kate felt the sincerity of his words. Luke Bowden was an honest man who was not the type to boast his conquests to others. "I hope you believe me when I tell you that you're the first man who's touched me in years, Luke, ever since my husband marched off to war and never came back."

He moved a hand to the side of her face and kissed her again…so gently…then grinned teasingly. "Oh, I can tell by your eagerness," he joked.

God, how she loved his smile. "I'm sure we will be doing this all night," she said, "so I hope the promise you made that first time still holds."

"What promise was that?"

"That you will still respect me in the morning."

He kissed her and moved between her legs, already able to move inside her again. "I'll always respect you…morning, noon, night…together or apart," he told her between rhythmic thrusts.

Their lovemaking started all over again, deep and wild and throwing all caution to the wind that howled outside. Kate chose to not think about his last words—*together or apart*. It hurt too much to face what that might mean.

TWENTY-FIVE

THEY MADE LOVE AGAIN, THEY ATE, LUKE CHECKED ON the horses, and they made love again. They slept...a sleep interrupted by making love yet again sometime deep in the night. The sun was already shining brightly when Kate rose and wrapped herself in a blanket. She put another log on the fire, although she could tell it was a little warmer outside by the fact that the cabin was bearably warm in spite of how much the fire had died down. There was still coffee in the pot, so she left it beside the fire to keep warm.

She glanced at a peacefully sleeping Luke, wondering how long they had slept. They probably should have left earlier for Lander, and she wondered if she should wake him. She would rather stay right here, make a home for Luke and never leave—but that was wishful thinking. He'd not made one promise, and she'd not asked for any. He'd called her beautiful, strong, and brave. But he'd not said that he loved her, even though he knew that she loved him. Physically, she felt satisfied, fulfilled, ravished. They were two adults who'd needed this kind of togetherness, ached to fulfill natural desires too long neglected. Luke seemed to understand that, and she felt no worry over whether or not he still respected her, even though she'd never in her life behaved this way, not even on her wedding night. She'd never wanted and taken Rodney with as much passion as she'd felt for Luke Bowden. Maybe it was because she was a mature woman and not the inexperienced younger woman who'd married Rodney Winters. Or maybe it was because Luke was, in a sense, forbidden. They hadn't taken any wedding vows, and they hadn't known each other long enough to even consider it. What they'd shared simply *was,* with no obligations, no regrets, no promises. Luke wasn't the type of man to brag about it or laugh at her because of it. His discretion and respect for her reputation was one of the things she loved about him.

She turned back to the fire when she thought she heard something, a shuffling sound on the sagging front porch of the little cabin. She hurried over to a window and thought she saw a shadow. Something, or someone, was moving around outside.

"Oh my God!" she whispered. She grabbed Luke's rifle from where he'd left it against the wall by the door and hurried over to where he still slept.

"Luke!" she said softly, nudging his arm with her foot. "Luke, wake up!"

He stirred and looked up at her.

"Someone is outside!" she told him, setting his rifle against the fireplace.

Luke threw off his blankets and jumped up, grabbing his long johns and quickly pulling them on. He moved his arms into the sleeves and buttoned the bottom half of the underwear. He blinked and shook his head, running a hand through his thick, disheveled hair. He yanked his six-gun from its holster, which hung over a nearby chair. "Take this and get over in the corner behind that stack of wood," he said, indicating a pile of wood near an old, broken down cook stove. He reached for his rifle. "I'll—"

Before he finished talking, a shot rang out, breaking a window. Kate screamed, and Luke spun around, blood spewing from a gash on his left side. He hit the floor.

"Luke!" Kate screamed again. Her first reaction was to go to him, but she noticed him quickly scoot his body over to cover his rifle. "Get their attention," she thought she heard him say, the words groaned in pain.

Another bullet shattered a second window. Kate kept hold of Luke's revolver and hurried around a dusty, wooden table, that and two chairs being the only furniture in the cabin. She headed for the wood pile. Just as she did so, someone managed to kick open the door in spite of the wooden bar that held it fast. Another shot came through the first window as Kate managed to duck behind the pile of wood.

"Come on, boys! The door is open!" someone shouted.

Five men barged inside. Luke remained still.

"You killed him!" Kate shouted, deliberately stepping out from her hiding place to keep them from checking Luke's body and finding the rifle. *God, don't let them find out Luke is still alive,* she prayed. She purposely dropped the blanket she'd wrapped around herself, revealing her nakedness, then quickly picked it up to cover herself, pretending it was all an accident. Immediately, she had the rapt attention of all five men. They were a mixture of sizes and ages, but all smelled of unwashed bodies.

They were unshaven, their clothes dirty, and a couple of them had no teeth. She could only hope Luke really was still alive and that this would give him a chance to get hold of his rifle.

"Well, well, well," the big man who'd broken down the door said in a gruff voice. He grinned, looking her over hungrily. "Leave the blanket off, lady."

Kate had kept hold of the blanket enough to cover her bottom half and the revolver in her hand. "I'll do no such thing!" she answered, hoping that refusing the man's order would keep their attention. She didn't even look at Luke, afraid that if she did so, the others would look, too, and see he was still alive. Or *was* he? Nothing but horror awaited her if he wasn't, and she wondered if she should shoot *herself* with the six-gun in her hand.

"Jesus, Mark," one of the others commented, "she's prettier than any of them damn whores in Lander."

"Fresher, too," a third man added. "She's only been had by one man, I'll bet." The one who spoke looked young, maybe still in his teens. "I'll bet her husband is the only one who's had at her. I'm thinkin' it's time she found out the pleasure of *more* than one man, especially a hard, young buck like me." He licked his lips and moved closer.

"She's mine first," the big, slovenly man called Mark told him. "The rest of you can hold her down and watch. I'm figurin' you'll jack off over that before you even get your chance at fuckin' her."

Kate felt ill. Luke had told her to get their attention, and she'd certainly managed to do that. Not one of them was watching him. In fact, two of them had stepped right over his body as they walked closer to her.

Should she start shooting now and take the chance of being killed before these men even touched her? Maybe so. Right now, death sounded more pleasurable.

"Get…get out of here!" she demanded.

They all laughed.

Mark spoke up. "Jimmy, it's a good thing you seen them horses in the shed out there." Kate guessed him to weigh at least two hundred fifty pounds or more. "If we hadn't come this way and decided to steal them horses and that nice young bull out there, we would have missed the biggest prize of all. She just might bring good money at Della's whorehouse down at Hole in the Wall."

He put his revolver in its holster and unbuckled his gun belt. "Let's find out how much she's worth." He stepped closer to Kate. "You've been fresh-fucked, ain't ya? You still achin' for a man?"

"You disgusting, filthy, fat bastard!" Kate shot back, determined to keep all eyes on her.

Mark stepped even closer, and the other four did the same, a couple more of them actually holstering their revolvers.

"You'll take back your words when we take turns shovin' somethin' in that smart mouth!" Mark sneered.

Kate noticed Luke roll off his rifle. The minute he moved, she raised her six-gun and fired through the blanket, putting a bullet in Mark's huge belly.

Instantly, the room was full of gunfire. Luke's rifle exploded—one shot, two shots, three shots. One of them went into Mark's back, and he fell forward, landing right at Kate's feet with her bullet in his belly and Luke's bullet in his back. Two more men went down at almost the same time that Mark fell. A fourth man cried out from a bullet Luke put through his rear end as he ran out the door, while the fifth man dived through a window, screaming when a piece of glass dug a deep gash in his thigh and then his foot.

Kate just stood there a moment before looking down at the blanket she still held. The end of her smoking six-gun stuck out through a burn hole in the blanket that was also still smoking. The heavyset Mark lay on the floor in front of her, a bloody hole in his back. As he fell, he'd hit his head on a chair, and the chair was now flipped upside-down. Kate wasn't sure if he was dead or just unconscious. Two other men lay sprawled on the floor, the teenaged boy still holding the gun he'd pulled but never fired. Luke's shots had been too fast for him to react quickly enough.

Luke grunted as he got to his knees. Kate's stomach tightened at the sight of blood on the left side of his long johns. He stumbled to the bodies, kicking each one. He noticed Mark stir, and he pointed his rifle at the man's head and fired.

Kate jumped and gasped at the sight. Luke had blown half the man's head off without an ounce of hesitation.

"Fucking bastard!" he growled. He looked at Kate. "You okay? Bullets were flying everywhere. Please tell me you aren't hit."

A trembling Kate shook her head. "I'm all right, but you're bleeding, Luke."

"I'm too fucking mad to care!" He wavered a little. Kate quickly managed to wrap the blanket more fully around herself and stepped over Mark's body and the teenager's legs to get to Luke, gun still in hand. "Let me bandage that wound, Luke."

"Not yet. You stay right here." He stumbled to the door.

"Don't go out there!"

"I have to make sure they leave. Watch the ones inside. Make sure they're all dead before you lay down that pistol." He managed to get to the broken door and outside to see the other two men riding away, leading three other horses with them—horses that belonged to the three dead men. He could see his own horses were still in the lean-to. He half wilted against the doorjamb and looked at Kate. "At least they didn't get our horses. They took just their own."

Kate ran up to him, and he moved an arm around her. "You sure you're okay?" he asked.

"I'm fine, but you're hurt! Please come over and lie down on the blankets, Luke! I'll heat some water."

"It's okay. Just bloody. I know how a bullet feels inside you. I think this one went all the way through."

"Let me look at it!" Kate helped him step over Mark and lower himself to the blankets. He reached for her hand and squeezed it. "You sure you're okay?" he asked yet again.

"I'm sure."

Luke shook his head, putting a hand to his side. "You did good," he told her. "I can't believe how quickly you picked up on what I said. I wasn't sure you even heard me."

Kate took a moment to sit down beside him. "Dropping the blanket was the hardest thing I've ever done." She put a hand to the side of his face and kissed his cheek. "I was so scared you were passed out or dead. I don't even want to think about—"

"*Don't* think about it." He kissed her lightly. "Dropping that blanket would have kept my attention too."

Kate broke into tears. "What an ugly ending to what was a beautiful night."

Luke brushed away her tears. "We make quite a team, don't we?" he said.

Kate couldn't help shedding more tears. "I'm sorry," she told Luke. "I cry when I go through something like this. My God, Luke, they saw me naked." She curled into the blanket. "And now I've killed another man!"

"You just wounded him. *I'm* the one who finished him off. And the son of a bitch *deserved* it!" He grimaced. "Give me a towel to hold against this wound. I can slow down the bleeding while you dress and go get Red. Tie a rope on him, and tie the other end to the feet of each of these dead bastards and drag their bodies outside. Get them out of here for now, and I'll take care of them later. I hate that the other two got away. That's not good. We'll have to keep our eyes open when we leave."

Kate straightened, wiping at her tears with the blanket. "I should tend to that wound first."

"No. Leave my rifle near me." Luke stroked her hair. "I need you to be the brave, able woman I know you are, Kate. I need you to get dressed and get these bodies out of here. Check on the horses. Keep a gun with you."

Kate nodded. "I will." She rose and retrieved a towel for Luke, then set a pan of water on the hot coals in the fireplace. She quickly dressed, her stomach still upset at Mark's filthy words and the thought of what would have happened to her if Luke hadn't been able to grab his rifle and move fast. How he did it with a wound in his side, she couldn't imagine. Pushing aside the horror of five men gawking at her nakedness, she did everything Luke told her to do. Just as she'd suspected, it was warmer outside than when they got here last night.

She led Red to the front of the cabin and, one-by-one, she tied a rope to each dead body and dragged it outside until all three men were out of the cabin, leaving behind a floor covered with blood stains mixed into dirt and dust. She put Red back into the shed and looked around to make sure the other two men weren't coming back. She saw no one. She quickly grabbed some gauze, a towel, and some whiskey from their supplies before hurrying back inside the cabin to dress Luke's wound. He was lying flat, still holding the towel to his side. She offered him some laudanum but Luke refused, wanting to be alert in case the others returned.

"While you were taking care of the bodies, I managed to sweep what was left of that fat bastard's brains into the fireplace," Luke said.

Kate shivered and grasped her stomach at the comment.

"I'm damn sorry, Kate," Luke lamented. He grimaced with pain, and Kate drew a deep breath and reminded herself this was no time to give in to the horror. She grabbed the whiskey and poured some on Luke's wound, wincing when he cried out with pain. She picked up the gauze and began wrapping it around his middle. "That never should have happened," Luke told her, managing to sit up so Kate could more easily dress the wound. "Normally, I would have been more aware. You damn well wore me out last night."

Kate felt her cheeks flushing. "I didn't mean—"

Luke put his fingers to her lips. "I didn't exactly object," he told her with a sly grin.

Their gazes held, both realizing the same thing. They had to get themselves to Lander.

"Let's rest from this for a couple of hours and then get to town," Luke said. "We can still make it there by dark."

Kate finished wrapping the wound and rose to get Luke some clean long johns. "What about the dead bodies out there?"

Luke ran a hand through his hair again. "I can't lift them. That might make this wound start bleeding worse." He took the underwear from her and managed to get to his feet.

Kate helped him step out of the bloody long johns and step into the clean ones. She found it incredible that she could look at all that was man about him without embarrassment. He'd invaded her in just about every way possible, and she didn't blame him or hate him. Again, their relationship felt more like husband and wife than just friends. Everything she did for him was in a wifely way, trusting his judgment and orders, caring about his physical welfare, wanting to feed him and keep his clothes clean and mended.

"We'll leave the bodies outside where they are for now," Luke told her as he finished dressing by himself, wincing with pain with every movement. "Once I get you to Lander, I'll find some men who are willing to"—he buttoned his pants, then grimaced as he stretched out an arm to put it in the sleeve of a clean shirt—"come back out here with me and help me bury the bodies. We'll have to look out for the other two. They might have ridden to Lander."

Kate began packing some of their things, all but the blankets and a couple of biscuits she'd heat for breakfast. "I think they were already on an early-morning journey to Lander when they noticed our horses in the shed," she told Luke. "They probably stopped to see if they could steal them, and maybe one of them looked in the window and saw us lying together."

"Could be, but the two who rode away headed back south, not north," Luke commented. He set the overturned chair back on its legs and sat down gingerly, taking up a cigarette from two he'd left on the table the night before. "Light a stick for me, will you?"

Kate held a small stick into the fire and brought it over to him, the end burning. He used it to light the cigarette and handed it back. "Let's eat and rest a bit, then get going."

It all happened as it should. They ate, drank coffee, and tried to rest but couldn't. Too much had happened, and three dead bodies lay outside. Kate brushed her hair and finished packing everything. Luke helped as much as he could.

They walked outside and to the horses. Luke winced as he finished tying Kate's bedroll onto Jenny. They led the horses out of the corral, and Luke glanced at the dead bodies lying a few yards from the cabin. He let go of Red's harness and turned to Kate, grasping her arms. "I'm sorry about all of this, and not just what happened this morning. I'm sorry about *everything*. I hope you believe me when I say none of this...I mean...in a way I took advantage of you. I—"

Kate put a hand to his lips. "I know you would not have touched me if I didn't want you to, but I didn't *want* to resist. You've done nothing but save my life and protect me and care for me, Luke Bowden, from the first day I found you until now. And yes, I saved your life, too, but out here everything we do is called survival. I wanted your horse and your food and water. What I did wasn't without its own selfishness."

Luke grinned. "Being able to breathe instead of choke to death would have been worth you cutting me down, even if you had taken Red and ridden off. I wouldn't have hated you for it."

Kate smiled through tears as she ran her hands over his broad shoulders and down his solid arms. "Neither of us could help the situations we were in, Luke. And if we part ways after this, I won't blame you, but there won't be a day that goes by that I won't think about you and pray for you...and miss you." Her eyes teared as Luke pushed a piece of her hair behind her ear, then leaned forward and kissed her forehead. He stepped back.

"Let me help you up," he told her.

"No. You shouldn't strain yourself." Kate reached up and grabbed Jenny's pommel. She put her foot into the stirrup, then grimaced from the pain in her leg as she started to pull herself up. Against her advice, Luke put a hand on her rump and gave her a push. "Luke Bowden, I told you not to help." She adjusted her dress and looked down at him. "Promise me that when we get to Lander, you will see a doctor and get that wound properly cleaned up and taken care of."

He patted Jenny. "I promise, but it really isn't all that bad. At least we got the bleeding stopped." He rubbed at the wounded area. "Right now, I have to mount up on Red, which won't be easy." He walked up to the big roan gelding and put a foot into the stirrup, then groaned as he pulled himself up and managed to throw his leg over the horse. He sat there a minute to let the pain subside, then picked up the reins to the lead pack horse and started off.

Kate looked back at the sagging little cabin with its broken door and broken windows...and three dead bodies lying near the hitching post out front. What happened there last night, and what happened before that in the golden grass of this wide, lonesome country, all seemed like a distant dream now...a wonderful, magical, beautiful dream.

Again, as when she looked back at the cave they'd shared, she felt a stab at her heart. This could be the end of the best and the worst events of her life. This could be a trip back to reality...and the awful loneliness she'd known before finding a stranger hanging from a tree.

TWENTY-SIX

THEY RODE QUIETLY THROUGH LANDSCAPE THAT seemed too violent for its dead silence, heading down embankments that led to dry gulches, back up the other side into more yellow grass. Kate began to appreciate how hard it must have been for Luke to get to Lander and back to her as fast as he did. She couldn't imagine making the ride from the cave all the way to Lander in just one day, and then making it all the way back the next day. Realizing how difficult that had been was just more proof of what a good man Luke Bowden was.

They rounded grand mesas that made her feel like a tiny, unimportant speck of dust against the magnificent endlessness. They'd stopped only once to eat and relieve themselves and water the horses, then kept riding. It was nearly dark when Kate saw the dim street lanterns in the distance.

"That's Lander," Luke told her. He'd ridden most of the way half bent over and holding his side. Kate was worried about him. "You be sure to see a doctor right away, Luke." She looked backward once more as they headed into Lander. The cave where so much had happened to them seemed so far away now. And the cabin where they'd spent such a passionate night together was now a distant dream that had been spoiled by the intrusion of the man named Mark and his men.

Now she would lose Luke. Of that she was sure. He'd be around other men and women and saloons and drinking and gambling. To her, everyone here would be a stranger not to be trusted, and Luke would not be at her side constantly. In places like this it was easier for men to mix and mingle with others than for a woman alone. And once a man got drunk, *everybody* was his friend, and she was pretty sure Luke could put down whiskey as good as the rest of them.

Luke ordered her to ride up beside him. "We'll put the horses and my bull in the stables this side of town," he said. "I'll see if we can rent or borrow a wagon to put all our supplies in. We'll take that to the rooming house I told you about. I told Nora to save you a room. Come morning, you can visit the bathhouse run by Betsy Heater. It has one area that's closed off just for women, so you'll have some privacy. You can clean up there in a real bathtub." He gave Kate a smile. "I'm told Betsy will even wash your hair for you, and she knows how to do hair up with combs and such. I'm guessing I won't recognize you when she's through with you."

Kate wondered if Betsy Heater did more for men than let them bathe. She told herself it didn't matter. She had no right being jealous of other women. She couldn't lay any claim to Luke Bowden. "A real bath and washing my hair sounds wonderful," she told him aloud. "Just don't you forget to see a doctor about that wound."

"Yes, ma'am. That's about the tenth time you've told me."

"Are you taking a room at the same rooming house as I am?"

Luke shook his head. "I'd better not. It wouldn't look good, us riding in together and then taking rooms at the same house."

"But this is outlaw country," she reminded him. "Who will care?"

"It's more to keep dirty thoughts out of the minds of most of the unruly, disrespectful men around here. If they think you're easy, they'll take too much for granted, and you won't be safe. I want you to be careful and trust no one but me. Keep that extra handgun with you wherever you go and keep it beside your bed at night. And don't be afraid to use it. There's no law out here to say it's right or wrong."

Kate's heart fell a little. He was telling her he *wouldn't* be in her bed and wouldn't always be around to protect her. *For how long? The whole winter?* Was he telling her this was it? That he'd stay away until spring, or even find someone to help her in the spring so that he could go on farther west in a day or two instead of waiting around for her? She fought an unexpected panic at the thought that this man would ride on and she'd never see him again. It wasn't supposed to matter…but it *did* matter! Yet she couldn't tell him. She'd promised what they'd shared was just a necessary but passing thing…that he was free to go his merry way if he chose.

Don't leave me, Luke! She wanted to shout it, but she held her tongue. Still, how was she going to sleep tonight, with strange people and strange noises all around her...and in bed alone?

They rode down a dirt street churned up from yesterday's sleet storm, horse dung mixed in with the mud. A couple of men rode past them, nodding to Luke and looking Kate over with curiosity. Was she a whore? She was sure that's what they were wondering, and it gave her the chills.

Luke rode into the town stable and spoke with a man there who called himself Big Jim. *Big* certainly did not properly express the man's size. Kate figured him to be at least six feet seven inches, and he had big arms and a barrel chest. But it wasn't his size that drew attention. He smelled so bad that Kate didn't even need to get down from Jenny and stand close to notice. He had a thick beard and bushy eyebrows, and he wore patched cotton pants and a dark shirt that needed washing.

Big Jim spoke with Luke a moment, then went inside a barn while Luke helped Kate down from her horse.

"Go on over there on that boardwalk beyond the stables," he told her. "It's too dirty here, and there is too much horse dung. How's that leg?"

"My leg is no longer the problem," she answered. "What about you and that wound?"

"I'll be okay, but I have to say that I'll be glad to find a bed and sleep for about three days. Trouble is, I have to ride back for those bodies tomorrow, so I'll be gone for a couple of days once I get you settled."

"Luke, that's too much riding too soon."

"I'll manage. The bodies need to be buried, and right now I'm not strong enough to dig three graves. Besides, I want to report what happened so if those other two show up, men around here will know what happened and who's telling the truth. There might be men in town who knew those men I shot, and they might not be happy about it." He put a hand on her shoulder and urged her out of the corral. "Go on now, before your skirt picks up some of this mud and mess."

Kate turned and walked several yards away to the boardwalk. Minutes later, Big Jim came out of the barn leading a draft horse hitched to a flatbed wagon. He proceeded to help Luke unload the pack horses and reload all the supplies into the wagon.

"The lady that runs the boarding house—her name is Nora Keil," Big Jim told Luke. "She has a big shed out back where she stores folks' supplies for 'em. Most of them that comes through Lander is on their way someplace else, so they need to store their things unless they have their own wagon. Even though, in a town like this, you gotta guard your wagon all the time, so lockin' your things up in Nora's shed is a little safer."

"I know," Luke told him. "I've already met Nora and had her save a room for Kate."

Big Jim rattled on about the town and those who lived there. He and Luke decided that saddles and tack would be left at the stables along with the horses. Big Jim and Luke talked about cost, and Luke asked a lot of questions about who would guard his stock.

"Hey!" Big Jim suddenly declared. "You're that

fella that was here a few days back huntin' them men who hanged him, ain't ya?"

Luke nodded. "That's me."

"Yeah. I remember now." Big Jim glanced over at Kate. "So, the pretty lady over there is the one you was talkin' to that there Jake Harkner about—the lady that saved you. Jake said somethin' to me about it that next mornin' when he lit out of here for Colorado—him and that friend of his, Jeff somethin'.""

Big Jim nodded and waved to Kate.

Kate smiled and nodded back, thinking how anyone could smell the man from a mile away. She waited, looking up the street as Luke dickered more over the reassurance that Big Jim would guard the animals well. It was growing darker, and already Kate could hear the clinking of distant piano music, most likely coming from saloons. Laughter from both men and women filled the air, and she even heard a gunshot.

"That was some shoot-out you had," Big Jim was telling Luke. "Some men are still talkin' about it. One man told me about how that Harkner fella shot a man who was fixin' to put a hole in your back. He's kind of famous, you know—five thousand dollars on his head someplace back east, I think. You're lucky he took your side. I wasn't here to see it all, but I sure wish I would have been."

"Well, I'm sure there are plenty of men out here who are wanted for something back east," Luke answered as he rearranged a few things in the wagon. "Harkner isn't the only one."

"Maybe not, but he's the most famous one on account of how good he is with them guns. Any lawman or bounty hunter who'd dare come here lookin' would wish he'd stayed home," Big Jim answered, letting out a hardy guffaw. "Ain't that right, Luke?"

Kate turned away. Was she really going to spend the whole winter in this wild town? What on earth would she do? Would Luke stay, or go? With all the drinking that went on, he could end up killed in a fight before winter was over. For the past several days they had lived in total quiet…just her and Luke and seldom any other noise than the whinny of a horse. This was different, and there were plenty of things here for a man—women and gambling and whiskey and probably even jobs. But Lander was definitely not a place for a woman like her. Luke had said there were a few wives here who had followed their husbands west because of being wanted somewhere for committing a crime. She supposed it was possible some had actually come out here to settle because everything was more or less free. There was certainly plenty of grassland for grazing, and there was no law, no set borders. Men made their own rules and claimed their own piece of land. And those who disobeyed the rules died. Even Luke had lived by those rules when he came here and hunted down the men who'd tried to hang him.

Luke came up behind her and grasped her arm. "Wagon's ready," he told her. He helped her walk to the loaded wagon. "Big Jim said that Nora over at the boarding house has a shed out back where she stores belongings for people who are just traveling through—so that's where we will put most of this stuff. Once I get you set up with a room, I'll go see the doctor. No sense in me cleaning up yet because I'm heading right back out in the morning." He helped her climb up into the wagon seat, then did the same. He picked up the reins and got the horse into motion, heading out of the corral.

"Luke, let someone else go after those bodies. You're hurt."

"I'll be all right. They might not understand exactly where the bodies are. Once you're settled, I'll find a couple of men in one of the saloons willing to make the trip for a little money."

"But you might not be able to trust them. You might get out of town and they could kill you and take your horse and your money."

"I'm a pretty good judge of men, Kate. You know that by now. You have to stop worrying."

The wagon bounced and rocked through mud and over large stones. Horses tied to hitching posts lined the main street. They passed numerous businesses, including a millinery. Luke had to slow the wagon once when two brawling men came barging out of a saloon and into the street, falling together right in front of the wagon. A crowd followed, including a couple of women in dresses cut so low their breasts practically spilled out of them. As most watched the fight, a couple of drunk men came closer to the wagon to look Kate over.

"Hey, mister, is she for sale?" one of them asked Luke. He reached up to put a hand on Kate's leg. In an instant, Luke pulled his revolver and cocked it, aiming it at the intruder.

"Get your hand off her or I'll blow your head off!"

Kate shrunk a little closer to Luke.

"Sorry, mister. I just figured—"

"You figured wrong. This is a respectable lady on her way to Oregon. I intend to make sure she gets there safely!"

The man backed off, and the fight moved to the other side of the street. Luke holstered his gun and whipped the horse into motion again. "I guess I don't need to tell you not to go out at night," he told Kate.

"You certainly don't." Kate closed her eyes and put a hand to her forehead. "Luke, how can I spend a whole winter here?"

"It's not as bad as you think. By morning, most of the drunks will be passed out and you can go wherever you need to go in complete safety."

"And where will *you* sleep?"

Luke grinned a little. "Big Jim has a couple of little cabins out behind the stables that he rents out. One is empty. The man says it has a pot-belly stove that I can use for heating *and* cooking. It has a cot and a small table and one chair. That's good enough for me."

So, they would be separated that way all winter. At least he hadn't said he'd be sleeping above the saloons, and not alone. Kate had grown so used to traveling and camping with him that she hated the thought of being apart now. And she worried that the more they were apart, the more sure he would be that he should move on without her come spring. "But Big Jim smells so bad," she argued. "If that place smells like him, *you* will smell like him."

"He lives in the stables. I'll probably have to clean the cabin up a little, but he said he never sleeps in there. He'd rather make money renting it out. I'm sure it's okay."

It seemed he had everything planned already. *Please don't leave me!* Kate wanted to shout. *What am I doing here? What will happen now? You're leaving in the morning. Will you keep riding and never come back?* What did she really know about the man after all? Yes, he was good and kind and generous and a wonderful lover. But he was as unsettled as the wind. Maybe it wouldn't bother him at all to leave her now. He seemed relieved to be in Lander and around other men.

Luke pulled the wagon in front of a clapboard two-story house painted white. A small picket fence surrounded it, and the door was painted blue. A sign out front read *Nora's Place.* Luke turned to Kate and took her hand.

"Look, it's important for a woman to keep a good reputation in places like this, Kate. That's why we'll be sleeping on opposite ends of town. The men around here will need to understand I'm just someone you hired to get you to Oregon after your wagon train was attacked and destroyed. Once men understand you are a decent woman and not here to work in the saloons, they will leave you alone and I won't have to worry so much about you. Maybe you could even get a job teaching a few kids to read, or at one of the supply stores or the millinery. There *are* usually some good people in places like this—those who run businesses or farm or ranch outside of town. You'll be okay."

Kate couldn't help having to blink back tears. "But we've been taking care of each other all this time. I know the understanding has always been that we'd lay up for the winter and go our separate ways, but now that it's becoming more real, I feel like I'm right back where I was...no one but me."

"Kate, except for the next couple of days, I'll be right here in town," Luke assured her, "at least long enough that you will make friends and learn who you can trust. You can send someone for me any time, day or night. But we *have* to stay apart, for your own protection. Besides that, we both need time to think and to know what we really want."

And I'm not young enough for you, am I? Kate thought. *I'm just a woman you've befriended...a woman you care about and respect...but I'm not wife material. I'm just a lonely widow who needed a man's touch.* Kate quickly wiped away more stubborn tears over his remark, *At least long enough for you to make friends.* That meant he did intend to leave Lander, at least for the winter. She quickly wiped away the tears. "I think I'm just overtired," she told Luke. "I hope I do get a room, because I think while you're gone the next couple of days, I'll do nothing but sleep."

"As well you should." Luke looked around before putting an arm around her and kissing her cheek. "I'm not abandoning you, Kate. I'll check on you as soon as I get back. In the meantime, I'm sure Nora will be glad for your company. She can show you where to shop and where that bathhouse is. Maybe you can even help her with cleaning and laundry. You just need something to keep you busy the next five months or so. I'll do the same. We both knew it would end up this way."

Kate nodded again. Why was parting so much easier for a man? Maybe because men were so self-sufficient and needed no protection. They were their *own* protection. __

"We had better see about a room and unload my things," she told Luke. She wanted nothing more than to throw her arms around him and beg him to sleep with her tonight...but everything had changed, and the longer they were here and leading separate lives, the more they would pull away from each other and go their separate ways. It was already happening. *I love you, Luke Bowden. I will always love you.*

TWENTY-SEVEN

THE LAST THING LUKE WANTED TO DO WAS GET BACK on the trail. He felt sick at leaving Kate behind in a strange, wild town full of strange, wild people. He'd never been so confused over his own feelings in his life. He'd been so sure of how much he'd loved Bonnie. Coming home to find her married to his brother was the most devastating event of his life, even worse than all the killings during the war, the bullet wounds he'd suffered then, and now the one in his side, which was hurting more than it should.

He'd not gone to the doctor first as he'd promised Kate. He'd been too damn tired and just went to the stables to sleep. Now he worried about the tenderness in his side this morning. For Kate's sake, he'd wanted to head to the cabin extra early and get those men buried soon enough to make it back to Lander by nightfall. He wanted to be close by Kate these first few days in case she needed him for anything, so there was no time to see a doctor before leaving.

He rode with Big Jim and a young man called Blaze. Big Jim liked the kid and had asked him to come with him and Luke. Blaze was maybe twenty and an orphan who'd gotten into trouble back in Philadelphia and came west "for the hell of it." He was good-looking and likeable but a little cocky.

Luke lit a cigarette. "I want to thank you two for helping me," he said aloud after inhaling. "I'm still worried about the two men who got away. They might not want to let this go."

"Well, if they come to Lander, you'll find men who'll back you up," Big Jim told him. "Like that Jake Harkner did when you went after them that hung you. We might all be a bunch of no-goods, but most in town won't be happy about them men trying to defile that nice lady you brung into town."

I defiled her enough myself, Luke thought, guilt burning through him. *Shit, what if I got her pregnant? I made her no promises, and she didn't ask for any.* That's what bothered him most. Kate Winters wasn't like most other women. Most would figure a man owed them something for what had happened between them: money, property, a wedding ring, *something*. Kate had asked for nothing.

The events that had led them to be together seemed so impossible…the timing of it…the way they just seemed to fall into step with each other. Comfortable, that's what it was. Too comfortable for strangers, their lovemaking too natural, too intimate, and too beautiful.

"I reckon if them men show up in Lander, we'll have us a hanging," Big Jim said, interrupting Luke's thoughts.

"Suits me just fine," Luke told him. Strange, how a

man could kill ten others in war, but in time of peace he could hang for killing just one man...or for stealing a horse. He wondered how these men...and Kate... would feel if they knew he'd accidentally killed a kid in the war—a boy only about ten years old. That was the main thing that kept him running...from himself and from memories. He had no right to ever be happy. Ever. Even when he had plans to head for California and raise cattle, he meant to do it alone, not with a woman or a friend or anyone else. After killing that kid and then losing Bonnie, he had no incentive for marriage or happiness or children of his own. He wanted to believe that what happened with Kate was just long-neglected manly needs and nothing more. And he wanted to believe that Kate's reaction was simply that of a lonely widow who had no one to care about her. She surely didn't know her own mind. He needed to convince her that she shouldn't depend on a man like him. She deserved better.

"Pretty country," Blaze commented.

Luke kept the cigarette between his lips. "Big," he answered. He studied the scattered boulders he and Kate had passed on their way to Lander. Had he really just ridden through here yesterday with her? Everything that had happened to him since the day she'd cut him down from that tree seemed unreal now. In country like this it was hard for a man—or woman—to stay in touch with reality, which was all the more reason not to take any of it too seriously. He felt as though he was living in a land of "in between"...in between the Civil War and Bonnie and where he was supposed to go from here. He used to think he was in control of his life, but right now he seemed to have no control at all.

"How far we got to go?" Big Jim asked.

A sharp pain moved through Luke's side. He winced from it but said nothing to the other two men. "Half a day, maybe. This is the third time I've been through here in just a few days. There's a cabin a few miles ahead. That's where the bodies are."

"How'd those men get the drop on you?" Blaze asked.

I'd just finished a full night of having sex and was worn out, Luke thought. "We were extra tired," he answered aloud. "We went through an awful lot after that hanging, and Mrs. Winters was recovering from a badly infected leg and I'd been doing most of the work. She got the wound in her leg from fending off a man who attacked her while I was in Lander that first time, when I was looking for those men who hanged me. So the poor woman had a bad time of it. When we found that cabin on our way here, we just sort of collapsed and slept too hard. Before that we stayed in a cave, not very comfortable for a woman. She's not used to this life, this land, the ruthlessness of some men. It's all been real hard on her." He drew deeply on the cigarette and almost groaned aloud from pain in his side again.

They rode on in silence, Luke wondering what Kate was doing now. Was she helping Nora? Was she at the bathhouse? Or was she still sleeping, like she'd said she might do? Last night in a tiny cabin behind the stables he'd slept alone, wishing Kate was in his bed.

"How come that gunslinger, Jake Harkner, helped you against those men who hanged you?" Blaze asked.

Luke shrugged. "I guess because he recognizes honesty in a man and he believed my story," he answered, beginning to sweat from hiding his pain.

"What's the man like? I heard he's unbeatable with a gun."

"Seemed nice enough. He has a wife and kids, believe it or not, but he's wanted back east, so it's hard for him to be with his family."

Blaze raised his chin confidently. "A reputation with a gun wouldn't bother me one bit," he told Luke.

Luke cast him a scolding glance. "Kid, if you want to dig your own grave, go ahead," he said to the young man. "I much prefer not getting into that situation at all, but sometimes it can't be helped. As for me, I'm actually better with a rifle than a six-gun. That's how I killed the men who hanged me, and how I killed those we're riding out to bury."

"I prefer my six-gun," Blaze answered arrogantly. "I wonder how fast that Jake Harkner is."

Luke had to grin at the boy's stupidity. "You go against a man like that and you won't live to see twenty-one," he said. "When Harkner shot that man up in the balcony behind me, I never saw him draw. If you want to push up daisies, you just try your hand at a man like that. Otherwise, you'd best keep practicing for a long, long time. Men like Harkner have an instinct most men don't, and he doesn't even need to aim. He just thinks about where he wants the bullet to go, and it goes there—know what I mean?"

Blaze frowned. "I guess."

Luke winced with pain again. Just talking was beginning to be an effort.

"You and Mrs. Winters really goin' your separate ways come spring?" Big Jim asked.

Luke felt a tug at his heart over the man's question. "That's the plan," he answered. "Kate has family in Oregon. After I take her there, I'm headed for northern California—good land there for ranching and farming." He crushed out his cigarette against a canteen and threw down the stub. "Let's get this over with." He urged Red into a faster gait.

A couple of hours later they camped again, ate, rested, then continued their journey, reaching the cabin around mid-afternoon. Luke could smell the bloated bodies on a south wind before he even reached them. The crazy weather had warmed up again, but there was a hint of cold in the wind. "Wish I could help you boys, but my side is hurting more," he told the other two. "I'll add to your pay by buying you a meal and drinks when we get back to Lander. I'd like to get back by tonight, but now I'm not so sure. My side is hurting pretty bad. I might need to rest overnight—depends on how fast we can get these men buried."

They drew their horses closer to the bodies, and all three riders curled their noses, although Luke was surprised Big Jim could smell the dead men above the man's own odor. Big Jim and Blaze dismounted and took short-handled shovels from where they'd tied them to their gear. They started digging one big hole for all three bodies, while Luke dismounted and fished around in the dead men's pockets for identification. He felt ill at the stench, but he felt it was important to prove these men's identities and also prove he'd not robbed them of anything. He wished they had suffered more before they died. They deserved a slow death for what they tried to do to Kate.

As he glanced up at the cabin and its broken windows and door, memories of what he and Kate had shared there brought on doubts and indecision over what he should do about their situation. If Bonnie hadn't destroyed his ability to trust women, it would be a little easier to decide what to do about his present confused emotions.

Blaze and Big Jim kept digging for nearly an hour, glad the ground was still warm and fairly easy to dig out once they got through the thick sod. Once in a while a large rock got in the way, bringing on a string of cursing from both men. Luke kept the papers he'd found on the men and looked them over. The big man had a card in his pocket on which someone had printed Mark Heller. The younger man actually carried a birth certificate that read Johnny Reed, and the third man had a receipt in his pocket for a new gun that had been sold to a Ben Lake. He told their names to Big Jim and Blaze. "Either of you know any of these men?"

Big Jim shrugged. "Well, their bodies are so bloated and blue, I can't recognize any of them on sight, especially the big one. Half his face is gone, but I've heard of a Mark Heller," he answered. "Ben Lake, too."

Luke took hope in Big Jim's answer. "I don't trust the two who got away not to make more trouble if they see me again," he told Big Jim. "Where are they from? Did you see them often?"

"Not often," Big Jim answered. He stuck his shovel

into a pile of dirt. "But I think they work at a ranch west of Lander called the Lazy T. Ranch hands come and go, though. They might never go back that way again. You said you found their tracks before you left here, and that they headed south, not north."

"That doesn't mean they won't still head back to that ranch some other way so they could avoid me," Luke said. "They must have realized we were headed north for Lander, and they didn't want to run into me. They were both injured, and they knew I'd be out for blood."

"You goin' after them?" Blaze asked him.

"I'm thinking I will. I don't want to worry all winter about running into them by surprise in Lander or worry they will catch sight of Kate Winters again and maybe bring her harm out of spite. When a fly lands on you, you don't stand there and let it bite. You kill it."

Blaze grinned. "Smart thinking. You have my help if you need it."

"Thanks." Luke shoved the identification papers belonging to the dead men into his saddlebags. He stood back while Blaze and Big Jim dragged the bodies to the open grave and shoved them into it. "We'll carve their names into some wood and find a way to nail it up over the grave," Luke said. "None of them deserves a respectful burial, but I was raised to believe someone should speak over another man's grave."

Blaze and Big Jim grimaced at the smell as they started filling in the hole. Luke tried to remember how many men he'd killed since he'd marched off to war and left Bonnie behind. He likely had no chance of making it to heaven now, especially since killing had become easier for him.

They finished the burial and stuck a crude wooden cross into the dirt. The three men removed their hats, and Luke spoke the words. "Lord, do whatever you want with them." *I know what I want to do with the two that lived.*

That was all he intended to say. He turned toward his horse. "I'd rather head back a ways before we make camp," he told the others. "I know you're tired, but a couple of hours' head start will help for tomorrow, and I need to get back and check on Mrs. Winters. What happened here left her pretty shaken, and even I would rather not stay in that cabin tonight. Besides that, I'm not feeling too good. I'm thinking I might need the doctor back in Lander."

"Whatever you say," Big Jim answered. "You're the one payin' us." He tied his shovel back on his horse, and Blaze did the same. Luke mounted up, grunting again at the pain in his side. "Damn," he muttered. He kicked Red into a fast trot. The memories from that cabin were too much…beauty and then ugliness. It seemed that everything about life had been ugly ever since he rode off to war.

They rode nearly two more hours before Luke could go no farther. He nearly fell off his horse, rather than making a normal dismount. As soon as his feet hit the ground, he went to his knees and vomited, realizing how right Kate had been when she'd told him to go see a doctor as soon as they got back yesterday.

"What's wrong?" Blaze asked.

"It's this wound in my side from the shoot-out at the cabin," he answered, grasping his side and falling over.

"Why, hell, Luke, you should have seen a doctor before we left," Big Jim said.

"That's what Kate told me, but…I thought…I'd be okay," Luke answered.

Blaze spread out some blankets. "You just lay down here, Luke. We'll make the fire and something to eat, and we'll get you back to Lander right away come sunup."

"Thanks." Luke thought how odd things were here in outlaw country. Blaze was a smart-ass kid looking to get himself killed some day in a gunfight. God knew what he was capable of. And Big Jim was an uneducated, unwashed, rather simple-minded man who probably didn't usually care much about another man other than someone to talk to incessantly. Yet right now they both seemed to really care what happened to him. Still, they'd probably rob him blind if he died out here.

He fell asleep. Or did he pass out? He only knew that when he woke up before dawn, he couldn't move.

TWENTY-EIGHT

KATE FINGERED A BOLT OF CLOTH, DECIDING THAT IF she was going to stay in Lander the whole winter, she needed more than the two dresses Luke had bought for her. She'd always made her own dresses, and considering that she was a good seamstress, she decided that might be a way to make money over the winter. There was surely a need for mending pants and shirts, and to make new clothing for both men and women.

Before he'd left her the night before last, Luke had given her money to buy whatever she might need. She was determined to find a job and pay him back for everything he'd done for her. After that, she would pay for her own needs. After all, if they were going to live apart and eventually go their separate ways, she needed to fend for herself. If she had a job, she could even save some money so she wouldn't arrive in Oregon penniless. She wouldn't want to be a burden to her brother-in-law and his family.

She studied a lovely mint-green cotton material dotted with tiny pink flowers. If she could buy or rent one of those newer sewing machines powered by a foot pedal, she could make all kinds of clothing, maybe even new dresses for the woman who owned this shop. They could be sold here for a commission. She took the bolt of cloth to the glass counter behind which an older woman was rearranging some hair combs.

"I'd like six yards of this," she told the woman.

The short, gray-haired clerk straightened. "Certainly, dear. I saw you come in but I had to go into the back room for a few minutes. You're the woman who came into town two nights ago with that hanged man, aren't you?"

Kate smiled. "Well, he was not exactly hanged. He is still alive."

The woman laughed. "Oh, but the whole town knows what happened to him. They are still talking about the shoot-out he had with the men who'd tried to hang him." She looked Kate over. "You're the woman who saved him, aren't you?"

Kate was amazed at how fast news traveled in this remote town, but then she figured gossip was probably a form of entertainment here. *I saved him and fell in love with him,* she wanted to answer. "I just did what any decent person would do," she replied. "He was still alive when I cut him down, so I helped him recover."

"The hanged man—what's his name?"

"Luke Bowden."

"Yes! He told a couple of men after that shoot-out here that he had to hurry and get back to the woman who'd saved his life. He bought a good deal of supplies before he went back for you. In fact, that dress you are wearing came from this very shop. He brought a…

well…a woman from one of those saloons to try it on, said she was about your size. He was right. It fits you beautifully! And you look very nice, dear, for what you've been through."

"Well, I didn't look so nice when we first got here," Kate explained. "It's a wonder what a real bath and washing your hair can do for you. Mrs. Keil—that's who I'm staying with—walked me to the bathhouse this morning and then here. Betsy at the bathhouse did my hair up for me. I haven't felt this human since I was first stranded in the middle of nowhere, before I found Luke."

"I find it amazing that you survived," the woman told her, shaking her head. "By the way, my name is Esther Pierce. My husband and I own this store."

"And I am Mrs. Kate Winters, as you apparently already know. I'll be here in Lander until spring. I'm headed for Oregon to live with my husband's brother and his family. My husband was killed in the war."

Esther shook her head. "Too many good men died in that war," she told Kate, "including my own son."

"Oh, I'm so sorry!"

"My husband and I came out here to get away from familiar things back in Missouri. Figured the challenge of life in this land would keep us busy and keep our minds off of losing our son."

"I can understand."

Esther began cutting the bolt of cloth.

"Mrs. Pierce, I am wondering if you might need some help," Kate asked. "I'm an excellent seamstress, and I thought maybe I could make new pants and shirts for men and dresses for women, and you could sell them here and give me a commission. It must take weeks to months to get in new shipments of supplies and cloth and the other things you sell."

The woman nodded, her gray eyes showing her delight. "Yes! I do a lot of my own sewing, but it's hard to keep up and also run the store. My husband is full of arthritis, and it's hard for him to stock the shelves and such."

"Do you have a foot pedal sewing machine?"

"Yes, I do."

"I'm able to come here and work several hours a day," Kate said, "if you will let me. I don't know anyone in town, and Luke is also going to look for work, since we can't leave until spring."

"I'd be glad for the help, but you must be careful around here, Mrs. Winters," Esther told her. "It's a dangerous place, that's certain. But most of the men in these parts recognize a good woman, and they don't bother the store owners, because without us, they wouldn't have the things they need." She began folding the material. "A lot of them are thieves and killers, but out here they live by their own code. If a good man or woman is wronged, the wrongdoer pays for it. That's how it is in places like this. No lawmen are needed, and those that come here don't last long."

Kate shivered. "So I've heard."

Mrs. Pierce wrapped the cloth in brown paper. She tied it with string and handed it to Kate. "You come by in the morning, dear, and I'll show you the sewing machine and tell you what's needed. In your spare time, you can use it to make your own dresses."

"That's kind of you."

Esther patted her hand. "There are several families here, Mrs. Winters—even some children. You'll be fine."

"That's good to know." Kate took the package and headed out, not quite so afraid to be walking alone. Nora had taken her around town yesterday and introduced her to a couple of wives of men who lived here—one family because the husband was wanted, another because they had moved here to open a general store.

Some had hope that Lander would one day be a town of law and order, but Kate doubted that would happen any time soon. For the past two nights, she'd heard nothing but saloon ruckus and occasional gunfire. Yesterday morning, she and Nora had stepped over the bodies of two men passed out from drink. Kate still wondered how she would get through an entire winter here, but she had little choice.

She headed down the boardwalk for Nora's rooming house, happy for the new material and anxious to start on her new dress. Now that she looked and felt like a normal woman again and had a job, maybe she could get over all that had happened and start over.

Someone suddenly rode up beside her. "Mrs. Winters!"

Kate turned, realizing she'd not brought her revolver with her. She clung to her package as she looked up at Big Jim. Her heart tightened at the worried look in his eyes. "What is it, Big Jim?"

"It's Luke, ma'am. I've been ridin' around lookin' for ya'. That wound in his side, it's worse. He's at the doc's now, and he can't move. Doc says it's bad infected."

Kate put a hand to her chest. "Can't move?"

"No, ma'am. You want I should take you over there?"

"Yes, please!" In spite of his foul odor, Kate walked around and raised her arm. Big Jim grabbed it and helped her up onto the back of his horse. He headed down the street toward the doctor's office. "Luke was supposed to see the doctor before he left," Kate told Big Jim.

"He didn't do it, ma'am. Said he figured he was okay."

"But he promised me."

"Men in these parts ain't much for keepin' promises, Mrs. Winters. Not much for goin' to doctors either."

"Hey, whaddya' got there, Big Jim?" a man in the street called out. There came some hoots and whistles.

"I got me a fine lady," Big Jim told them, "and the next man who gives her a hoot or a whistle will get my fist in his face."

Men backed away, and Kate quickly surmised that no one wanted to get into a fight with Big Jim. He rode up to a sign that read Physician and helped her down.

"Take this package to Nora's Place," Kate told him, handing up the wrapped dress material she'd purchased. "And thank you for coming to find me."

"Yes, ma'am. I hope Luke will be okay. We got him here fast as we could."

Kate rushed inside the small doctor's office to see Luke lying on a cot, looking far too pale. She rushed to his side and knelt beside him. "Luke!"

He did not reply.

TWENTY-NINE

KATE LOOKED UP AT THE SLIM, GRAY-HAIRED MAN with bloodshot eyes who came out of a back room carrying a towel. The sleeves of his white shirt were rolled up to his elbows, and his black pants were held up by suspenders. He smiled at her, revealing a missing eye tooth.

"I'm guessing you're Kate Winters," he said. "Big Jim said he was going to find you. You must be the woman who saved Luke from a hanging."

Kate wondered when people were going to stop referring to Luke's hanging and the fact that she was "the woman who'd saved him." "Yes," she said, rising to face the man. She smelled whiskey on his breath when he came closer and put out his hand.

"I am Doctor Richard Gray," he told her, "and I served with the Union. I tell people that, because some who believe in the Confederacy won't let me touch them."

"It makes no difference to me," Kate said. "My husband died fighting for the Union."

"In that case, I am at your service, and I assure you

that I am very accustomed to bullet wounds and infections and how to treat them."

"Perhaps you are, Doctor Gray, but your drunkenness might render you incapable of proper care. Mister Bowden means a lot to me, and I want him to have the best care. You, sir, reek of whiskey."

The doctor grinned with a bit of shame in his eyes. "I am not drunk, Mrs. Winters. I admit I have a hangover, but I am never drunk this time of morning, and I am sober enough to do what is needed. If you feel you must, you are perfectly welcome to sit with Mister Bowden and help me with him."

"I would like that."

Luke groaned, and Kate looked at the doctor pleadingly. "How bad is he, Doctor Gray? Big Jim said Luke couldn't move!"

The doctor nodded. "He can't for now, but I think that will improve as the infection subsides. He is not paralyzed, Mrs. Winters. He is simply in a lot of pain. He has a clean bullet wound. By clean, I mean the bullet went right through the flesh. I don't think any vital organs were affected, but bullets can carry germs like anything else. After all, men load bullets into their guns with their own hands, and Lord knows where those hands have been." The man wiped at his forearms with the towel. "The medical industry is proving more and more that infection often comes from wounds that aren't cleaned up good enough, or that become infected by germs on dirty hands. I cut into the wound a little and cleaned it out, then dumped a lot of whiskey into it. Whiskey still seems to be the best cure for infection. I stitched the wound and wrapped it. Now we wait."

Kate felt pain in her chest at the thought Luke could die. She'd seen too many men die from simple wounds when she helped nurse some of the soldiers who returned home during and after the war. It still made her sick that she couldn't have been with Rodney when he died, couldn't hold him once more or tell him she loved him.

Doctor Gray pulled a wooden chair over next to Luke's cot. "My wife is in back. Would you like some tea or something?"

"Not right now, thank you." Kate sat down in the chair and grasped Luke's hand. "He's so hot! Can you bring me a pan of cold water so I can keep cool cloths on his head?"

"I'll have my wife bring what you need."

Kate blinked back tears. "How much pain is he in?"

"Well, right now he's full of laudanum…at least as much as I could get down his throat. He was already close to unconscious when Big Jim brought him in. It took them all day to get here, so I couldn't treat him as quickly as he *should* have been treated. I'm guessing when the laudanum wears off, he'll be in considerable pain. I'm afraid I can't guarantee that what I did was enough, Mrs. Winters. He's in bad shape, and we all know how infections this bad usually turn out."

Kate fought not to weep openly. Luke had been adamant they should appear to be just friends, but she wasn't sure she could keep up the front. This was her brave, handsome, able Luke, who'd saved her leg and probably her life—who'd carried her around and tended to needs no stranger should have to tend to. This was the man who'd come back for her, bringing her creams and dresses and combs and most of what a woman needs besides food and water. He'd defended her in that cabin, made sure she was comfortable once he got her to Lander…and this was the man who'd made love to her, every touch respectful and adoring…the man who'd not told anyone or bragged about it once they got to town. He'd kept his promise to be discreet.

"He promised me he would come and see you to have his wound cleaned up better before he left yesterday," she told the doctor. She squeezed Luke's hand. "Why didn't you keep your promise, Luke? *Why?*"

"I expect he figured he was okay," the doctor said. "I'll go get my wife. Her name is Emelia. We came out here after the war, like so many others did. Like Esther Pierce and her husband, we lost our only son and that changed everything for us. We had to get away from familiar things."

Kate kept hold of Luke's hand and lowered her head, pressing the back of his hand to her forehead. "I think just about everyone out here came because of the war," she said, "as did I…and so did Luke." How could Bonnie hurt him the way she had?

She heard a door softly close and looked up to see the doctor had left the room. She leaned closer to Luke, taking the moment of privacy to kiss his cheek, his forehead, feeling terror at how hot he felt. "Don't you dare die on me, Luke," she said softly into his ear. "Who will take me on to Oregon? You're the only man in this whole great big land that I trust to truly protect me with his life." She lightly touched the scar on his neck. "And I didn't save you from a hanging to watch you die this way."

He groaned again, but she couldn't tell if it was from pain or if he was trying to say something to her.

"I'm going to stay right here with you," she told him then, "just like you stayed with me when I was hurt."

The door to the back room opened again, and a woman of perhaps fifty years old came into the room carrying a pan of water. She looked haggard and sad and had too many lines in her face that were accented when she smiled at Kate.

"I'm Emelia Gray," the woman told Kate. "My husband said you want to sit with Mister Bowden for a while and try to keep his fever down."

"Yes, thank you."

Emelia set the bowl on a nearby table. "Just don't overdo yourself, dear. From all I've heard, you've been through a lot yourself." She dipped a washrag into the bowl and wrung it out, handing it to Kate. "I promise I will help my husband take good care of him. Mister Bowden seems like a fine, honest man who didn't deserve that hanging and certainly doesn't deserve this."

"He *is* a fine man," Kate answered. She folded the towel and laid it across Luke's forehead. "And like most men out here, he's had an unhappy past, and he suffers from things that happened in the war."

Emelia walked around and put a hand on her shoulder. "And you're all he has—and he's all *you* have."

Kate nodded, then realized Emelia Gray understood more than most. Kate turned and looked up at her. "Mrs. Gray, we aren't married or—I mean, we are just traveling companions. We met quite by accident, and after what happened with my wagon train, I needed someone to help me get to Oregon. I was lost and had nothing to my name but the clothes on my back." She turned back to press the towel on Luke's forehead. "I wouldn't want anyone to get the wrong idea about our relationship, but Luke has helped me so much, so I care about him."

Emelia squeezed her shoulder. "Mrs. Winters, I'm a woman, too."

Kate realized what the woman was trying to tell her, and she couldn't hold back her tears any longer. There was a distinct possibility Luke could die. Her shoulders jerked as she quietly sobbed.

"I know loneliness and sorrow, Mrs. Winters," Emelia told her, "and I know that out here people do things they would never do under normal circumstances. I've seen total strangers marry out of the simple need of a woman alone with children to raise, and a man who needs the company of a woman and her cooking and sewing and canning and laundering and making a home…and all the other things a man needs a woman for. It's just a fact of life, and men get lonely, too. Out here not many people worry about how things look. Everyone knows that for a woman alone, life is just too hard and too dangerous, especially if she has children with no father."

Kate wiped at her eyes and re-folded the towel, bathing Luke's face with it. "Luke worries about my reputation and doesn't want some of the less understanding men here in Lander to get the wrong idea about me. He's been so respectful."

"Well, while you are in here, you are allowed to

cry all you want and show your feelings all you want. I hardly think the two of you are fooling anyone, but just knowing what an able man Mister Bowden is, and knowing he is determined to protect you, will keep most of the less respectable men away, I assure you. There are a lot of no-goods in Lander—in all of this outlaw country—but most of them are respectful toward women. They aren't all like those no-goods who attacked you. It's just wise to stay off the streets at night when a lot of them have been drinking. After dark, and after drinking a good deal of whiskey, even *I* look beautiful to some of those men."

Kate smiled through tears and looked up at her. "You *are* beautiful!"

Emelia took a clean handkerchief from a pocket of her dress and handed it to Kate. "I am gray and wrinkled and thick-waisted," she said with a twinkle in her blue eyes, "but thank you for the compliment. You, on the other hand, are quite lovely, and you're new in town. You need to still be a little careful. Let my husband walk you to and from the boarding house. And since Mister Bowden is so concerned about your reputation, you should probably go back to your room there tonight and every night. My husband can come and get you mornings. I'm afraid he often needs to walk off a hangover anyway." She took the washrag from Kate and rinsed it in the cool water again, then handed it back. "Richard drinks, but he's a very good doctor, I assure you. He drinks at night so he can sleep better… since losing our son. He treated Jimmy himself, but our son still died. It was the kind of wound no man would have lived through, but it still haunts my husband."

"I'm so sorry," Kate told her.

"Life goes on, Mrs. Winters."

"Please call me Kate."

"And you may call me Emelia." The woman patted her shoulder again. "You stay here as long as you want. Just be aware that men come in and out with wounds from fistfights and gunfights and such. We might have to move Mister Bowden to a spare room in the back, as we have only two cots here for treating others. Our living quarters are also in the back. You may eat with us when you need to." She walked toward the back of the room. "I have some things that need doing. I'll bring you some tea in a little while."

"Thank you so much. I wasn't sure there were many women in this town other than…well…those who live above the saloons. But now I've met Nora Keil and Betsy Heater and Esther Pierce, plus you."

Emelia paused. "Well, between you and me, Betsy Heater used to work above the Royal Flush Saloon, but she decided to make her money running a legitimate bathhouse, although it seems to be quite popular with men who don't usually bathe as often as they should."

Kate drew in her breath and met the woman's gaze. Emelia grinned. "That's just life out here. You'll get used to it." She left the room, and Kate put the cool rag on Luke's forehead again.

"So, Luke Bowden, you cleaned up good before you came back to the cave. Was it at Betsy's place?"

What a strange turn her life had taken…nursing a man who was in many ways still a stranger, yet she'd slept with him. She wasn't so different from women like Betsy.

Maybe that's all I'll end up being to you. In the spring, we'll go on west together and part ways, and no one will ever know what we shared. The problem is, how will I go on without you?

THIRTY

For five days, Luke lay in waves of fever and pain, hardly aware of his surroundings. Mourning the fact that the infection that raged within would likely bring his death, Kate could do nothing more than keep bathing him with cool water. She sat with him day after day, praying for him and force-feeding him, hoping the food would stay down, because it usually didn't.

A glimmer of hope for answered prayers came on the sixth day, when Luke's fever finally broke, and he actually fell into a genuine, hard sleep. Kate sat at a table nearby with her head down on folded arms, nearly asleep herself when she heard Luke say her name in a quiet, weak voice. She looked over at him to see recognition in eyes that were clear rather than bloodshot from fever.

"Luke!" She hurried to his bed and sat down on the edge of it, reaching out to touch his face. "Your fever is finally gone! I was afraid it would come back, but I think you've finally conquered it." She grasped his hand. "How do you feel?"

"Hungry."

His response filled Kate with hope that this man who meant so much to her was actually going to survive the awful infection. "*Hungry?*" she asked with a smile. "That's wonderful! It's a sign you're finally getting better."

"What the hell happened?" His voice came in a near whisper, as though it took all his strength just to talk. "The last thing I remember is talking to Big Jim...around a camp fire, I think...after we buried those men."

"If you're talking about the night before they brought you back here, Luke, that was seven days ago. This is your sixth day here at the doctor's office, and you're lucky you're alive."

"Seven days!" He tried to rise, but Kate pushed him back down.

"Luke, you are going to have to lie here a few more days. You don't want to do anything to aggravate that wound. Doctor Gray had to cut it open and drain it and stitch it. You've had an infection that went through your whole body. You've been very, very sick. Everyone, including me, thought we were watching you die." Kate leaned close and kissed his forehead. "You have no idea how happy I am that your fever is gone and you seem to know your where-abouts. The doctor said a fever suffered so long could have affected your brain."

She straightened, and Luke put a hand to his eyes. "My God. I'm starting to remember now. I threw up a lot, didn't I?"

"That was just your body's way of getting rid of the infection."

Luke felt under his blankets. "And I'm damn... naked."

"There was no sense dressing you when you were vomiting all over everything." Kate grasped his hand and squeezed it. "I guess now we've traded places nursing each other, haven't we?"

"And I suppose you have been with me...this whole time?"

"Most of it. The doctor walked me back to the boarding house every night. Sometimes Big Jim walked me." She leaned closer. "And guess what? I talked Big Jim into going to the bathhouse. He's a little more bearable to be around now."

Luke smiled weakly and looked her over in a way that reminded her he knew every inch of her body. "You can be pretty convincing yourself...when you want to be."

Kate felt the sweet urges Luke Bowden had a way of easily stirring. "And so can you, Mister Bowden."

Luke closed his eyes. "Yeah, well, there has been nothing sweet or convincing about me...these past few days." He let go of her hand and rubbed at his eyes. "Jesus, I'll never live this down. I'm sorry...for what you must have put up with."

Kate reached out and smoothed back his hair. "You couldn't help it, Luke, any more than I could help all the things you had to do for me when my leg got infected." She kissed his forehead again. "And you have to stop almost dying on me, Luke Bowden. You're one tough man, but this terrible infection might have been avoided if you'd seen the doctor before leaving, like I asked you to."

He winced as he shifted in bed. "But I felt okay. I didn't figure…it would matter." His voice was already sounding a bit stronger.

"And you are such a typical man, thinking he doesn't need any help. I know now what a long ride that is back to that cabin. It was too much too soon after being wounded."

He frowned. "You aren't safe, Kate. Those other two are going to come here looking for me…maybe for *both* of us. They'll figure they have…unfinished business with you. I have to get up and get dressed… go after them." He tried to sit up again.

Kate forced him back down again. He was so weak it didn't take much. "What are you talking about? Those other two men rode off and—"

"No! You don't understand." He sighed deeply. "My God, I have to get out of this bed." He met Kate's gaze. "I meant it. You aren't safe. Didn't Big Jim tell you?"

Kate frowned. "He told me he knew who the other two men might be because of the identifications of the other three. He said something about the Lazy T Ranch, but he said that's miles to the west of here, and there was no sense trying to find those two. He said they likely never even went back to the Lazy T… said you found their tracks and they headed south, not north."

"I don't trust them. They know we can identify them and what they did. They would have defiled you in the worst way and then probably killed you."

"Luke, what are you telling me? Are you actually going after those men?"

"I *have* to. There's no law out here, but there *is* such a thing as outlaw justice. What those men intended to do to you is something a lot of the men in Lander won't put up with now that they know you and know all the details. I have to at least ride out to the Lazy T…see if they went back there. They probably did, because they will be branded horse thieves if they don't. Their mounts probably belonged to the Lazy T. Stealing horses is as bad as killing a man out here. They could be hanged." Luke tried to sit up yet again, and again Kate pushed him back down.

"Luke, please calm down. Everything is fine for now. I'm all right, and Big Jim is keeping an eye on things."

"Shit!" Luke lamented his weakness. "I have to get out of this bed. I don't plan to spend the winter here wondering when those two will come to town and recognize me, probably shoot me in the back, knowing I'm a witness to what they did at that cabin. And that means *you're* in danger, too."

"Luke, you've already had two brushes with death. You can't go riding out to that ranch."

"I can't let this go. I'm betting I can find a couple of men who will go with me to look for those two."

"And living here doesn't mean you have to become an outlaw yourself. That's how you're talking."

"Out here, who cares? I already *am* on the wrong side of the law in some ways. That hanging changed my attitude on trying to do things right. And I'll have help. Those men who attacked you are the kind of men even most outlaws don't like." He took hold of her hand. "Get the doctor. I need to talk to him."

"He's in the back." Kate rose. "Luke, I don't like the way you're talking."

"I promised to get you to Oregon safely. Getting rid of those two...will help ensure that. I might not find them at all, but I have to try."

His voice was growing weaker again, worn out by his spurt of awareness and energy.

"Then just get some rest for now," Kate said. "And try to eat. You'll never get out of this bed if you don't start eating. It's the only way to get your strength back. Tomorrow I promise to help you clean up, and I'll shave you. And you will eat some more. Just promise me you won't try to get out of bed by yourself yet."

"I don't have much choice," he answered. "I already...need to sleep again."

"I'll get Doctor Gray," Kate said. "And as soon as you're fully awake again, I'll bring you some soup and we'll see if you can keep it down." She started for the doctor's living quarters.

Luke spoke up. "Kate."

Kate turned.

"Thanks for staying and...helping take care of me."

She walked back to the bed and knelt beside it. "How could I *not* help, after all you did for me?" *I love you so! I was so terrified you would die.* "And by the way, I took your advice about getting a job. As soon as you're a little better, I have one waiting for me at Esther Pierce's clothing store. I'm going to make dresses and men's pants and shirts."

He closed his eyes and shifted in his bed again. "I'm glad you've found something to get you through the winter."

Without you? Is that what you mean, Luke? He was different. Harder. She could already see it and feel it. This country…towns like this…the injustices he'd suffered…the war…Bonnie…those things took away the tenderness in a man. Marriage and settling were not on his mind now. Maybe he never *would* have thoughts like that for her. *I promised to get you to Oregon,* he'd told her earlier. So, that was still what he planned to do—get her to Oregon and then be on his way.

She stood up and leaned over him, kissing his cheek. "Just sleep now, Luke. You need real sleep even more than you need food. Let your body mend, and be thankful you're even alive." She could tell he was already drifting off.

"Make sure…Big Jim watches out…for you," he said, before his breathing became deeper as exhaustion took over.

Kate waited and watched, making sure he'd fallen asleep and wouldn't try getting up again. *Thank you, Lord*, she prayed. He seemed likely to completely recover now. She just wished he'd stop talking about going after the two remaining men who'd attacked them at the cabin.

She loved him more than ever.

I can't make any promises.

Kate blinked back tears and reminded herself she'd accepted those words and had no right expecting anything more.

THIRTY-ONE

KATE WALKED TO THE SHED BEHIND NORA'S ROOMING house and used the key Nora gave her to open the shed door. The weather had turned much colder, and she needed her winter coat. She stepped up onto the shed's wood floor and held up a lamp to see better. Inside, the shed was divided into several bin-like sections, most of them filled with saddles and tack, small barrels of flour and sugar, and carpet bags full of extra clothes, blankets, and even rifles and boxes of ammunition. The contents of the bins changed constantly as miners, business men, settlers and such came and went.

Right now, most of the bins were empty. Winter had already set in, and most of those who'd spent the summer here had headed south, wanting to avoid the fierce mountain winter likely to come soon. It was unlikely any newcomers would show up again until spring. Supply wagons had come through Lander a couple of weeks earlier, bringing food, ammunition, whiskey, cloth, and other supplies people would need to get through the winter. Any day now it could snow to the point where no one could get in or out of Lander. The "big lonesome" would be even more silent and vacant.

Kate walked to Bin Number Two, where hers and Luke's things were kept. She felt a stab at her heart when she saw the saddle Luke had bought her to use on Jenny. She hadn't even seen or ridden the pinto mare since she and Luke had arrived over a month ago and put the horses up at Big Jim's stables. She missed the horse, missed the cave, missed being around Luke every day, and missed the woman he'd brought out in her—the one she'd again buried so she could pretend she was just fine on her own.

Her heart ached at the memories. She missed being just Luke and Kate. She missed the old coffeepot and the smell of Luke frying bacon. She missed the man himself, his touch, being carried in his arms when she couldn't walk, his wonderful smile, and everything else about him.

It had taken Luke longer to get his strength back than he thought it would, but he was healing well now, eating like most men ate, his appetite fully returned. He was her strong and sure Luke Bowden again, but he wasn't the same man he'd been at that cave. He'd grown more distant, insisting that's how it had to be while they were here. At his request, she'd stayed away while he healed. Other than one lunch together, she'd not seen or talked to him. And at the lunch, he'd not even hinted at wanting her again the way he'd wanted her that night on the trail to Lander and again in that cabin.

The intrusion of those ranch hands at the cabin and Luke's wound had ruined the magic of that night

together. Now they lived their own lives in civilization, if living in Lander, Wyoming Territory, could
be called civilized. And in spite of the lawless type of
people who lived here, Luke was determined there
should be no rumors about the two of them.

Kate believed it was more than that for Luke. She
sensed he truly *wanted* to pull away, *wanted* to not care
too deeply. He wanted them to be more like strangers
again by the time they left in the spring. He wanted
to erase the memories and all feelings. It was easier
that way. He was not ready to marry again. He might
never be ready. Bonnie had done that to him.

I'll never trust another woman, he'd told her...
somewhere...sometime.

He still slept at Big Jim's stables, but Kate feared he
was beginning to spend some of his nights in rooms
above the saloons. She never asked, but he was a man,
after all. The thought of other women touching him
made her ill. Luke Bowden belonged to *her*, but she
knew he didn't feel the same way and probably never
would.

She touched the Mexican saddle blanket they'd
used over Jenny's saddle so she could ride more
comfortably after they left the cave. She remembered
the touch of Luke's hand on her leg when he helped
position her foot into the left stirrup...remembered
the thrill of being in his arms when he lifted her off
the horse and down into the grass...what it was like
the first time he made love to her somewhere under
the big sky. Maybe he thought he could still have sex
with her on their way to Oregon, where he would just
leave her and ride out of her life.

"Not again, Luke," she said softly. "If we do that all over again, I'll never be able to watch you ride away." She had to harden her heart to the realization that what they'd done was just something they'd both needed to do. The only way she could live with their secret was that Luke kept his promise never to talk about it, even in their private conversations. At their lunch, he'd discussed working for Big Jim, had asked about her work, had sometimes tossed her a compliment about how she looked.

You look extra pretty today, he'd said. But always, when he complimented her that way, she felt he was leaving his sentence unfinished. She felt the *un*spoken words…*for a woman your age.*

Now all she heard from others was that Luke spoke only of revenge. He was still determined to find the remaining two men who'd attacked them. He was a different man from the one she'd cut down from that hanging tree, and being around the kind of men who lived in Lander was having its effect on him. She was fully aware that since getting on his feet again, he'd started drinking a little too much and talking to men about going after the ranchers who'd nearly caused his death and who'd meant to put Kate through something *worse* than death.

Kate blinked back tears as she searched through their belongings.

She recognized the small flour barrel Luke had brought back to the cave with so many other supplies and all the wonderful things he'd purchased for her. She saw a couple of their canteens, their blankets… the blankets they'd slept on together…the blankets they'd made love on. She spotted a leather satchel that belonged to Luke, and she couldn't help opening it.

She found a shirt inside, and she took it out and pressed it to her face, breathing in Luke's scent and realizing she never should have let him make love to her. She'd set her own trap because of her need and weakness, but no other man in all these years had brought that out in her. She cried into the shirt, then reluctantly put it back, tempted to keep it so she could sleep with it at night in her lonely room at Nora's.

No. That would only make it harder to forget what must be forgotten. She placed the shirt back, then noticed a pocket watch in a corner of the satchel. She'd never seen Luke carry a watch. Why did he leave it in the satchel when there were times it could be very useful? Curious just to see it, she took it out and popped open the cover.

"Oh, Luke!"

Inside was the picture of a very young woman, perhaps seventeen or so. *It must be Bonnie.* She was beautiful, young, with dark hair and eyes, tiny and well-dressed with lace and ruffles and a bit of her bosom showing at the square neckline of her dress. Her smile was sweet, and her eyes big and dark. Was she smiling for Luke in the picture? Looking at it tore at her heart to think how a proud and happy Luke Bowden must have felt when he excitedly rode home from war to marry the beautiful young Bonnie, only to find her living with his brother and tending a baby.

"I'm so sorry, Luke," she said softly. She knew now why he didn't carry the watch. And she also knew she could never take the place of someone so young and lovely, someone Luke had probably known all his life, someone he grew up with back in Ohio and who he thought would wait for him when he rode off to war.

She closed the watch and put it back, then latched the satchel. She found her coat, the dark-blue one with white buttons Luke had bought for her. Again, memories from the cave returned. She felt totally out of control of her own life. She wanted to go back home and find Rodney there waiting for her, along with her father and others from the days when there was no war but only friendships and enjoying normal, everyday life on the farm...back in Indiana...places she would never see again.

Maybe it *would* be best to go to Oregon and Rodney's brother and his family...familiar faces from days gone by. For now, *Luke* had become the familiar face, but he would end up going out of her life as fast as he'd come into it. She had to face that cold, hard fact.

"I'll have a word with you, lady!"

A man's deep voice startled Kate out of her thoughts. She gasped and turned to see a grizzly-looking old man standing at the entrance to the shed. She backed away, pressing her coat close. "Who... who are *you*? What do you want?" She'd left her six-gun in her room, never expecting some stranger to show up in the shed.

"Name don't matter. I'm here to deliver a message." The man stepped farther inside and walked closer to Kate.

"Get out of here!"

He grabbed her arms in a vice-like grip that startled her. She didn't expect so much strength from such an old man. His pale-blue eyes glittered with meanness. "You tell that son of a bitch you've been travelin' with and probably fuckin' that he'd better shut his yap about comin' after Benny and Henry out at the Lazy T. He's lookin' to get his head blown off!" He shook her slightly. "You understand me, lady? If Luke Bowden thinks he's protectin' your honor, we all know different! Benny and Henry looked in the windows and they seen what was goin' on between you two, and you was full nekked when they went in that cabin, just standin' there *beggin'* for it! And now we know you two weren't even *married*!"

"You're hurting my arms!" Kate told him, trying to jerk away.

The man squeezed even tighter. "You tell that Luke Bowden what I said! I'm the owner of the Lazy T, and my men have told me about Bowden's threats to come out to my ranch and kill some of my men! Now, I'm tellin' *you* that if Luke Bowden or any of those other men come out to the Lazy T makin' trouble, they won't be ridin' back here. They'll all be *dead*! You got that?"

Terrified, Kate nodded. "Yes," she answered, hardly able to find her voice.

The man suddenly backhanded her. Kate went sprawling onto the dusty wood floor.

"Hey, what's going on in here!"

Kate recognized Nora's voice. She rolled to her knees to see the man who'd attacked her run out the door, pushing Nora aside as he did so. Nora quickly ran to her side. "Kate, who was that? What happened?"

Kate picked up her coat and held it tight against her. "Go get Luke," she told Nora.

THIRTY-TWO

KATE SET DOWN A CUP OF TEA AND WRAPPED HERSELF tighter into her coat. She'd put it on right away after her attack, shivering from shock more than from the cold. She'd left the shed and was back in Nora's kitchen, but she still felt the need to wear it. Somehow it made her feel calmer to be wrapped in its warmth.

She heard the front door open and slam shut, heard the thud of a man's booted footsteps and the softer, quicker footsteps of a woman. She put a hand to her right cheek, which still stung from the old man's blow. She knew by the footsteps that Luke was here, with Nora obviously hurrying behind him. He appeared at the kitchen doorway.

"I'll leave you two alone," Nora said. She closed the kitchen door behind Luke, and Kate heard the woman's soft footsteps as she walked away.

Immediately, the small kitchen was filled with Luke's virile presence—and his anger.

"Kate!" He pulled up a chair beside her. "What the hell happened?"

She didn't look at him. "Luke, it was probably nothing. I mean...I don't want to start a war."

He grasped her arm, a bit too firmly. "What *happened*?" he demanded.

"Luke, you're hurting me. That man grabbed my arms so tight he left bruises."

Luke immediately let go. "Shit! I'm sorry. What did he do, Kate? What did he say?"

For some reason, Kate had trouble looking at him. After seeing the picture in the pocket watch, feeling the pain of missing him when she went through their things, wrapping herself into the coat he'd bought for her as though it would protect her because it was from Luke...it all brought to light how much she'd grown to love him. If she looked at him, he might see that. She stared at her teacup.

"I was out in the shed, looking for my coat," she explained. "An old man snuck into the shed behind me and said he wanted a word with me. He scared me to death, backed me into a corner, and said to tell you that you'd better...that you'd better shut your mouth about going after Benny and Henry out at the Lazy T. He said, if you do, you'll get your head blown off."

Luke pushed some of her hair behind hear ear and studied the bruise forming on her cheek. "That son of a bitch!" he growled. "Did he hit you more than once?"

I love the touch of your hand... "No." Kate fought tears. "Once was enough." An unwanted tear slipped down her cheek.

"*Look* at me, Kate!"

She still refused. "Luke, you just got well from a terrible infection that should have killed you. I don't want you to go looking for trouble again. You've been hanged, and you got in that shoot-out going after those men here in Lander, and then you got shot defending me against those men at the cabin and—"

"*Look* at me!" Luke demanded.

Kate quickly wiped at her tears. This would be easier if she didn't love him and didn't want him to wrap her in his arms right now and say he loved her, too. She sniffed as she turned and finally raised her eyes to meet his gaze. Why did he have to be so handsome? He was still vital enough to attract a younger woman...someone as young and beautiful as Bonnie. He was going to go after those men, and there was nothing she could do to stop him. She already knew that. He'd changed so much, was angry all the time.

"Have you told me everything?"

"Yes," she answered. "He backhanded me to the floor." She put a shaking hand to her cheek. "But I don't want you to go riding out there, Luke. Please don't."

She could literally feel his wrath as he pushed back his chair and stood up.

"Bastard!" he fumed. "I can't let this go, Kate. Surely you know that."

Kate shook her head. "I really wish you'd just leave it alone, Luke. I've watched you come close to death three times now. I can't go through that again!"

He paced. "I have help. A lot of the men in town have offered to go out to the Lazy T with me. I found out that other Lazy T men have mistreated some of the women above the saloons. We've decided to put a stop to it. Men out in these parts will stand up and fight for our women. What happened to you will give them even more cause to ride out to the Lazy T with me! At least now we have *names*! Benny and Henry. They obviously came back to the Lazy T, and they've given their version of what happened."

His comments about the women above the saloons made Kate want to ask if he'd slept with any of them, but she didn't bother to ask. It was none of her business. He was obviously doing all he could to distance himself from her, hanging out in the saloons, drinking and gambling. Maybe this angry man ready to kill was the *real* Luke Bowden, the one she'd not had time to get to know. And was she any different from those women who lived above the saloons, after what she'd let him do with her?

She looked down at her teacup again. "Luke, he said that those two men looked in the windows at the cabin. They saw what we were doing, and he said now that everyone knows we aren't married, don't bother defending my honor because I *have* no honor. He accused me of...the day of the shooting...of standing there naked...begging for those men to come for me. I'm sure that's what those men told him and others at the ranch when they got back." She looked up at him. "Don't go out there, Luke! They will just drag me through the mud and make it look like you shot them just to keep me to yourself. They might find a way to make *you* look like the guilty one, not them. If the men in town find out the truth—"

"Stop it!" Luke told her, his eyes on fire with rage. He marched back to the chair beside her and sat down, turning it to face her more fully. He grasped her hands.

"Don't you dare hang your head, Kate Winters! Nothing those ranch hands say will change the mind of one man here in Lander about you being worthy of their defense. So don't go around hanging your head, understand?"

She looked away again. "Luke—"

"Don't say it, Kate!" He squeezed her hands. "I want you to know that I've already made up my mind. When this is over, I'm going on to Atlantic City. It's only a few days southwest of here, so there is still time to get there before the really deep snows set in. I only came to Lander because it's a little farther north and that much closer to Oregon. I'll come back here for you in the spring. All our things are here, our horses… everything. I *have* to come back. For now, I'm just taking Red and one of the pack horses. I can get anything else I need in Atlantic City. It's bigger than Lander—"

"No!" Kate met his gaze again. "What if you decide not to come back?"

"Didn't I come back to that cave?"

"But you were gone from the cave only a day or two, and you knew I could die if you didn't return. This is different. I have help now, and even friends. And you're talking about five or six *months* away! You have no obligation to come back, Luke, and you will already have a head start for California."

Luke sighed and leaned closer. "Kate, I owe you my *life*. I'm not going to abandon you after what you did for me, let alone what you put up with nursing me back from death when I had that infection. And I already told you I need to come back anyway, for the rest of my things. As far as protection, you're already established here, along with Nora and Esther and even Betsy, and there are a few other women here, wives of businessmen and even wives of some of the outlaws. The men here will protect you now, especially Big Jim, who already promised me he'd keep a special watch on you. That was my main concern, and with me gone there will be no question about your respect. It's best this way, Kate, for your reputation and for *both* of us to have time to think about…you know…about how we feel about each other."

But it's not best this way! I said I only acted out of need, Luke, but I acted out of love. She studied his dark eyes. *But you don't love me, and you told me so. You're just giving me time to forget you.* It wasn't his fault she'd lost her heart in her need to be a woman again. Such things didn't mean the same thing to a man.

"I don't want you to ride to that ranch, Luke. It's too dangerous."

"I'll be all right. And while I'm gone, I'll rest easy knowing you have a job for the winter, a nice woman to stay with, the protection of every man in this town, and you'll be warm and well fed. When I come for you in the spring, you will be rested and ready to make the trip to Oregon. You can look for a man who isn't half outlaw and who already has a job or owns property…maybe even a widower who needs someone in his life again, which is exactly what you're looking for."

I've already found the man I'm looking for. Why couldn't she make herself say it? She pulled her hands away, hating what his touch did to her. She couldn't tell him her real feelings because he had to feel the same about her. She didn't want a marriage of obligation. She didn't want him just feeling sorry for her... marrying her and then meeting some young woman and wishing he'd waited. She scooted back her chair and stood up. "I suppose you're right about staying away," she told him. She walked to the kitchen window and looked out at light snowflakes that drifted on a gentle wind. *But it will be such a long, dark, lonely winter without you.* Maybe not seeing him for weeks or months would help her get over him. The way they'd met, the things they'd been through, all were circumstantial and proved nothing in the way of love. "I'll worry about you traveling in this unpredictable weather," she told Luke. "The tops of the mountains out there are already white with heavier snows."

"I'll go straight south to Atlantic City. I'll make it okay, and I'll leave as soon as this thing at the Lazy T is finished. The ranchers there have caused other problems, and with no law out here, men have to keep the peace their own way."

Kate felt him rise from his chair and walk closer. He put his hands on her shoulders, turning her to face him. Kate tried to ignore the broad, powerful shoulders, the full lips and thick, rather shaggy hair, the air of "man" about him. "Promise me you won't end up like them, Luke. You're too good of a man to turn to the outlaw way."

"I'm just doing what needs to be done," he said. "I'm not going out to rob a bank or steal some man's cattle and horses."

Kate smiled weakly. "I know. I just...I've seen the

good in you, Luke Bowden. No matter what happens between us, I don't want to see that goodness fade away."

"It won't. Just tell me one thing, Kate. Tell me I didn't…get you in a bad way."

Kate looked down, a mixture of embarrassment and desire making the color rise to her cheeks. "No." Oh, how she wanted him again. She was tempted to ask him to sleep with her this very night, before he left for Atlantic City. She put her hands against his chest. "Promise me that you *will* come back in the spring. I don't trust anyone else to get me to Oregon."

"I'm a man of my word. You know that. But for the next few months, being apart is the only way we will find *ourselves* again and know what we really want. Don't ever feel used or ashamed, Kate. You're one hell of a woman who deserves the best, and the shape I'm in right now, I'm not the best at all."

You're everything I want in a man. But I'm not going to beg you into my life, Luke Bowden.

"I'll go talk to the men who said they'd help me. We will probably leave in the morning for the Lazy T."

"Please don't let this be just about me. It embarrasses me, Luke."

"It *isn't* just about you. The tension between men here in Lander and those out at the Lazy T has been building for a long time, and bored men in places like this itch for a fight, so we might as well get it over with. I don't doubt some of the men in town will come riding back with Lazy T cattle and horses." He grinned and leaned down to kiss her forehead. "Are you sure you're okay? Do you need to see Doc Gray?"

She shook her head. "No. I'm fine." Kate stepped away and folded her arms, wrapping herself into the coat again. "Thank you for this coat, Luke. It's really lovely."

"And so is the woman wearing it."

Kate looked up at him, and for a moment, she thought she saw the spark there she'd seen that first time he took her in the wilds of the Outlaw Trail.

"I just might come back and find out you've found some man you care about and married him," Luke told her, "and that you don't need me at all."

Like what Bonnie did to you? Kate wondered if she should just debase herself and tell him he was the only man she needed and wanted, and that he could have her all he wanted any time. She shook her head. "I highly doubt that." She touched his arm. "Be careful, Luke. Don't do something to get yourself hurt or killed and leave me stranded in this wild, lawless place forever."

He leaned down and kissed her cheek. "Don't you know by now that I know what I'm doing?"

Kate searched his eyes. "I only know that I can't stop you—not from going out to that ranch, and not from leaving Lander once this is over. That's the part that scares me the most."

He touched the deep red that was turning to a bruise on her cheek. "Between me and the other men in this town, Kate, no one will ever hit you again," he said. "That's one thing I *can* promise.

Kate couldn't hold back her feelings any longer. "I need a kiss, Luke. Brazen as that sounds, I can't let you leave me for months without another kiss, because

I…I wasn't going to say it, but I love you. Why *not* say it? You already know that I love you. I miss what we had, even it if was only for a few days and even though I know I'm not marriage material and even—"

Luke put his fingers to her lips. "What makes you believe you aren't a woman worth marrying?"

Kate leaned forward and rested her head on his chest. "I'm sorry, but when I went to that shed to find my coat, I found a leather bag of yours and—I know I shouldn't have—but I looked inside. I found the pocket watch—the one with Bonnie's picture in it. She looked so young and so beautiful, and that's the kind of woman you should look for when you are ready to start life over." She felt Luke stiffen a little, but then he pulled her into his arms.

"Kate, Bonnie has been out of my life for a long time. I was younger then and thought youth and beauty meant everything." He reached under her chin and made her look at him. "And you have the beauty, in more ways than just looks. You're a beautiful woman in your strength and your ability to survive. You'd make a wonderful wife. But I have so many doubts, not about you but about myself. I never said I would only settle for a woman like Bonnie, and I never said I didn't love you. But I need to go away and sort things out. Being away from you is the only way I can know this is what I want, and I have to learn to trust again. Neither one of us is in any shape to have our hearts broken all over again."

Kate grasped his hand and kissed it. "It's too late for that—at least for me, Luke. My heart is already full of love for you, and I don't need time or to be apart from you to know these feelings will never change. But you do what you have to do. I'm old and wise enough to understand." She looked up at him, and in the next moment he was tasting her mouth in a sweet, tender kiss that led to wrapping their arms around each other with great passion, the kiss growing deeper.

Kate whimpered in the glory of the delicious kiss, a kiss she'd needed for so long. Still, she felt his lingering anger, the battle going on inside this man. Yes, he was probably right. He needed to go away.

Luke finally released the kiss and pushed her slightly away. "Not this way, Kate. I don't want to do this to you again. I can't stay away if I'm worried I've left you in a bad way. You think you can't have children, but you don't know that for sure and I'm not going to sleep at night wondering. I have to go, Kate. If I stay here, we'll keep doing this and we'll never know if it's real. Tell me again that you understand."

Kate couldn't help the tears that formed in her eyes, but she nodded and pulled even farther away from him. "I understand," she said softly.

"I *will* be back, Kate. We just both need some breathing room."

Kate felt sick inside. "Just go then. God be with you, Luke. I don't want you to go to that ranch first, but if it will settle your restless, angry spirit, then go." She met his gaze. "Just be careful. Don't try to do it all on your own. Let those other men help you."

Luke looked her over in that way he had of making her want him again, but then he turned away. "I'll be back, Kate. That's a promise." He opened the kitchen door that led into the hallway, then looked back at her once more before walking out. He left, closing the front door behind him softly this time instead of slamming it.

Kate folded her coat closer and walked back to the window, still wondering if she would really ever see Luke Bowden again. The window faced away from town, and in the distance, she saw two men riding in the foothills, one of them leading a pack horse. It reminded her of traveling with Luke, two strangers, yet deep friends…two lovers, yet Luke wasn't sure he was in love at all. She hardly knew who she was anymore or where she belonged. Luke was just a man who'd come into her life under the strangest of circumstances, a man who would have meant nothing to her in an ordinary life…yet she wasn't sure how on earth she would ever be able to forget him…or stop loving him.

"Stay away as long as you need, Luke Bowden," she said softly. "You could come back two years from now, and I'd still be here…waiting."

THIRTY-THREE

KATE STOOD ON THE BOARDWALK WITH ESTHER, BOTH women shivering into their coats. Esther's Clothing was only three buildings down from The Royal Flush Saloon, where a good twenty-five men had gathered for the ride to the Lazy T. It seemed half the town was up in arms, and Kate felt responsible for all of it. What if one of the men who'd decided to join Luke was hurt or killed when they rode out to make war on the Lazy T? Worse, what if Luke himself was killed? He would be a prime target.

"They'll be on the lookout for us," Luke yelled, "and I'm told by those of you who have seen the Lazy T that we have to ride through a canyon to get there. Keep an eye out, because there will likely be men hidden up in the rocks! I want volunteers from this posse who are willing to go up into the rocks and try to climb around behind the Lazy T men and keep them busy while the rest of us ride like hell through that canyon!"

About five men raised six-guns and rifles. They cheered and whooped. "We'll get 'em, Luke!" one of them yelled.

All the men preparing to ride out with Luke had gathered around him in front of the saloon, and some of were obviously already looking drunk, even though it was only nine in the morning. Practically every hitching post anywhere near the saloon was crowded with their horses.

"This is going to be bad," Esther commented softly.

"I know, and I feel so responsible," Kate told her.

Esther patted her arm. "The way I hear it, Luke Bowden was going to go there anyway to find those two men who got away after that attack on you. Luke is doing this just as much for himself and his pride as he is for you. This isn't your fault, Kate. Luke is out for revenge, plain and simple, just like when he came here after those men who tried to hang him. What happened to you yesterday just strengthened his resolve, and it made the rest of those men mad enough to join him."

Men were agreeing with Luke when he said it was time to end the threats from Lazy T men. They raised fists and guns in support, several of them firing shots into the air.

"No one man has dared to try doing something about those men on his own," Luke shouted, "but if we ride out there in force, we can end their constant threats and abuse, especially toward the women of Lander!"

A number of men in the crowd shouted their own ideas for how to get through the canyon. Kate noticed three women with painted faces who were wearing colorful satin dresses were mixed into the crowd. Her insides burned when one of them, a blond-haired, buxom beauty, made her way to stand beside Luke. She grasped his arm as he continued shouting orders, then leaned up and kissed his cheek. Luke turned and kissed her on the lips, then turned his attention to the crowd of men again, encouraging them to ride with him to the Lazy T to avenge what happened to "Mrs. Winters."

Kate closed her eyes and struggled with a jealousy that she really shouldn't be feeling. Had he been sleeping with that blond woman? Was that why it was easier for him to ride out of her life than it was for her to *watch* him ride away? Why were men allowed to sleep around without retribution, while women had to always guard their reputations and live without a man's affection if they weren't married?

Men began mounting their horses while Kate grappled with seeing that kiss. In her case, it wouldn't matter if she *was* allowed to sleep with any man she wanted. She *didn't* want any other man but Luke. She didn't want to believe he'd kissed that woman because he had any feelings for her. Maybe he *wasn't* sleeping with her. Maybe that was just a good-luck kiss.

She told herself none of it mattered. The fact remained that in spite of what feelings they might have for each other, nothing Luke Bowden did was any of her business. All that mattered at the moment was that Luke was deliberately riding into danger. He could be killed by a bushwhacker hidden in that canyon. She didn't want him or any of these men to be killed or wounded because of her, but she suspected a lot of them were joining Luke just for something to do. There certainly wasn't much in the form of entertainment in places like this, and with winter setting in, few of them would consider riding into the big country beyond Lander to steal cattle or rob a bank just for excitement.

God only knew what some of the men yelling and drinking and mounting their horses today had done in their pasts. Yet there was this odd good side to some of them. They could rob a bank and kill innocent men in doing so, yet they would turn around and risk their lives for a woman, or even another man they hardly knew.

"I've never seen such stark contrasts in the nature of men as there is in this country," she told Esther. Both women continued watching the wildly excited men.

"Oh, yes, you see all kinds out here," Esther said. "But when you think about it, you can find mean and nasty men who abuse women anywhere and among *all* classes. You don't have to come to outlaw country for that."

"Yes. I never thought of it that way." *And you don't have to stay in your own hometown to find good men. Sometimes you can find a good man in the most unlikely places.* Kate thought how, back home in Indiana, she'd lived in the same town all her life, a town where everybody knew everybody and knew who was good and who was bad. Yet she'd come out to a new land, and within a few days, she'd fallen in love with a complete stranger.

The men were growing even more restless. They continued shouting and whooping it up, firing off more gunshots, causing some of the horses to whirl in place or rear up from all the noise. Some of the men leaned down from their saddles and kissed the women, and some rode past the clothing store and tipped their hats to Kate.

"Ain't no son of a bitch from the Lazy T gonna come here and bother you again, Mrs. Winters," one man told her before charging away.

Most of the posse thundered past, still yelling and sounding like a bunch of wild animals. The street quickly became a churned-up mess of mud and snow. Seconds later, Luke rode up to Kate and nodded. "Big Jim is bringing my pack horse along," he said. "Remember everything I told you, Kate. I'll be back."

Don't go! Please don't go! "You be careful," Kate said. "I don't trust any other person to get me to Oregon."

Their gazes held. Was there something more he wanted to tell her?

"I'll get you there." Luke smiled rather sadly, then kicked Red into a hard run in order to catch up with the other men, who, even in the distance, were still whooping and cheering and shooting off their guns. Kate watched him, wondering if she'd seen Luke Bowden for the last time. She ached to feel him hold her once more, taste his kiss once more, feel his big, muscled body lying on top of her once more, invading her once more. She wanted him so badly that her head ached.

Shaking her head, Esther walked back into the store as Kate turned to watch a couple of stragglers mount their horses and head out after Luke. That's when she noticed the blond woman Luke had kissed walking her way.

Kate considered going back inside the store and ignoring her, but jealousy mixed with curiosity made her wait. The woman shivered into her shawl when a quick, cold wind hit her face. She wore a pink satin dress that had seen better days, and the deep-pink paint on her lips looked out of place as she walked closer. Kate couldn't help thinking she'd be prettier if she left the paint off. Hard living and the gaudy paint made it impossible to tell her age. Eighteen? Twenty-five?

The woman stepped to within three or four feet from Kate, squinting from a bright sun that temporarily broke through the snow clouds above and gleamed against the white snow on the ground and on rooftops. "You're Kate Winters," the woman said matter-of-factly.

"Yes."

"I'm Sienna."

Kate nodded. "Is there something you want?"

The woman sauntered even closer. "Luke Bowden is a damn good man."

"Yes, he is."

"Not bad-lookin', either," Sienna said with a sly grin.

Kate grasped the collar of the blue coat Luke had bought her and pulled it tighter around her throat. "And?"

"He loves you, you know."

"What?"

"He *loves* you. He's just afraid to tell you or admit it to himself. That woman Bonnie hurt him real bad, and it's hard for him to trust another woman."

"He *told* you he loved me, or are you just assuming?"

"He came to me one night for...well...you know." She smiled.

Kate felt her cheeks flushing from anger. "Yes, I know."

"And you're jealous as hell."

Kate struggled with an urge to hit the woman. "What is your point, Sienna?"

Sienna shook her head. "My point is that if you're so damn jealous, then you must love the man."

"I'm not so sure that I do."

"Yes, you are." Sienna laughed lightly. "Look, Mrs. Winters, he didn't sleep with me. He *wanted* to. He even paid me. But he said he couldn't because somebody else was on his mind. And when a virile man like Luke Bowden can't perform, I get curious. We ended up just talking, and he told me about that Bonnie woman and about you and how you saved his life and all. And then he told me what happened between you and him, and how it was just something you both needed but he said that now he can't forget it…said you were a good woman…and maybe he was in love with you but he's scared to death of being hurt again. Don't you know that's why he's leaving?"

Kate frowned. "Yes, I do. But why are you telling me all of this?"

"Because I'll bet you think he will forget about you if he goes away and will decide he doesn't love you at all."

"I have considered that. I'm not exactly the age most men look for in marrying."

Sienna shook her head. "He thinks you're beautiful. He told me so. But he's giving you a chance to find somebody else, a chance to be sure he's what you want, just as much as him needing to be sure about you."

"He thinks I might find another man? In *this* town?"

Sienna threw her head back and laughed. "Sure. There are some good men here. Some of them will want to court you. Luke wants to see if you will wait for him. After what that woman Bonnie did to him when he came home from the war, he doesn't trust *any* woman. But with you—he said you're the first woman who's come along he feels like he *can* trust. He just wants to be sure."

Kate hated the thought that this woman knew everything. She scowled at her. "I'm not sure he would want you talking about him or talking about what he and I shared."

"Don't worry. I haven't told anyone else, not even the other women. Luke told me not to, and women like me know when to keep our mouths shut. It's just that I like Luke, and I want to help. You admitted to Luke that you *do* love him, didn't you? Poor Luke is afraid that will change if he goes away, like it did with Bonnie. He wants to find out if you'll see other men while he's gone, maybe even marry someone else on account of you're alone."

Kate raised her chin. "That's ridiculous!"

"Not to Luke. What Bonnie did really hardened him on women, and out here, loneliness can make a man or woman do strange things. Luke is just guarding his heart, Mrs. Winters, and making damn sure the next woman he loves won't break it all over again. That's why he hasn't out and out said those three words—*I love you*—yet." Sienna shivered into her shawl again as the sun disappeared behind dark clouds.

"I just wanted to be sure you understand what's going through Luke's mind and heart right now, because I think you're a really nice woman and that you probably love that man a lot. He needs to go away and think this out, but when he comes back, you two need to stop dancing around each other. Besides, Luke needs you in more ways than one. He's wrestling with other demons."

"What do you mean?"

"I mean that on top of the hurt caused by the woman he loved, Luke is haunted by the fact that he accidentally killed a young boy in the war."

Kate put a hand to her chest. "He never told me that!"

"He didn't want you to know."

"But he told *you*."

"I don't matter to him like you do. He's been running from it ever since. Going home to find Bonnie married to his brother only added to his guilt. He thinks anything bad that happens to him is deserved punishment, including losing Bonnie. He figures he'll probably lose you, too, so he's scared to care about you." Sienna stepped even closer. "Look, Mrs. Winters, Luke has a lot of issues, and sometimes they come out in his anger, but the anger is at himself. It's why he went after those men who tried to hang him and why he's going to the Lazy T. Anger. A man has to *vent* that kind of anger, and he's afraid that if he stays with you, he'll somehow vent it *against* you in one way or another."

"But I would never blame him."

"That doesn't matter. *He* would blame *himself.* War does things to a man. Half the men in this big country are here because of that war. You're probably lucky your own husband *didn't* come home. He might have come home a changed man. Most men who marched off to that war were peaceful businessmen or peaceful farmers, and they ended up seeing more blood and more dying and more horror than they knew could be possible. They were forced to kill soldiers on the other side who were hardly more than fourteen years old. And it wasn't always just battle they saw. Some saw rape and murder—watched once-ordinary men do things they never thought of doing in their normal lives."

"I'm aware of what war can do, Sienna."

"I'm just explaining the things Luke struggles with. Men open up to women like me because they know we won't be shocked, and we won't blame them or send them away."

"Nor would I. I thought Luke would understand that about me. I could tell there were times when he wanted to say something more, but he kept it all inside."

"His life and all his plans for after the war changed when he killed that kid and then came home to find the woman he loved married to his own brother. I think he's finally ready to love again…ready to settle down and put the war and Bonnie behind him. But it scares him, too."

Kate's heart beat so hard she wondered if Sienna could hear it. She felt like crying with relief. "He really didn't sleep with you?"

"No, ma'am." Sienna grinned. "Not that I didn't *want* to, mind you. He's a strong, good-looking man." She looked Kate over again. "They don't come much better than Luke Bowden. Hell, he's riding into danger right now just to protect your honor. He called you a good woman. I'm thinking he's right."

Kate quickly wiped at a tear. "You have no idea what your words mean to me."

"Oh, I have a pretty good idea. You and Luke are both stubborn and afraid to love again. I figured I'd come over here and tell you what a fool you are not to keep telling him how you really feel. I know it doesn't seem right to a woman like you to fall in love with a complete stranger, but that's not unusual out here. None of us lives by any rules, Mrs. Winters, and with all the dangers in lawless country, life can be too short to waste it letting pride get in the way of desire."

Kate wiped at another tear. "What about you? Why do you—"

"Do what I do?" Sienna interrupted. She laughed, a low, almost angry laugh. "When your father starts selling you to men at a young age, it's pretty hard to know anything about loving a man."

Kate took a quick breath in shock at the words.

"It's okay," Sienna told her. "Actually, I have a favorite client who wants to marry me. It's taken me eighteen years to understand anything about love. I'm thinking I'll marry the guy. He loves me in spite of what I do."

Kate nodded. "You *should* marry him, then."

Sienna nodded and smiled. "I'd better get going before your reputation is ruined just by standing here talking to me." She stepped back a little. "You think about what I told you."

"I will, but what if Luke decides he *doesn't* love me?"

"Lady, you need to think more positive. And by the way, I need some new dresses. I'll be by tomorrow, and you can take some measurements."

"I'll be glad to make some dresses for you."

Sienna nodded. "Good." She turned and sauntered away.

Kate watched after her, a mixture of joy and relief rushing through her blood. She'd learned something that helped explain why Luke had so much trouble committing to any feelings of love. He felt he didn't deserve to be happy.

Big Jim rode by on a big, black gelding. He held the reins to a pack horse. Kate recognized the horse as one of those she and Luke had used on their trip to Lander. It all seemed so unreal, yet in some ways *too* real. She looked up at Big Jim, and he smiled and tipped his hat to her.

"He'll be okay, ma'am," he said.

"Make sure of that, Big Jim," Kate replied.

Big Jim nodded. "I will, Mrs. Winters." He kicked his horse into motion and followed in the direction of the posse, which by now had disappeared into the horizon.

Kate watched after him and put a hand to the bruise on her cheek. Luke Bowden was doing this for *her*. What a fool she'd been. Of *course* he loved her! Why else would he care enough to ride into the face of danger and maybe even death, if she was nothing more to him than a casual acquaintance?

She walked back inside Esther's Clothing, finding it difficult not to burst into tears in front of Esther…tears of hope and joy. She prayed inwardly that after all she and Luke had been through, God would protect him now and through the winter. Most of all, she prayed God would bring him back come spring.

THIRTY-FOUR

LUKE FELT AS THOUGH HE WAS BACK AT WAR, WEARING a blue uniform and riding straight into a host of gray-clad soldiers. In his mind, the bullets spitting through the air from the rocks above were actually coming from rifles hidden in trees. Lazy T ranch hands yelling from above were southern soldiers giving out that chilling Rebel yell that meant he could die at any moment. The orders he shouted to the men from Lander came from a Union Lieutenant-Colonel named Lucas Bowden, whose responsibility it was to protect the young men under his orders.

"Charge on!" he heard himself yelling. He kicked Red into a hard run, and while some of the men with him dismounted and climbed into the rocks along the canyon to go after the shooters there, he and those who stayed with him barreled through the canyon toward the ranch beyond. Luke had no idea who fell and who was still on his horse. He only knew there were still riders behind him.

He'd seen women horribly abused in the war. Never again! He'd enjoyed killing those men at the cabin who'd had the same intentions for Kate, and he would enjoy killing the two ranch hands called Benny and Henry.

The shooting in the canyon faded as he and the others exited into wide-open land. Luke could see corrals in the distance, as well as a house and several outbuildings.

The Lazy T.

Luke glanced back to see a good fifteen men still with him, all whooping and hollering, guns drawn. He waved them on, and they charged through a small herd of cattle, sending the beef running in every direction. Men came out of the house and cabins, some dressed and ready, others still pulling on pants and coats... some armed and some unarmed. A lot of them, taken by surprise, were still barefoot. Luke suspected they figured that anyone coming for them would never make it through the canyon, nor would they come so early in the day. They also probably figured Luke wouldn't be able to gather so many men, certainly not half the town of Lander.

The element of surprise worked its magic. Luke shot down a man whose rifle was aimed right at him. The few wives and children of some of the ranch hands ran inside cabins, and the air was filled with gunfire and cursing. Fences were pulled down. Horses were run out of corrals and scattered. Luke felt a sting at the top of his left shoulder but paid no attention. He saw one of the men from Lander chase down a young man who was running. The runner turned and fired, and the man on horseback shot back. Blood instantly stained the front of the runner's shirt, and he went down.

Lazy T men began throwing down their revolvers and rifles and putting up their hands. Luke rode up to the runner who'd been shot and realized it was one of the two men he was looking for. He lay there looking up wide-eyed at Luke, who pointed his six-gun at him. "I went through hell from that gunshot wound I took from one of you," Luke growled, "and I know what you would have done to Kate Winters if you could have!" He fired, opening a hole in the man's forehead.

Luke turned Red and headed closer to the house, where several men stood with their hands up and surrounded by the riders from Lander. He charged into the gang from Lander and turned Red. "Anybody hurt or killed?"

"Don't know about them back at the canyon, but Toby over there took a bullet in the arm," one of them answered. It was Bill Pate, a bank robber from Illinois who was in love with a woman named Sienna. "I think that's it," Bill finished.

Luke reined in Red when the horse skittered sideways, as excited as the man who rode him. "Whoa, boy," Luke soothed. He scanned the faces of the men who stood there in the cold, some of them still half-dressed and shivering from the wind. He didn't see the second man he was after, but a mean-looking, hard-built old man caught his eye. The man stood on the steps of the sagging porch across the front of the main house. "Get over here!" Luke ordered.

The old man came forward, his dark eyes on fire with anger. "You got no right comin' to my place and killin' my men!" he spit at Luke.

Luke dismounted and charged toward him,

unbuckling his gun belt and throwing it down as he walked. "It's *you*, isn't it? You're the bastard who cornered Kate Winters and hit her!"

The old man clenched his fists. "That whore *deserved* it! She was *askin'* for what my men was gonna do to her back at that cabin! They *seen* you and her nekked together!"

The man hardly got the words out before Luke's big fist landed into the old man's mouth, splitting his lip and knocking out two teeth. The old man spit blood as he got to his feet. He barreled into Luke, knocking him down, and the fight was on. Men from both sides began shouting and circling the fighters, each man cheering on either Luke or the old man.

Luke was aware of Bill Pate picking up his gun belt and looking on with concern. He'd grown to like Bill, and real friendships were hard to come by in outlaw country.

Fists flew. Luke's rage over all the wrongs in his life and over what the old man had said about Kate knew no bounds. He quickly had the old man on the ground and landed a fist into his face and ribs and gut over and over until the man lay there like a rag doll. Finally, some of the men from Lander managed to pull him off.

"You're *killin'* him, Luke!" a man called Sam told him as Luke pushed back.

"I *want* to kill him!"

"Leave him be!" another yelled. "He already looks half dead. Let him suffer! He won't give us any more trouble after this!"

It was only then that Luke realized his hands hurt

from all the pummeling, and that the old man represented everything Luke hated: the war, Bonnie, his brother, himself killing that boy. Panting, he backed away. His clothes were filthy from groveling in the wet dirt, and his left shoulder felt on fire. He realized then that he'd never even noticed this whole morning how cold it was.

"Luke, looks like a bullet might have skinned across your shoulder there," Bill told him, walking up and handing him his gun belt.

Luke grabbed the gun belt and strapped it on. He looked around at all the men. "Where's the other man who was at that cabin? I know all of you know who I'm talking about. Their names were Henry and Benny. I shot one of them, a young man lying over there by that privy!"

A Lazy T man walked over to look, then turned to the others. "It's Benny! Anybody seen Henry?"

"He was back at the canyon," one of them answered.

"Let's go, men!" Luke mounted his horse and glanced down at the old man, who still lay unconscious, his face a bloody mess. He turned to one of the ranch hands who stood close by. "Is he the owner?"

"Erin Sanders," the man answered. "Yeah, he's the owner."

"You tell him he'd better not show his face in Lander again, and if any one of you men makes trouble for Mrs. Winters or for anyone else in town, you'll regret it. The men in Lander will be watching you!" Luke turned Red and started off. "Let's go check on the men in that canyon." He charged Red back toward the canyon, a myriad of emotions running through him, his hands aching and his shoulder burning. His jaw hurt from one of Erin Sanders's blows, and his heart ached over what Sanders had said about his men seeing Luke and Kate naked together. It made him sick that the men heard it that way, even though he had no doubt they'd suspected all along.

He wondered when it happened, when he'd grown so defensive and angry and in need of revenge for the smallest of wrongs. He didn't used to be this way. If he could stop thinking about that little boy he'd accidentally killed in the war, stop thinking about seeing men's legs and arms cut off while they screamed in sickening horror, stop thinking about going home to find Bonnie holding a baby fathered by his own brother, maybe he could be the Luke he used to be before all that happened. Now he'd taken advantage of a good woman, taken his pleasure in her without telling her he loved her. Kate had told him it was all right, but he knew in his heart it wasn't. He wished he could get rid of all this anger and start over. Maybe spending the winter in Atlantic City would help. Maybe he would go back to Lander in the spring and Kate would be waiting for him, just for him, the way Bonnie should have done.

They made it to the canyon. One man from Lander was dead, another only slightly wounded. Three Lazy T men were being held at gunpoint. A fourth lay dead. It was Henry Kline, the second man Luke had searched for.

Luke saw Big Jim waiting for him in the distance

with the pack horse Luke would take to Atlantic City. He looked around at the men from Lander.

"I want to thank all of you," he said. "Some of you have become good friends. Watch out for Kate Winters for me."

Most of them nodded and promised to do just that.

"I'll be back come spring," Luke told them. "If Kate has been hurt or abused, whoever did it will pay."

"Ain't gonna' happen," Bill told him. "You can bet on it."

Luke nodded. "Thanks." He turned Red and headed for where Big Jim waited with the pack horse. His heart felt heavy at the thought of not seeing Kate for months, but he had to get away. He had to know if he really loved her…and if she really loved him. He had to know he could trust her.

He rode up to Big Jim and took hold of the rope to the pack horse.

"You look like you need doctorin'," Big Jim told him.

"I'll manage."

"Don't forget how sick you got from that other bullet goin' through you, Luke."

Luke felt around his shoulder. "It's just some skin shaved off, I think. I'll pour some whiskey on it. The bullet never went through on the inside."

"If you say so." Big Jim shook his head. "You sure you don't want to just go back to Lander now and marry that woman?"

Luke smiled sadly. "Part of me wants to, but I can't, Big Jim. I have my reasons." He nodded to the man. "You keep an eye on Kate for me."

"You know I will. Did you get the two men you were after?"

Luke nodded. "I did." He turned Red and headed south, intending to stay far to the west of that cave, and away from that cabin where he'd made love to Kate Winters. He couldn't stand remembering. He urged Red into a faster trot, feeling strangely unsatisfied and wondering why people said revenge was sweet. It wasn't.

THIRTY-FIVE

KATE CAME TO ENJOY HER JOB AS A SEAMSTRESS FOR Esther. It kept her occupied, and the women in town loved that they could have new dresses without having to wait for the spring shipment from the east. Kate had even made friends, especially, and surprisingly, with Sienna, whose last name she didn't even know. Sienna never spoke it, and Kate decided not to ask questions. In places like Lander, last names didn't matter.

Today was gloomy and deeply cold. She sat near the pot-belly stove in Esther's kitchen. The woman's husband, Deter, had ridden out to a hillside a couple of miles north of Lander, where there were actually some trees that could be cut down for wood. Big Jim and two other men had gone with him, taking a wagon they would use to haul firewood to town. Esther had invited several of the women to her house for tea and pie, telling them to bring whatever hand sewing they were working on.

It felt good to get together with other women. When first coming to Lander, she'd thought it was just a small cow town full of outlaws. But in these long winter months of being alone here, she'd enjoyed these sewing parties, as Esther called them. She'd also made friends with Betsy Heater and used her bathhouse often...always wanting to be clean in case Luke decided to come back earlier than planned.

She kept telling herself not to get her hopes up. Even as she sat now in a sewing circle with Esther, Emelia, and Nora, plus two of the wives from town—Lynn Tibbits and Darlene Knight—her thoughts were on Luke. Christmas had come and gone, and Lander remained buried in snowstorm after snowstorm. At night, she seldom even heard the tinkle of piano music from the saloons because the deep snows insulated the sound, and the saloons had to keep the full front doors closed against the cold. She'd visited Big Jim at the stables a couple of times, just to see Jenny and Luke's other horses—a way of reminding herself he had to come back just to get his stock, if for nothing else. Scout had grown into a huge bull that looked intimidating but was as gentle as a cat. The bull even liked to lick her hand. Visiting the stock comforted her. The animals belonged to Luke, and being with them helped her feel closer to him.

Esther poured more hot water into Kate's teacup while Kate showed Darlene the best way to darn a sock. Through her visit with the other women and all the conversation, she still thought about Luke, wondered if he was all right. After the shoot-out at the Lazy T, Big Jim had returned to report that Luke did indeed ride on to Atlantic City, even though his fingers were swelling from a fistfight with old Erin

Sanders and his shoulder was injured. Did Luke even make it there?

She could still remember the talk when the men returned that night.

What a fight! Luke shot down two men, and he beat ole Erin Sanders near to death!

Kate couldn't help believing that the Luke who went plowing into the Lazy T, killing men and beating on others, was not the real Luke. Deep inside, he was a peaceful man, and she had no doubt that he wanted to live that way again.

Luke Bowden is some man, another told Kate. *He went chargin' in there like a she-bear protectin' her own. Ma'am, he stood up for you with nothin' but total respect. We're all lookin' out for you now, so you can just rest easy.*

Men did watch out for her, almost to the point of annoyance. Kate wondered if it was mostly because they were afraid of having to answer to Luke Bowden if something happened to her. A few had dared to ask her to accompany them to a town dance in one of the stable barns in January, a party to celebrate the new year. Kate decided they were just being nice and didn't harbor any romantic thoughts for a woman they figured belonged to Luke Bowden. Even so, she'd turned them all down and went to the celebration alone, helping serve punch and cake and accepting only a few dances.

She'd not heard a word from Luke. He hadn't even contacted Sienna. Either he thought this way was best, or he'd never even made it to Atlantic City. She blamed it on the weather. Winter had come raging into western Wyoming shortly after Luke left, so maybe messengers simply couldn't get through. A wild, windy snowstorm had buried them around mid-October, and the weather hadn't let up since then.

Was the entrance to the cave where she'd fallen in love with Luke Bowden also buried in snow now? There was a lonely grave out there…a grave where a man she'd shot lay dead. How long ago was that? It seemed like a couple of years already. A mass grave holding three men lay near that cabin…the cabin in which she'd let Luke make love to her with total abandon, fiery passion, and deep desire.

So many memories…such crazy, unexpected twists to what was supposed to be a journey to Oregon to meet with family. She wondered if she would ever get there after all. This aloneness might be permanent. In spite of all the hope Sienna had given her, she still wondered if Luke would want her when he returned, *if* he returned. He could easily make arrangements for someone to bring Scout and his horses to him—or even sell them for him. Come spring, she had to know if he was even alive or dead. He'd told her she could have everything he owned if he died, and for all she knew, that's what had happened. The thought of it made her feel ill. Maybe what they had shared was just another event in her lonely, confused life.

February brought a break in the weather, and some of the deep snows that had imprisoned the citizens of Lander within the town's borders began to melt. All knew more wicked winter storms would come over the Rockies and blast away at them again, but today was sunny, the thawing ground very sloppy with mud that literally sucked at feet and hooves and wagon wheels.

"If you do it this way, the darned spot will be flatter and won't irritate your husband's feet," Kate told Darlene with a smile, telling herself maybe she should forget about Luke and figure out how she was going to get to Oregon in a couple more months.

"Oh, I see! This does work better," Darlene said.

Women chitchatted about husbands and children and the weather. Outside the kitchen door, someone stomped snow off booted feet and knocked on the door. All six women looked up, and Nora grabbed a six-gun and put it in her lap.

"Who is it?" Esther called.

"It's Big Jim, ma'am. Got a note here for Mrs. Winters."

Women smiled excitedly. The tiniest diversion from the norm was cause for excitement. Lynn Tibbits giggled, and Nora gave Kate a teasing look as she nodded.

"It's from Luke, I'll bet," Darlene said with a smile.

They all waited anxiously as Esther got up and opened the door. Lynn's new baby girl began to fuss, and Lynn stuck her foot out to rock the baby's cradle. Her other daughter, now two years old, sat in a corner of the room playing with a doll. She totally ignored the fuss.

Esther opened the door, and Big Jim handed her an envelope, peeking inside as he did so and nodding to the other women. "Afternoon, ladies."

They all nodded in reply, every one of them anxious for Esther to close the door and cut off the strong body odor that came rushing in when she'd opened it.

"A messenger brought this to me this morning,"

Jim told them all. "He brung some newspapers, too, and a few other letters. He's been to Atlantic City and decided to take advantage of this break in the weather and bring some things up to us. Drove a sled all the way here. He headed right back. Wants to get to Atlantic City again before more bad weather sets in."

Esther took the note. "Thank you, Big Jim."

"It's for Kate," the man said excitedly. "Anybody want to guess who it's from?"

All the women smiled. "We're pretty sure of that," Nora told Big Jim.

The man tipped his hat. "Mrs. Winters, a lot of the men down at The Four Aces will want to know how Luke is doin', if that note is from him. Will you let us know?"

"Of course," Kate answered. She could hardly calm her heartbeat. Finally! News from Luke. She fought the dread that it could be bad news instead of good. Maybe someone from Atlantic City had written the note *for* him, letting her know that Luke Bowden had been killed.

"Thank you," Esther told Big Jim.

"Yes, ma'am." He turned and left, and Esther closed the door. All the women waved their hands over their noses.

"Thank God he's gone," Lynn said. "Much more of that smell could kill my baby."

They all laughed at the remark, and Esther handed the note to Kate. "I know that whatever is in that note is none of our business," she told Kate, "but please just let us know if it says Luke is all right."

"I will." Kate took the letter with a shaking hand.

"Naturally, I hope it *is* good news. It could be nothing special at all. We all know how poor men are at writing letters."

Kate clung to the letter and rose from her chair, using a kitchen knife to slice open the envelope, which read only "Kate Winters." She breathed deeply before pulling out the single-page letter inside and unfolding it. She took it into the parlor to read alone.

Kate,

Sorry this is so late. I'm okay. I could have come back during this break in the weather, but I promised to keep my jobs till spring, and you know me—a man of my word. I am working as a bank guard, and at night I keep the peace in the biggest saloon in Atlantic City. I think about you all the time and I miss you and worry about you like a husband would worry about his wife, so I guess maybe that's what you should be, if you will have me.

Kate's heart skipped a beat. She read the line again...*if you will have me.* Was he indirectly proposing to her? Luke was that kind of man, never one to come right out and speak his feelings.

Kate continued reading.

I've been a fool in a lot of ways, but I've had to wrestle with something I did in the war and learn how to live with it. Kate, I killed a young boy. It was an accident, but it was still my bullet that killed him. That and what happened with Bonnie left me real angry inside and scared to love ever again. Sometimes drinking covers up the anger, and sometimes it makes it worse, so I promise not to drink, except maybe once in a while with friends.

Kate smiled at his attempt at finding an excuse to occasionally imbibe. She wanted to jump up and scream out that Luke Bowden had mentioned marriage, but she feared a broken heart later. He could change his mind before he returned, and she didn't want to risk the embarrassment. He was, after all, an independent and unsettled man. Her whole being ached to hold Luke right now, to hug him and hug him. But for all she knew, he'd been drinking when he wrote the letter and feeling sentimental from whiskey.

She moved to the second page of the letter.

I plan to come back in March. We will decide things then. I just hope I come back to find you still love me and haven't found someone else. I promise that's okay. I wouldn't blame you. Leaving did just what I thought it would. It opened my eyes. I never thought I could miss someone so much when I've only known that person such a short while, but I guess God knows when something is right and when it's wrong. That thing at the Lazy T left me knowing that revenge isn't always satisfying. Only the love of a good woman is satisfying. And you're that good woman. If I've already lost you because I left, I can only blame myself, not you. God bless.

Luke

Esther peeked inside as Kate folded the letter. "Are you all right, dear? Is the letter from Luke?"

Kate nodded. "Yes. He's fine. He says he'll be here by the end of March." A tear slipped down her cheek, and Esther came into the kitchen and took a chair beside her.

"What is it, Kate?"

Kate wanted to tell her that in so many words Luke had asked her to marry him. "I'm...I'm just relieved he's all right. He's working as a bank guard." She sniffed and pulled a handkerchief from her dress pocket. "It's just so good to hear from him," she continued. "I've been worried about him, so this letter makes me feel much better."

"Oh, that's good, dear," Esther said. "You should go back into the kitchen and tell the other women Luke is okay. And maybe you can find a way to write back to him and have someone take a letter before the next big storm moves in."

Kate nodded. "Yes, I think I will." *And I know what I will say,* she thought. *Dear Luke. No, you haven't lost me, and yes, I will gladly be your wife.*

THIRTY-SIX

MARCH CAME AND WENT, AND LUKE DIDN'T SHOW. Now it was May. *May*! Luke was two months late, and Kate feared the worst. She checked the supplies she and Luke had stored in Nora's shed to make sure no mice had gotten into them. She packed her own extra clothing and some bolts of cloth into the same supplies, making ready for when Luke would come to take her to Oregon. She'd hardened her heart against expecting anything more from him, just in case he'd changed his mind about wanting to stay together. He'd only said "if you'll have me." He never actually mentioned marriage in his letter, and so many things had gone wrong since she left home for Oregon that she was hesitant to think she could find real happiness again, in spite of Luke's letter. She was glad now that she hadn't mentioned his hint at marriage in that letter. It would spare her the humiliation of having to admit Luke had changed his mind.

Tomorrow Lander would hold a spring dance. The whole town would attend, she was sure, along with new arrivals. Esther had told her that usually, even some of the worst and unkempt of the men in town bathed and shaved for the dance, including Big Jim.

Women were already cooking and baking for the event. A piano had been dragged out of The Royal Flush saloon and that, combined with a man who wasn't all that bad playing the fiddle, would provide music for the dance. Kate could just imagine what a wild event it would probably be.

A few men had already started slow-cooking a side of beef. Kate could smell it in the air—a wonderful smell that woke up a person's stomach and made them hungry, not just for the beef, but for all the other food that would be served…biscuits, pies, cookies, cakes, potatoes cooked a dozen ways, churned butter, gravy, vegetables, fried chicken, sweetened dried apples, and just about anything and everything a person could want in the way of a meal.

Kate would help with all of it, but she would attend the dance with a sad and worried heart. Had Luke changed his mind to the point of deliberately not returning at all? Or was he dead? The latter made her feel ill. Should she stay here and keep waiting? Or was it time to move on, time to find someone else to take her to Oregon? She'd written her brother-in-law to tell him she would arrive "sometime before July."

She realized now that if she did leave, she would miss her women friends here, and she'd even miss some of the men. They had all been good to her. She'd be leaving behind a lot of people who'd befriended her and cared about her. And she'd be leaving behind memories—glorious, salacious, beautiful but painful memories. Leaving would mean never seeing this place, or these people, or this big, big country again—never seeing Luke Bowden again. Still, maybe in Oregon she could turn her upside-down world right-side up again. Maybe Luke had just been a stepping-stone to leaving the past behind her.

Every day she cleaned up and dressed, hoping this was the day Luke would come back. Today she wore a sky-blue cotton dress with a tiny, white-flower design and white lace trim. Betsy had piled her hair into red curls into which she'd wound and twisted more of the same white lace, and tiny gold earrings decorated her ear lobes. She looked down at her black, high-button shoes, bought for her by Luke Bowden. He'd offered her everything that was his if he should die. He'd sent her that letter, saying how much he missed her. Why would such a generous man who apparently loved her simply go away and never come back? There could be only one answer, and now that the danger of avalanches, spring snowstorms and flooding from spring runoff had passed, she decided she would send someone to Atlantic City to find out what had happened to Luke. She could make no decisions until she knew the truth, even if she learned Luke had gone on to California.

She had her own place now, a small cabin the men had built for her behind Nora's place. The cabin was another reason she hated the thought of leaving. Those who'd built it—*a bunch of no-good outlaws,* Big Jim had called them—had even hung a dinner bell outside her door and rigged the cord to hang inside the main room of the cabin, right beside the door, so Kate could pull it if she needed help. She still couldn't get over the fact that those men had been kind enough to think of such a thing. All of them had done the work "for Luke." Always "for Luke." Even her own waiting was "for Luke."

She fought tears as she left the storage shed and headed to her cabin. Lost in thought, she didn't see him right away…a man standing beside a big red horse outside some fencing that housed a small horse stall. The same men who'd built her cabin had also built the horse stall and corral so she could keep Jenny nearby.

At first, Kate thought maybe she should ring the bell for help, but it only took a moment to realize who was standing here.

"Luke!"

Tossing aside all pride and all worry she might make a fool of herself, she ran to him, arms out, joy in her heart, not caring about his reason for coming so late. Was that love in his eyes? Had he really come for her?

She threw herself into his arms, and those arms came around her in just the way she'd dreamed—protectively, lovingly, the embrace of a man who'd missed her just as much as she'd missed him.

"Kate." He said nothing more for the moment, but the way he spoke her name told her everything. He breathed deeply as his lips caressed her neck, her throat, her face, her eyes. "My God, Kate, you smell so damn good, just like I remembered." Her hair, her forehead. "And you're even more beautiful."

He met her lips, and he tasted like Luke, he smelled like Luke, he held her like Luke, he kissed her like Luke, with hungry lips that knew how to stir every deep desire a woman could experience.

"I'm so sorry," he told her. "So sorry. Please tell me there is no one else."

"Of course there's no one else," Kate told him. More kisses. "I would have waited forever for you."

"I was so afraid you'd give up on me."

Kate put her head on his shoulder. "Luke, why would I do that?"

He hugged her close, her feet still off the ground. "Because part of me *wanted* you to give up on me. The short time you knew me, I didn't exactly show you my best side, Kate. I was always angry and full of a need for revenge. I killed so many men, and I used you like the women over the saloons. That was wrong, Kate. I knew it was wrong, and I didn't care. I haven't cared about much of anything since I killed that kid in the war and then lost Bonnie."

Kate kissed his neck, and he lowered her to her feet. "Luke, you aren't the only one who needs to get over things that happened because of that ugly war. It took me years to get over it, too. And I didn't think I could love another man, but then you came along. The way we met was crazy, but I think God had a purpose." She leaned up and kissed the lingering scar on his neck, remembering that first day and how afraid she was of him. "What did you mean about wanting me to give up on you?"

Luke leaned down and kissed her hair, then drew her close again. "I couldn't get back in March because of the weather, Kate. Atlantic City was absolutely buried in snow. Not even horses could get through it. One man tried to get through for supplies, and horse and man both died." He grasped her arms and pushed her away slightly. "The rest needs forgiving, Kate. April came, and I could have left, but that damn voice of doubt left over from Bonnie told me to wait a couple more months—to test you out and see if you really would wait, or if you would find some other man. I'm so damn sorry I did that to you."

Kate shook her head and closed her eyes. "Oh, Luke, I was going crazy with worry, and my heart was breaking. I thought, if you were alive, you'd gone on to California and I'd never see you again." She reached up and touched his face. "You shouldn't have doubted me, Luke Bowden. I'm not young and petulant like Bonnie was. I'm not a kid who thinks she needs taking care of and who would turn to any man for it. When I love a man, Luke, I love him in every way possible and with my whole heart, and not just any man will do. When we made love, it was so much more special than just satisfying baser needs."

Another kiss.

"It seemed like we were sharing souls," Kate told him, "sharing our spirits, even sharing all the bad memories, both of us trying to erase them through each other. A woman can't throw that aside and just turn to another man for those things. That kind of lovemaking is special, Luke, and in my heart I wanted *you* to feel special. I wanted to relieve the pain of bad memories, and I needed the same."

Luke took hold of her wrists and kissed her hands. "You should be furious with me for putting you through the worry of these last couple of months. I could at least have sent someone with a message— some kind of excuse for not coming back yet—but

I knew if I did, you'd for sure wait. I wanted to see what you would do not knowing, and that was mean of me. It's just an example of how I can be a real ass sometimes, Kate."

She couldn't help a smile. "*All* men can be real asses sometimes," she told him. "You think I don't know that? Look what I've been through. Look around you in Lander."

Luke grinned. "They took good care of you, though, didn't they?"

"Yes, they did." Kate turned and nodded toward the cabin. "They built that for me, alarm bell and all."

Luke put an arm around her and began walking her toward the house. "I came in the back way. I wanted to see you before I went into town. But back before I left for Atlantic City, I talked to Big Jim about investing in the livery and expanding it. We'll raise horses and cattle and herd them down to Cheyenne to meet the train. Now that the Union Pacific is finished, we can ship cattle all the way to Omaha and Chicago." His arm tightened around her. "I want to stay right here in Lander, Kate. We've both made some pretty good friends here. Why should we go any farther when we already have people here who care about us? And we would both have jobs and do okay."

Kate stopped walking and looked up at him, folding her arms. "Would you mind explaining why I should just accept that and stay here because you say so?"

Luke put his hands on his hips. "Because wives generally stay with their husbands, don't they? If the husband says, *This is where I'm going to live and work*, the wife usually accepts that and sets up housekeeping."

He glanced at the cabin. "And we already have a house, it seems."

Kate frowned. "Is that your way of proposing? It's not very romantic."

Luke laughed lightly. "Another sign of me being an ass." He took a deep breath and removed his wide-brimmed hat, then bent down on one knee, and with his free hand, he took hold of Kate's right hand. He looked up at her. "Kate Winters. Will you accept the name Kate Bowden and marry me?"

Kate couldn't help the tears that came to her eyes. "Luke, what if I can't have children?"

He only grinned. "If we have babies, that's fine with me. If we don't, I'm okay with that, too. All I care about is how much fun it will be trying to *make* those babies. In fact, answer me quick, because I hope that, like me, you want to catch up on a few things as soon as we go inside that cabin. And tomorrow, we're getting married, come hell or high water. Can you think of a better way to do it than during the spring dance?"

Kate studied his handsome smile and the way the wind blew his shaggy hair in ten directions. She'd often wondered if the wind ever stopped blowing in high country. She answered him through tears. "No, I can't think of a better time to get married."

Luke's grin widened as he rose. "I love you, Kate." He leaned down and met her lips again, sharing a salty kiss. Kate remembered cutting him down from that hanging rope, struggling through the snow with him, waking up in that cave to find herself half naked under a blanket, the way he'd kissed her in the middle of the night in that cave, the first time they made love in the tall grass under a big sky, and the wild night of sex they'd shared in that old cabin, and the way he'd risked his life to protect her. She couldn't imagine a better man to protect and provide for her, or a better man to lie with in the night. Luke Bowden might be good at a lot of things, but making love to a woman had to be right at the top of the list.

Luke picked her up in his arms then. "Show me your cabin, woman."

Kate pulled the combs and ribbons from her hair and let it fall out long, the way he liked it. "What about Red? You haven't unsaddled him yet."

"That poor horse has been through hell with me. He'll understand."

Kate laughed through her tears and put her head on his shoulder as Luke carried her inside and to her bed. He dropped her onto the bed and crawled onto it himself, his big frame covering her. "May I take your clothes off, ma'am?"

Kate smiled and reached over her head to grasp the brass bars of the headboard. "You may do anything you want, sir."

Luke leaned down and tasted her mouth in a kiss that told her this was going to be a long, delicious day...and night.

EPILOGUE

IT WAS A DOUBLE WEDDING. LUKE AND KATE. SIENNA and Bill. A traveling preacher performed the ceremony, and no wilder celebration ever took place than that day in May in Lander, Wyoming Territory, Outlaw Country. And no wedding reception anywhere could possibly have involved more drinking, more dancing, more screams and laughter, more shots fired into the air, more gambling, more drunken fist fights or more business for the prostitutes than the marriage of Luke Bowden and Kate Winters.

Beyond all the yelling and piano music lay the silence of the high, lonesome country beyond the remote little town of Lander—the silence around a lonely, dead tree where a piece of frayed rope still dangled—the silence of a small cave where coyotes were digging through the bits of food someone had left there…before winter.

AUTHOR'S NOTE

I hope you have enjoyed my story. If you want to read more about the outlaw Jake Harkner, be sure to pick up my Outlaw Hearts series of books—*Outlaw Hearts*, *Do Not Forsake Me*, *Love's Sweet Revenge*, and *The Last Outlaw*.

In all of my Men of the Outlaw Trail books, I will be mentioning characters from several of my older books, and you will then be able to read about them and their own stories. There is nothing I love more than writing about the "bad man with a good heart." Every story I write is based on real historical events and locations and is a story of pure, beautiful love set against the challenges of settling America's "Old West."

ABOUT THE AUTHOR

USA Today bestseller Rosanne Bittner has written and published seventy novels over the past forty years. Rosanne's first love is American history, the Old West, and Native Americans. Her well-researched books cover real events and locations from all facets of the birth and growth of America. She has won numerous writing awards, including a RITA nomination from Romance Writers of America for *Song of the Wolf* and a WILLA award from Women Writing the West for *Where Heaven Begins*. She was named "Queen of Western Romance" by *Romantic Times Reviews*, who nominated her second Outlaw Hearts book, *Do Not Forsake Me*, for Best Western Romance for 2015. Most of Rosanne's novels have garnered over 95 percent five-star reviews from Amazon readers and great reviews from *Publishers Weekly*. Rosanne belongs to several historical societies and is an active volunteer in a home-town charity organization. She and her husband of fifty-four years live in southwest Michigan.

rosannebittner.com
rosannebittner.blogspot.com
rosannebittner17@outlook.com
Twitter—Facebook—Goodreads/Sourcebooks/Amazon

ALSO BY ROSANNE BITTNER

Outlaw Hearts
Outlaw Hearts
Do Not Forsake Me
Love's Sweet Revenge
The Last Outlaw

Christmas in a Cowboy's Arms
Longing for a Cowboy Christmas
Wildest Dreams
Thunder on the Plains
Paradise Valley
Desperate Hearts
Logan's Lady

PATHFINDER

Return to a time when the West was wild with
Anna Schmidt's Cowboys & Harvey Girls series,
inspired by real-life pioneering women

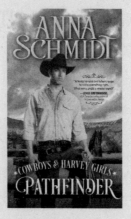

When Captain Max Winslow first sets eyes on no-nonsense
Harvey Girl Emma Elliot, he knows that anything between them
would be impossible. She's a realist embracing what the future
holds, while he's a dreamer, determined to preserve the West he
once knew. And yet something about Emma's strength of will
calls to him. It isn't long before Max must decide: is there room
in his dream for love, or will his resolve to hang on to the past
jeopardize their future?

"Truly enlightening."

—*Fresh Fiction* for *Last Chance Cowboys: The Rancher*

For more info about Sourcebooks's
books and authors, visit:

sourcebooks.com